Johanna Coco is finally h   r
beloved grandmother's func   .1
she's stayed away to begin with—Charlie McCallan. Her high school
sweetheart is now divorced, and no longer the skinny boy Johanna once
loved. Hometown handsome and dependable as always, Charlie is the
kind of man she needs to lean on as she and her sisters grapple with their
grief—as well as the mystery of their long-missing mother, Carolina. But
Johanna's heart isn't only haunted by her ghosts; it's haunted by what
happened between her and Charlie…

Charlie is determined to do things right this time, and he has to do it
before Johanna vanishes from his life again. First he needs to prove to her
that the past is past, and they can overcome it—no easy task when he's up
against the ghosts lingering in her life, trying to convince her that happily-
ever-after is not in the cards for any of the catastrophe-prone Coco sisters,
least of all Johanna. But her fearless first love is ready to do whatever it
takes to win her back—ghosts be damned.

Visit us at www.kensingtonbooks.com

Books by Terri-Lynne DeFino

Bittterly Suite Series
Seeking Carolina
Dreaming August

Published by Kensington Publishing Corporation

Seeking Carolina

A Bitterly Suite Romance

Terri-Lynne DeFino

LYRICAL PRESS
Kensington Publishing Corp.
www.kensingtonbooks.com

First Electronic Edition: October 2015
eISBN-13: 978-1-61650-768-8
eISBN-10: 1-61650-768-3

First Print Edition: October 2015
ISBN-13: 978-1-61650-769-5
ISBN-10: 1-61650-769-1

Printed in the United States of America

For my dollbabies~women of words, sea breezes, and chocolate cake.

Acknowledgements

I have heard it said writing is a solitary effort. We sit at our computers for hours at a time, oblivious to the world going on around us in favor of the one in our heads, one peopled by men and women of our own creation. Solitary? As a famous wizard once said, just because it's happening in your head, doesn't mean it isn't real. Our worlds, our characters, the events we write are very real. We make them real, we hope, for our readers. Solitary? Hardly.

We also have editors and copy editors and cover artists. Whole teams work on bringing our novels from files in our computers to books winging their way out into the world. Without my editor, Penny Barber-Schwartz, Bitterly, Connecticut and all its inhabitants would not be in this book, at this time. For that, darling Penny, not only I, but my characters thank you.

Thanks to my sisters in romance, the members of CoLoNY. Not only did you help birth The Bitterly Suite, but you have encouraged, supported, and celebrated with me every step of the way.

As always, thanks to my brilliant dollbabies, women who are not just a week on the beach, writing, eating cake, and laughing. They are the core of my writing life. We don't see one another but a week every year, but they are with me every day. Hands on my shoulder. Whispered words of encouragement. Messages on Facebook.

And though it's going to make her blush, I want to especially thank Sharon Struth. She is kindred of a kind one doesn't find every day. Thanks, Shar—without you, I wouldn't be writing this acknowledgement in the first place.
Last, as always, thanks to my Frankie D. He knows why.

Chapter 1

Twelve Drummers Drumming

Snowflakes do not fall; they dance. Will-o'-the-wisps in Les Sylphides. White on black. The poet wind scatters them and they twirl amid the tombstones—stately guardians dressed in gray—and fall, at last, to sleep.

Disturbing that slumber is a sacrilege, I know, she cannot not bring herself to commit.

No matter the cold.

No matter the dark.

No matter she is trespassing after cemetery hours. She will stand perfectly still until she is another guardian among the stones.

* * * *

Rough hands chafed warmth back into Johanna's hands, her arms. "Are you crazy?"

The masculine voice mumbled words she did not care to decipher. He was right. She was crazy. Crazy as a loon. Mad as a hatter, as a Cheshire Cat. Crazy as…

She closed her eyes, unwilling to finish the unkind, if accurate, thought. Trembling, drifting, all she wanted was to sleep.

"Oh, no you don't. Get up. Walk." He jammed a shoulder under her armpit and hefted her upright.

Johanna's feet moved of their own accord, half-dragged, but they moved. "Where am I?"

"Bitterly Cemetery," the man answered, "doing your best impression of a snowman…woman."

Oh. Right. Farts. She pushed feebly out of his arms. Her knees buckled, and she was grateful he hadn't let go. "I can walk on my own."

"I'm sure you can. Normally. Come on. I've got the heat blasting in the truck. Get warm, and I'll take you home."

Johanna let him help her. Bitterly, Connecticut was way too nice a town to allow miscreants. Everyone knew everyone and had most of their lives. This was no one to fear, even if he did frequent cemeteries after hours rescuing would-be popsicles from certain frostbite.

Her head began to clear. Memory edged around her trembling, the cold, her grief. The man scooted her into the truck, closed the door and came around the driver's side. "There's coffee in the thermos next to you."

"No, thanks."

His cell blipped and he turned a shoulder to answer it. Charlotte someone. She apparently wanted pizza.

Johanna tuned out, instead warming her hands in the hot air blasting from the heating vent. She thawed. Her trembling eased. Two days trying to get there in time, and she'd failed. Again. Was there no end to the ways she would fail her grandmother? Her sisters? She fought the tears rising up like rebels and failed at that too.

He handed her a crumpled tissue.

She snatched it from his hand, relieved it was only crumpled. "Thanks."

"No problem."

"I wasn't trying to freeze to death or anything. I was just paying my respects. I missed the funeral."

"I know."

"I'm sure the whole town knows." Johanna yanked off her hat, tried to smooth down static curls. "Well, the snow isn't my fault. The whole Northeast is covered. My car wouldn't make it and I couldn't rent an SUV and I'm damn sure not going to attempt these roads in anything else, so I had to take a train and then no one answered their cell phones. I had to walk from——"

"Jo."

She startled silent. Squinted. He pulled off his snowcap and a flop of auburn hair tumbled out. His beard lit a brighter copper than his hair. Eyelashes and brows arched over hazel eyes. A face she knew, despite the years. Johanna's heart stuttered. "Charlie McCallan? For real?"

"Took you long enough."

"You…you don't look…" She pulled at his beard. "You've grown up."

"It happens to boys when they turn into men." He laughed. "They get hairy."

He wore thick workman's overalls and a down jacket, but he was obviously and most certainly no longer the bony kid she'd once shoved into the lake.

She flexed thawing fingers. "It has been way too long, Charlie."

"I thought maybe you'd show up for the twentieth reunion."

"Twentieth?" Johanna slumped. "Really?"

"Last Thanksgiving. You should have come. Fifty-eight of the...what was our class? Ninety-something?" He shrugged. "Whatever it was, we had a good turn out."

"I don't remember getting the invite."

An eyebrow lifted, but Charlie only shifted into gear.

Tires crunched in the snow. The packing sound reminded Johanna of riding with Poppy in his ancient plow, making safe the streets of Bitterly through the long, snowy winters. Outside the warm cab, in this new winter, flurries drifted.

Charlie-freaking-McCallan. Of all people.

She had known him as unavoidably as she did everyone else in Bitterly—the ghost-white kid whose parents were caretakers of the town cemetery. They'd grown up together, largely circled in and out of friendship, until the summer they were seventeen.

The heat in the truck was becoming oppressive. Johanna unzipped her coat. "Working the graveyard shift? Pun very much intended."

"I don't really work the cemetery anymore. Mom and Dad retired, turned it over to the town. I fill in once in a while, doing maintenance."

"No one knows this place better than you." Johanna blew her nose. "And Gina? How's she?"

"In Florida with the yoga instructor she left me for."

Again her heart stuttered. Johanna loosened her scarf. Gina had been nice enough, pretty enough, and got pregnant senior year and ruined everything.

"And your...daughter, wasn't it? You had a few more, too."

"Charlotte," he answered. "She's good. I've got five kids. Two daughters and three sons."

"That's a lot of kids."

He chuckled, his eyes straying from the road to look her way. "It is. They also require a lot of pizza. Mind if I stop on our way past?"

"Oh, sure. No problem. Thanks, by the way, for..."

"No worries."

They drove in silence, the ineffectual wipers slapping a rhythm to go with the crunching tires. He pulled into town following the same trek

Johanna had made from the train station. She hadn't earlier noticed the faux-gaslights wrapped in pine and holly, the trees lining the Green, the candles in every window. Neither had she absorbed the olive oil boutique or the wine bar on either side of the pizza place that had once been the only restaurant in town. She'd been too furious that none of her sisters picked up her call. Her numerous calls.

Johanna sighed. The window fogged. Charlie was nice enough not to ask what was wrong. He could guess, and he'd probably be right. He pulled up in front of D'Angelo's Pizzeria, and left the truck running.

"I'll be right back."

She waved him away. The waft of cold air he let in made her shiver, but it felt good. Bracing. Clarifying. She opened the window and let the falling snow hit her face. Remembering. Johanna hated to remember. It was her number one reason for staying far away from Bitterly. The door opened and reason number two slipped into the truck, stretching nearly across her to set the pizzas down on the back seat. His jacket fell open. He was definitely not the skinny kid she'd pushed into the lake. He smelled good. Pizza and something musky.

"Sorry. They're hot."

She closed the window. "Does your father-in-law still make the pizza?"

"No. Gina's parents sold the place and moved to Florida about six years ago. But the pizza's still good."

"Smells it."

"You want to—"

"No, no. Thanks. I have to get home. My sisters will be waiting."

"Okay." He put the truck in drive, pulled carefully back onto the road. "It was good to see Nina. I see Emma and Julietta around town, but I don't think I've seen Nina, well, probably since I've seen you. Your grandfather's funeral, right?"

Eight years. Had it really been so long?

"I suppose so," she said. Eight years since she'd seen Gram and Emma in the flesh. She had nephews she'd never met. Cyberworld made staying in touch so easy. Video-chatting, instant messaging, texting. Nina lived in Manhattan. They met now and again for dinner or a show. Julietta had come down to Cape May a few times to help out with the bakery. But Gram…?

Tears again. She hated them, fell victim to them more often than she could count and they never did her any good. Ever.

"Hey, it's all right."

"No. It's not. But thanks."

Charlie fell silent.

Johanna blew her nose on the now-shredded and soggy tissue he'd given her for all the good it did. Covertly wiping her fingers on the inside of her coat pocket, she hoped his kindness held out and he'd pretend not to notice. "Town sure has changed a lot." She cleared the frog in her throat. "I never thought it would happen."

"It's all because of the expansion up at the ski slope. Slopes, now. Five different trails. Remember how rinky-dink it was? Bonfire in an old garbage can? Bales of hay as stops at the bottom of the hill?"

"And the tow rope that shredded our gloves." Johanna laughed. "I vaguely remember one of my sisters telling me about the changes."

Charlie paused at the red blinking light at the edge of town. "Now it's the Berkshire Lodge with ski lifts and instructors and a lodge where you can buy a seven-dollar hot cocoa. Tourists love it. After the expansion, the whole town started to surge. Remember the lake?"

How could I ever forget? "Yes."

"It's a country club now, one most residents in Bitterly can't afford to join. Pisses me off I can't bring my kids to swim there."

He drove out of town and into the farmland where the house Johanna and her sisters grew up in straddled the county line. Snow-humped fields and white woods preserved the country feel of her childhood, even while quaint road signs boasting names like Country Farm Lane and Flirtation Street indicated new developments set back from the road. There had been nothing out here when she and Nina first arrived at the house on County Line Road. She'd been just shy of four, and now remembered little of the children's home in Massachusetts, or adjusting to the doting grandparents she came quickly to love. But Johanna remembered New Hampshire. Mommy. Daddy. When there were so few memories to hold on to, it wasn't hard to hold them tight.

"Don't go into the driveway," she said as he was about to do so. "It doesn't look like it's been shoveled."

"My truck can make it."

"No." She grasped his arm, gave it a friendly squeeze. The windows in the house were dark, all but the one around back. The square of light on the snow peeked around the corner, a crooked finger beckoning. She imagined her sisters gathered at the table in the kitchen. Drinking tea. Or wine. Trying not to speak unkindly of their errant sister who missed Gram's funeral.

"Thank you, Charlie." Johanna looked for the door handle. "I don't know what I'd have done if you didn't show up."

Charlie reached across her, flicked the perfectly integrated handle she wouldn't have found in a thousand years of trying. The door swung open, letting the cold swirl in.

"Lucky for me I did."

"For you?"

He smiled. "You'd have come and gone before I ever knew you were in town. I'm glad I got to see you, Jo."

"Same...same here." Johanna stepped out into knee-deep snow. "I'll be in town a few days. Maybe I'll see you around."

"Kind of hard to avoid it, in Bitterly. Get inside before you freeze again."

Johanna scooped up a handful of snow and tossed it at him before slamming the door. He laughed and waved and pulled away. The light was still on in the interior of his truck, alighting on his hair like sunshine on a copper kettle. She watched until the curve in the road took his taillights from sight.

"It really is good to see you, Charlie," she said to the falling snow. Whether she was pushing him into the lake or he was chasing her with a dobsonfly, they'd been friends first. Johanna turned aside those thoughts, and to the house instead.

Home.

The word sent disparate shivers into her core. White with black shutters and a red door. The farmhouse porch, empty now but for the ring of firewood between the front windows, usually boasted a number of rocking chairs and porch swings. She and her sisters never complained about summer assigned reading. Afternoons spent on the porch, Gram's lemonade popsicles melting down their fingers, was one of their joys of summer.

Wrapping her scarf more closely around her neck, Johanna trudged down the driveway and around to the back of the house. She hugged the wall, peeking through the window from the shadows, her heart hammering. There they were, just as she imagined them, sitting around the table as they had so many times during those years they all lived happily there.

Nina, a Wagner dream of Valkyries—blond and bold and brutal, her hands wrapped around a teacup as if she would crush it, or hold it together.

Emmaline, who, like Johanna, had inherited dark curls and cocoa-brown eyes from their mother and, unlike Johanna, was spared her frenzy.

And Julietta.

Johanna's brimming eyes overflowed.

Awkward even when sitting still, as blond as Nina without any of her beauty, Julietta was a sprite straight out of a fairy story, all arms and legs and ears. Thick glasses accentuated the enormity of her pale eyes. Perpetually childlike, ridiculously brilliant, Julietta was the one. And they all loved her best.

Johanna wiped her eyes with her scarf, her nose with the back of her hand. She gave up trying to pretend she hadn't been crying, hadn't been frantic and furious and ready to succumb to the madness always looming like tomorrow's shadows. Stumbling to the back door that would be open because the lock had broken when she was fourteen and never been fixed, Johanna Coco went home.

* * * *

The truck slid to a stop at the bottom of the hill. Charlie rested his head to the steering wheel. He breathed deeply, inhaling the aromas of pizza and Johanna. Memory sparked. Summer after junior year. Her body pressed to his. The music, and the crowd, and the sand beneath their feet. She had turned and smiled that earth-shattering smile when he slipped his arms around her waist, pulled her against him so she wouldn't get crushed by the head-bangers moshing outside of the mosh pit. Charlie remembered her leaning into him, her hands holding him in place, the sweetness of her perfume ignited by sweat, and the seemingly inconsequential moment of contact that changed his world.

Headlights approached. He lifted his head. A plow-truck going up the hill stopped. Charlie rolled down his window as the other driver did the same.

"You stuck, Charlie?" Dan Greene, best pal since childhood, leaned an elbow out his window. "Need a tow?"

"Nah, just taking a few minutes peace. The kids are home waiting for their dinner."

"What are you doing way out here?"

Charlie thumbed over his shoulder. "I just dropped Johanna Coco off. I found her in the cemetery."

"At this hour?"

"You know those Coco girls."

"I sure do. Too bad she didn't make it to the funeral."

"She tried. This damn snow—"

"Don't you be cursing my livelihood. This damn snow is taking my sister's kids to the beach this summer. Kind of ironic, huh?"

Their laughter faded into the night. Charlie felt suddenly drained. Tight as he and Dan had always been, he didn't have the words to express his sudden chaos of thoughts. Tapping the side of his truck, he waved and let up on the break.

"Right. See you, Dan."

"See you, Charlie."

The scrape of Dan's plow on the road vanished as Charlie's window went up, trapping the scent of pizza lingering. Johanna's, like the woman herself, did not. Wild as the Coco girls had always been, Johanna was the wildest. She left after high school and seldom returned. For Charlie, that had been a good thing. He glommed every bit of news, every shred of gossip over the years. Her travels. Her pie-in-the-sky business ventures. Lover after temporary lover she brought home to Bitterly, never the same guy two visits running. Seeing her was always hard, harder when he and Gina stopped getting along. Last time, when she returned to Bitterly for her grandfather's funeral, the twins were newborns, Charlotte, Will, and Caleb were still in elementary school and he was still married, happily-enough. That was eight years ago, and now none of those things were true. Johanna was home, for however long, and Charlie was not going to let her escape Bitterly without hearing the words he tried to tell her that summer night on the beach and hadn't stopped thinking since.

* * * *

Johanna woke, blinking away the bright sunlight streaming through lace curtains. Not the cluttered bedroom above the bakery, the one that always smelled of baking and the sea, it was yellow. White bookshelves. A desk under the window, and a Nirvana poster on the closet door. Her nose was cold but her body, warm under downy blankets. A heavy, scraping sounded somewhere outside. She pushed up onto her elbows.

Bitterly.

Home.

Her old room, bed, even the comforter.

Gram was dead.

"Farts."

Johanna flopped back into the pillow. The reunion with her sisters had been tearful, and comforting. Wrapped in their arms, she laughed at her fury, at the thought that they'd abandon her at the train station because they were collectively angry.

"Last we heard, you didn't think you were going to make it," Nina had said, thumbing tears from Johanna's cheeks. "After the burial, we all went out for pizza and didn't see you'd called until we were there. Charlie McCallan offered to go find you and bring you home."

"And here you are." Julietta had thrown her arms around her. "Oh, Jo! I'm so sorry. After all you went through to get here, you didn't even get pizza."

They talked long into the night. And they cried, none harder than Johanna. Emma and Julietta still lived in Bitterly and Nina made certain she returned home for every holiday. Only Johanna stayed away with a million excuses and none of them good enough to justify an eight-year absence.

The aromas of coffee and bacon crept into her room. More snow in the night kept Emma with them instead of going home to her husband and boys. It would be she doing up breakfast the way Gram always did. Johanna pulled back the covers and swung her legs out of bed. The nasty scraping sound outside continued. She looked out the window to see a plow clearing the driveway. Someone was shoveling the front walk. A shock of red hair had her throwing open the window to shout, "Good morning, Charlie."

The young man who looked up was not Charlie for all he looked like him. Exactly, in fact, like the kid she used to know. Her heart caught in her throat for the memories pelting. This room. That boy. But it wasn't Charlie, and everything was different now.

"Hey," he called back. "You looking for my dad?"

"I suppose I am."

"He's in the truck. Will's doing the back walk. I got this one. You'll be shoveled clear in no time."

"And you are?"

"Caleb. Which sister are you?"

"Johanna."

"The one who lives at the beach. Cool."

"It's far from cool, I assure you. Cape May is full of old people and tourists."

He laughed and waved and Johanna closed the window. If she could find the ingredients in the pantry, she'd make the boys her famous hot chocolate. She pulled on the thick robe perpetually hanging on the back of her door, wrapped it tight and followed her nose to breakfast.

Faded school photos lined the hallway painted the same yellow as her bedroom. Gram had let them each choose her own colors when Emma and Julietta came to them in the big farmhouse in Bitterly. Nina, a cool and sophisticated thirteen-year-old, chose blue with white trim. Emmaline, only six, wanted mauve and olive green. Head still bandaged and arm in a sling, Julietta's four-year-old love of purple and orange had been indulged. But Johanna, eleven and confused as to why they were decorating rooms when Mommy had once again vanished and Daddy was dead and now she had two little sisters as well as a big one, chose the soft, buttercream yellow.

"You?" Poppy had asked. "My wild Johanna? Not red or crazy-girl pink?"

He took her into his wiry arms, right there in the paint shop, when she started to cry. "It reminds me," she whispered against his neck. Of the house in New Hampshire, the one that burned. It reminded her of them.

He bought three gallons of the buttercream yellow.

"What? It was on sale. Half price," he told Gram when she scolded. He painted her room first, then the hallway. Last, because there was enough left over, he painted the room he shared with Gram.

"It reminds me too."

It was their secret. One of many. She suspected he had them with her sisters too, those half-truths more story than anything real, like Weiner-schnitzel, the little man who lived in his pocket, whose voice only she could hear.

Johanna stopped outside Gram's bedroom door, pressed her hand to the wood panel. She let her hand slide to the knob, felt the cool metal, let it go before any more memories got loose. Instead she hurried down the stairs, her feet thumping like when she was a kid late for school. Already there were her sisters, lined up at the counter like pretty maids in a row, sipping coffee. At the table sat Nina's husband, ridiculously gorgeous despite his dark hair sticking up in spikes, and the stubble of a man who needed more than one shave a day. Johanna stopped short of sliding across the polished wood floor into the kitchen the way she used to, but only because she wasn't wearing the proper socks.

"Hey, Gunner. I didn't know you were still here."

"I went to bed early so you ladies could have some time alone." He stood up and pulled Johanna into an embrace, kissed both cheeks. "Good to see you, Jo."

She tried to laugh. "It hasn't been that long."

"Almost a year."

"No it hasn't. Nina and I just…oh…" She pressed cool fingers to her burning cheeks. "I guess it has been a while. New Year's right?"

His smile crinkled in the corners of his blue eyes. "Right. Nina said you had a hard time getting here."

"It was insane. But I'm here now." She slipped one arm around his waist, the other around Emma's. "We all are. Gram would love it."

"Yes, she would have. At Thanksgiving." Emma slipped out of her embrace but kissed her cheek. "You're here now, and Christmas is in less than a week. You will stay, won't you?"

"I sup—"

"Good. Eat. I have to go. Snow day. Got to get home to the boys so Mike can go to work."

Johanna let her arm slip from Gunner's waist. Emma had every right to be upset, despite their tearful reunion. To go unchastised indefinitely was too much too hope for. She pulled out a vinyl chair and plucked a slice of bacon from the plate. Julietta dropped onto the chair beside her. "Emma's been cranky lately," she exaggerated a whisper. "I think she's prego."

"I am not cranky," Emma said, putting on her coat. "And I am definitely not pregnant."

"You and Mike not having sex again?"

Emma froze. Johanna cringed but Julietta sat poker-straight, head cocked and her expression concerned.

"Sex isn't the issue," Emma said, resuming her struggle with the zipper. "It's…nothing. Nothing that needs discussing now. Supper at my house tonight. Nina, you and Gunner, too."

"We'll be there."

"What about me?" Julietta asked. Emma kissed both her cheeks.

"You are a given, darling." She headed for the door. "Seven o'clock. Bring wine."

Gunner's cell rang just as Emma closed the door. Bits of her brother-in-law's hushed conversation drifted back into the kitchen. Nina poured another round of coffee before sitting down herself, her attention focused on her husband.

"He's going to have to leave," she said quietly. "It was nearly impossible for him to get out of the city to come here at all. Huge things happening at the gallery."

"How huge?" Julietta asked. "Da Vinci huge?"

"Not art-wise. There's been this firm out of Sweden wooing us for years. They want to buy us out, and I think temptation is starting to get to Gunner. If they succeed, the good news is neither one of us will ever have to work again."

"And the bad news?"

Nina smiled into her coffee. "Neither one of us will have to work again."

"How tempted are you, Nina?"

"I love the gallery. We've worked really hard all these years to grow it from that stinky little artist co-op into what it is now. But I'm ready to let it go, maybe travel a bit. I just don't think Gunner would last a year living the life of the idle rich."

The sisters ate and chatted, but Nina's attention remained on Gunner. When he came to the doorway and motioned her to him, she went without a word. The pair of them, arms around one another, shared the phone. Gunner's hand moved up and down his wife's spine, as unconscious an act as it was sensual. Johanna forced herself to look away, a little embarrassed and a lot envious.

"Could you imagine the world devastation should those two ever have kids?" Julietta was still staring in that unnerving way she had. No self-consciousness, no apologies. "We'd all have to wear sunglasses or suffer some sort of beauty-blindness."

"Is that like snow-blindness?" Johanna joked.

"No." Julietta snorted. "Photokeratitis is real. I made up beauty-blindness."

"Well, they're not going to have kids, so the world is safe."

"It's not too late. She's only forty-one."

Johanna let it go. Nina had vowed to never have children, to never pass along the genes they all inherited lest any child of hers suffer their parents' fate. Emma seemed determined to prove her sister's fears wrong with three sons in quick succession. And if Julietta's suspicions proved right, perhaps another.

Left alone with her youngest, unflappable sister, Johanna hedged. "So, Emma and Mike were having problems, you know, in bed?"

"It was a few years ago." Julietta bit into her toast. "When Gio was a toddler. She wanted another baby. He said they couldn't afford any more, and didn't trust her not to accidentally-on-purpose sabotage their birth control. So," she shrugged, "no sex was the only way to make sure it didn't happen."

"He didn't trust her?"

"I wouldn't have either. She really wanted another baby."

In the next room, Gunner and Nina were laughing. Julietta's attention diverted quickly, always too easily. She pushed out of her chair and joined them.

Johanna sipped at her coffee, basked in the sunshine coming through the big kitchen window and the sisterly gossip she didn't realize she missed. If I were in Cape May, she'd have already put in half a day of work. Sleeping in, having her breakfast made for her, indulging in chatting with these sisters she loved, it let her, if only for a moment, forget all the reasons she had for staying far away from Bitterly.

A soft knock on the back door opened her eyes. Charlie waved from the other side of the glass. She leapt too quickly to her feet and nearly spilled her coffee.

"All done?" she asked as he stomped his boots clean.

"Boys are just finishing up."

Johanna stepped aside to let him in. He put up his hands.

"I'll get snow all over the floor."

"Who cares? Get in here. And call your boys. I'm making them hot chocolate."

"No need to—"

"It'll take two minutes. Sit. Warm up. It's the least I can do. Okay?"

Charlie chuckled softly. "Sure."

Johanna called out to the boys who shouted in return. Head stuck in the pantry, she was relieved to find the ingredients necessary for a real cup of hot chocolate, and not the powdered stuff in an envelope.

"Help yourself to the coffee," she said over her shoulder, "unless you want hot chocolate."

"I'd love some. Thanks, Johanna."

He spoke her name softly, like a whisper before falling into sleep. Johanna stirred the melting butter and chocolate, added the sugar spoonful by spoonful. By the time she started incorporating the milk, she could speak without her voice cracking.

"Thanks again for last night."

"No worries. That reminds me—I have your backpack. You left it in the truck."

"Oh, I did, didn't I. Totally forgot about it."

"I'll have one of the boys get it." He passed behind her to call out to his sons.

Johanna shivered. Lowering the heat, she stirred as if her life depended upon it not sticking to the bottom.

Charlie peered over her shoulder. "Smells good. I don't think I've ever had anything but the packaged stuff."

"I doubt there's even any real cocoa in that."

"Probably not. You never struck me as the cooking type."

"I never was."

"But you own a bakery."

"An impulse decision, not a lifelong dream," she admitted. "I was vacationing in Wildwood, and decided to check out Cape May. I fell in love with the town, the Victorian houses and quaint shops. It's real old-world, you know? Even in the height of summer. When I saw CC's for sale, I..." She bit the truth off there.

Charlie answered for her. "You bought it."

She shoved him playfully. "I hocked everything I owned and mortgaged six of my nine lives, but I did."

"CC's, huh?"

"Cape Confectionary. It came with the name. CC's for short."

"Ah, I see."

"After all my failed attempts at earning a living, this one has turned out to be something good. Who'd have thought I would have a knack for baking? In the summer, I do breakfast and lunch too. It gets kind of crazy, tourists from all around the world there to see the famous Jersey Shore. It's like no place else on earth. You should bring the kids down."

Her cheeks were burning before the words were out of her mouth. Johanna took the pan off the burner, kept her back to him as she poured three mugs. Stomping on the small porch off the back of the house signaled the boys' arrival. Another moment and they were in the kitchen, stripping off snow gear in the boisterous way of young men.

"Caleb, Will, this is Johanna Coco. Johanna, two of my boys."

"Hi, again," Caleb waved, his smile wide. "We met through the window already. Here's your backpack." He retrieved it from the pile of coats and scarves. "Got a little snowy."

"Thanks." She held out a steaming mug. "I'll trade you."

He took it with an enthusiastic, "Thanks," and flopped onto a kitchen chair. His brother, dark-haired as Gina, did not share his enthusiasm, but he took her offering and sat beside his father at the table. Johanna placed the last cup in front of Charlie.

"What do we owe you gentlemen for your services?"

"This'll do." Charlie sipped. "Come on, Jo. It's a favor to friends."

"Last night was a favor," she said. "This is not. You have to let me pay you something."

"No I don't."

"Charlie."

"Johanna." He laughed. "Seriously. Don't make this awkward."

"Hey, I want some." Julietta blew through the room, took the pan from the stove. She poured herself the little bit left. "Dang."

"I'll make more, Jules."

"I was hoping you'd say that." Caleb raised his empty cup. "Ow! Quit it, Will."

"You're being rude."

"No, I'm not. It's a compliment. How's a compliment rude?"

Will rolled his eyes and shook his head. He reminded Johanna of Nina at his age, when anything and everything her sisters did was somehow embarrassing to her.

"If your dad won't let me pay you, then I think more hot chocolate is an absolute must. Will? You want some too?"

He looked into his cup. "Well, if you're making it anyway…"

Johanna started mixing ingredients again, silently happy to keep them around a little while longer. Her slip was already fading. As if Charlie would ever bring his kids to Cape May, of all places. As if anything about that teenage-summer still mattered to him at all.

"We always pay you," Julietta was saying. "Don't be stupid."

"This is different. Don't start with me, Jules."

"I'm not starting anything. You are."

"What are you, twelve?"

Johanna stiffened, but Julietta laughed and shoved him. "Then come to Emma's for dinner tonight. We're all going to be there. If you won't take money, we can pay you in food. My sister's as good a cook as Gram was."

"Thanks but—"

"Charlie, I can't take this much rejection in one day. You know I'm special that way. I'll square it with Emma. Come. It's the least we can do for all you've done the last few days."

Charlie's shoulders slumped but he smiled fondly. "All right. Thanks."

"Great. Be there at seven. Bring wine."

Johanna stirred and stirred. The action soothed. She poured out cups while the others chattered. Will and Caleb were trying to convince their dad to take them snowboarding. Charlie said Charlotte could do it. He'd already promised Tony and Millie he'd make a snowman with them. Julietta told the story about the time Emma went up the mountain on some school trip, and how she nearly killed herself and five others by falling in the middle of the slope. Their words were far away and apart, as if she were a ghost listening from the shadows in an altered world. Johanna tried to shake herself out of it. She hadn't needed this slip from reality in a long time. Of course, being in Bitterly would trigger it.

The scraping of chairs on the hardwood restored her hearing, her sense of place. Johanna found herself helping Charlie into his big jacket.

"Sorry about the floor." He pointed to the puddles around his sons' discarded boots. "I'll have the boys—"

"Don't worry about it. Julietta will do it."

"You sure?"

"I'll make her more hot chocolate."

He laughed, the corners of his eyes crinkling in deep creases there for as long as she could remember. Back then, they smoothed as quickly as they formed. Today, they did not, and Johanna liked it quite a lot.

"I'll see you later then?"

"Yup. Later."

"Come on, boys." Charlie was out the door before his sons could pull on their boots. Johanna bit down on her lips suddenly buzzing with words like—Stop. Stay. Do you ever think of me? Of that summer? It was so long ago, and they had been so young. In those sweaty months before Labor Day, Charlie McCallan made her happier than she ever thought she could be. And then it was over, just like that.

She dug into the front pocket of her backpack, pulled out two crumpled twenties and stuffed them into the boys' hands.

"Don't tell your dad."

"Wow," Caleb said. "Thanks, Johanna."

"Thanks," Will murmured, shoving the bill into his pocket.

Closing the door behind them, Johanna leaned against it. Dinner. With Charlie. She glared at her sister.

"What?"

"You know what. Heavens to Murgatroyd, Jules. I'm going to murdilate you."

"You're welcome." Julietta handed her the mug of hot-chocolate dregs, kissed her cheek. "And you can clean up the floor."

* * * *

Johanna lay alone, in the dark, supine on her grandmother's bed and a hand on her overburdened belly. Emma's famous macaroni and meatballs sat heavily alongside the pastries Charlie brought—recompense for having to bring his eight-year-old twins, Millie and Tony, to dinner when his older kids stayed late at the slopes. Johanna's middle nephew, Henry, had been thrilled. He and Tony were classmates, and though Millie was as well, she mostly ignored the boys to instead braid and unbraid the silky strands of Nina's golden hair. Nina happily took her own turns at Millie's thick, red curls and Johanna had to wonder if her sister's childlessness was the choice she always insisted it was.

Gio, the youngest nephew, pestered Henry and Tony, while Ian, the oldest, seemed to share a special bond with his Aunt Julietta. Most of her evening was spent helping the ten-year-old with his math homework. In the thick of it all, Johanna had felt as full of love as she had been of the food.

No one misses the funeral of a Sig'lian'. We make mean ghosts. Gram always said Italians loved a funeral; it brought family home, and brooked no excuse.

In the dark silence beyond midnight, listening to her belly gurgle along with the creaks and groans of the old farmhouse she grew up in, Johanna was wishing she'd taken her chances with the ghost. The sensation of being only a guest in her sister's home, in her sisters' lives descended. Being in Bitterly forced her to acknowledge all the good things she was missing to avoid the bad. Until coming home, she'd been happy in Cape May, in her bakery at the beach, with the hundreds of friendly strangers who populated her life.

Johanna groaned upright, and moved to the window. Outside, the moon shined brightly on the snow and the world existed only in shades of blue. Snow, snow, everywhere—snow. A cathedral of trees. A holy realm of ice. The only church she had ever needed.

She used to imagine her mother playing in the yard, building snow castles or chasing fireflies. But Mommy had never lived in Bitterly, a fact Johanna didn't know until Emmaline and Julietta came to live with them too.

Johanna turned away from the window, those thoughts. She moved about Gram's room by moonlight. It never changed, but for the buttercream yellow paint that had replaced Gram's more sensible white back when she and her sisters were small, and grieving. The dresser, oiled and smooth as honey, always scented with the lavender sachets kept in every drawer. Johanna opened the top one and breathed in, struck suddenly by the notion of getting rid of all the clothes. Who would have the heart to scoop the nightgowns from the drawers, the dresses from the closet, and haul them off to some charity? Johanna shuddered. She could not do it. She would rather burn everything, and that made her shudder again.

On top of the dresser sat Gram's jewelry box. Adelina Coco was Sicilian, but she was also a New Englander. One good dress and a pair of sensible heels was all she needed. The plain box Poppy had made for her one Christmas, when they were newly married and quite poor, was mostly empty. Johanna lifted the lid.

The ribboned lock of Carolina's dark hair.

The crumbling letter Johanna knew by heart.

The gold Virgin Mary medal Gram never took off, along with her wedding rings and Pop's.

And the locket.

Johanna's breath caught in her throat. She had forgotten about this talisman, this magical thing. Picking it up by the chain, she let it twirl in the moonlight.

"It belonged first to Poppy's grandmother," Gram had told her. "Her own *nona* gave it to her when she left Sicily for America to be married. See the initials? FMC. That is for Florentina Coco."

"What does the M stand for?"

"Maddelena, I think. Do you want to hear the story or ask questions?"

"Hear the story. Please."

"Good girl. Back then, when someone left the old country, those left behind knew it was for good. Florentina's grandmother had already lost many sons and many grandchildren to America. But Florentina was her favorite, I am told, and so she put something very special inside the locket before waving good-bye. Can you guess what it was?"

"A picture?"

"No, not a picture. She put a wish inside."

"Sure, Gram."

"You don't believe me? You doubt it can be true? There was a time, Johanna, when we women still had our magic. It was a simple matter of course, and nothing at all extraordinary. That old woman put a wish into this locket as certainly as I am standing here telling you this tale. The locket has passed from daughter-in-law to daughter-in-law, from Florentina's down to me. The wish is still there, waiting to be used, because a wish can be scary to actually make, and no one has yet had the courage."

"Not even you?"

"Not even me. But you do, my Johanna. I have no daughters-in-law, so when I am gone, I give this to you. The wish will be yours to make."

The clarity of memory left Johanna trembling. She had been seven, and so fragile, always fantasizing about the fiery death she deserved, one that would have spared her all the pain that came after. Gram found her in a closet, curled into a ball and weeping. It was all her fault. If not for her, she and Nina would still be living happily in the woods of New Hampshire with Mommy and Daddy. Words would not come, not then and not ever, because they would have made Gram think Johanna didn't love her and Poppy, wasn't glad to be in school, relieved to wear clothes that were not stolen out of a drop-box she'd been lowered into because she was the smallest.

Johanna shuddered. To be so young and so confused, so full of grief and relief—tears started back then continued into the present. They had always been her way of coping. Cry enough and weariness overwhelmed the confusion, put it into perspective of a kind. The older she got, the better Johanna understood how the evasion of tears became the evasion permeating her life. She simply didn't know how to change it. Or if she wanted to.

Trembling fingers clicked open the locket. She saw the same faded photo, but not even a sparkle that could pass for a wish. Johanna touched the picture of Carolina Coco, young and smiling, her head thrown back. Just beyond the round of her mother's cheek was what Johanna always believed was her father's shoulder. Looking at it now, adult eyes focusing beyond the illusions of childhood, it was probably a wall.

"If there is a wish in here, Gram, why didn't you use it to make Mom well? Why didn't you use it to get her back?"

Johanna closed it, kissed it, and slipped it over her head again. Emma would want the medal. Julietta and Nina could decide on who got what rings. But the locket was hers.

Gram said.

* * * *

The letter is old and crumbling, and a lie. It speaks of love ferocious, one undefeated by time and distance—or locked doors and walls and razor wire that cuts deeply. Leaves scars that do not heal. It speaks of happiness, that false thing made of chemicals rushing through the brain and can be altered by more chemicals crushed and stirred into orange juice. It made promises that were lies before the ink dried on the page.

But I didn't know then. I did not know. If you ever believed all the other lies, please believe this one truth I was never able to speak.

Chapter 2

Eleven Pipers Piping

Gunner was already on his way out the door by the time Johanna found her way to the kitchen. Dashing about, stuffing things into his duffle, yanking his cell phone charger from the wall-socket, he called out to her as he hurried past.

"Nice seeing you, Jo. Keep Nina out of trouble. Ha, look who I'm asking. I'll see you at Christmas, right? We'll celebrate."

And out he went, snatching a kiss from Nina as he blew through the door. She watched him, her arms crossed against the cold coming in. Johanna went to stand behind her, rested a cheek to her sister's arm.

"Does this mean what I think it means?" Johanna asked.

Nina stepped back and closed the door. "If what you think is that the gallery sold? Yes. They made us an offer we'd be insane to refuse."

"Woohoo!" Johanna grabbed her sister's hands, bounced up and down. "How fantastic."

"I suppose."

"Nina, you're rich."

"I had plenty of money without selling it."

Johanna let go her hands. "I thought this is what you wanted."

"I did. I do."

"Then?"

Nina sighed, pulled a chair away from the table, and flopped into it. Johanna sat opposite her.

"I feel this...loss." Nina's lip trembled. She would not cry. Tears were Johanna's thing. Her elder sister had no patience for them.

"Is it Gram?"

"Sure. Of course. But it's more. We've sacrificed everything but one another to this dream of ours, and now it's gone. Poof. I think this must kind of be like what a mother feels when her kid goes out into the world."

"But like kids, you can still visit."

"It just won't be mine anymore." She shrugged, and like that, it was settled. "Gunner's happy, that's for sure. He's already planning what comes next."

"Of course he is."

"The man is perpetual motion."

"You married him." Johanna reached for her sister's hand. "Congratulations, Nina. I'm really happy for you."

"Thanks."

"We should go out tonight and celebrate, just the four of us."

"I'd like that." Nina squeezed Johanna's hand, and let it go. "My treat. I'll ask Emma what's good in town these days."

"D'Angelo's." Julietta swept into the room. Hair piled on top of her head, two crossed pencils holding it in place and glasses slightly askew, she poured herself a cup of coffee. "Why?"

"The gallery sold," Nina answered. "We're going out to celebrate tonight. And pizza isn't appropriate celebration food unless it's for a winning soccer season."

"Pizza is always appropriate."

"Only in your world, Jules."

"I live in the same world you do, and pizza is the perfect food."

"What makes me think that now Gram's gone, you are going to live on D'Angelo's pizza?"

Julietta only sipped her coffee. The fear was not a new one. Johanna had been thinking thoughts along those lines since she got the call that Gram was gone. Old as she had been, none of them expected her to die. Ever. She, Nina and Emmaline had lives outside of the old house, outside of Gram. Julietta worked from home, via the internet, as a freelance researcher. Gram cooked, cleaned, laundered, made sure her youngest granddaughter actually got dressed on occasion. It had been a running joke among them for as long as she could remember—without Gram, Julietta would be another Howard Hughes, toenails and all.

"How about Moose Tracks?" Julietta suggested. "It's a new place in Great Barrington. Opened up where the Thai place used to be. Remember it?"

"Vaguely," Johanna answered. "What kind of food?"

"Americany-bistroish."

"How do you know the place?" Nina asked. "Did you go with Gram?"
"Gram?" Julietta snorted. "No."

Johanna leapt off her chair to grasp her sister by the arms. "Did you go on a date?"

"Jo! You made me spill coffee on my sweatshirt."

"It's a sweatshirt, and it looks like it should have been washed ages ago. Come on, Jules. Spill it."

"You spilled."

"Don't pretend not to know what I'm talking about."

Her youngest sister dabbed at the coffee on her shirt with a dishtowel. Red splotches spread across her cheeks.

"I'm not that hideous," she murmured. "I'm thirty-two. A date was bound to happen sooner or later."

"Don't be ridiculous. You are beauti—"

"I'm not." Julietta's unblinking eyes met hers. "I'm smart. I'm occasionally funny. I'm weird. I am not beautiful."

Silence fell. Johanna knew better than to argue. So did Nina. Their youngest sister never understood the social niceties that required people to lie, even if it was to be kind. It made no sense and thus, she had no patience for it.

"So he took you to this Moose Tracks place?" Nina asked. "And you liked it?"

Julietta blinked, releasing Johanna from that piercing blue stare, and turned instead to Nina. "They have really good pizza."

* * * *

Moose Tracks was exactly the sort of place Johanna expected. Upscale, spare but with a nod to the outdoors—a pair of antique snowshoes on the wall, duck decoys on the rafters, a collection of hunting horns hanging over the bar. The food was of the artisanal variety, plow to plate and local. It gratified her to see Julietta's pizza was thin-crusted, oil drizzled, and loaded with arugula and goat cheese.

At least it was real vegetable matter and dairy.

"No, that's where Efan works," Julietta was pointing to the castle-like building across the street. "He's a teacher at the prep-school, not a waiter."

"I didn't mean to imply Evan is a waiter," Emma answered. "If you would tell us something about him—"

"It's not Evan. It's Efan. With an F."

"Okay. So what does he teach?"

"History, but he's an expert on Welsh folklore."

"Kind of a narrow expertise, isn't it?" Nina sipped her wine. "How did you meet him?"

"Why do you need to know all this?"

"We're curious." Johanna intervened. "Sisters are allowed to be. Required to be, in fact. Let's hear it."

Julietta put down her pizza. "Fine. You want details? I came up here because I needed a series of books I could only find available in the academy's library and ran into this guy. Efan. He saw the books I was pulling out and we started talking and got into a big discussion about *The Children of Dôn* and it got late and there are no visitors allowed on campus after seven so Efan suggested we come here and finish. He paid for dinner, even though I told him I could get it covered on my expense report. He laughed and said my candor was refreshing but he hasn't contacted me since so I suspect he got over it quick. Okay? Enough? Can I eat in peace now?"

Johanna exchanged glances with Nina, then Emma.

"Darling." Nina touched her sister's hand.

Julietta frowned but did not look up.

"Jules, does he even know your full name?"

She shrugged. "Maybe. I think so."

"Do you know his?" Johanna asked.

Julietta shook her head.

"So you are both Cinderellas waiting for someone to show up with a shoe." Emma picked up a piece of Julietta's pizza, took a bite. "Oh, Jules."

Julietta's shoulders slumped, and the red splotches of her cheeks deepened. She was shutting down to process troubling information. It might be days before she spoke to any of them again.

Johanna, at least, no longer tasted the food. "I'm going to the ladies' room. No one eat my food."

She checked her watch. Almost seven. She had ten minutes. Hurrying past the ladies room and out the delivery entrance, Johanna braced herself for the cold. She ran along the back of the businesses, past dumpsters and skids and a couple of guys smoking. She crossed the street at the corner and kept running straight through the wrought-iron gates of the castle-like academy. Leaning against the directory, she caught her breath.

Dining Hall? Or Library? Johanna took her chances with the library. It was closer, close enough for her to see the image of George Washington carved into the grey stone over the great doors. She made a shivering dash for it.

Warmth, and the papery-leather scent of books. Johanna had never frequented libraries, but the scent always made her think of September and school starting and those hopeful days when the academic slate was clean. She had another year to prove she wasn't a C student. By Christmas break, she'd always be lagging, all desire to catch up firmly behind her social life and the upcoming school play she always aspired to but never got a part in. Nina studied hard. Julietta didn't have to. Emma was hit or miss. Johanna was mostly miss and, come senior year, had simply been happy to graduate.

"Excuse me." She caught a librarian stacking books. "Do you know a man named Efan? He's a history teacher."

"Everyone in the library knows Efan," the young man said. "He practically lives here. What do you want with him?"

"Well, ah—you see..." Johanna blew out a breath. "Okay, I'll be straight. My sister met him here a couple weeks ago and they hit it off. Apparently, neither one of them gave any contact information."

"That sounds like Efan."

"They're a pair, I'm sure," Johanna said. "We, my sisters and I, are having dinner across the street, and I thought I'd take the chance of finding him, give him my sister's info. Is he here?"

He tilted his head, grimaced a little.

"I swear I'm not stalking him."

"How about you write down your sister's contact info and I'll give it to him?" He fished a pencil out of his pocket, handed it to her along with a scrap of paper from the pile on his cart. Johanna wrote down Julietta's email address, website address, and cell phone number. She handed it to the librarian.

"How do I know you're not going to chuck that the minute I leave?"

"How about I promise I won't?"

"How about you pinky-swear me?" She stuck out her pinky.

He laughed, and hooked his little finger around hers.

"Pinky-swear. But I can't promise he'll call or anything. Efan is...a little strange."

She let her hand fall. "So is my sister."

Johanna didn't bother taking the circuitous route back to Moose Tracks, but entered through the front door. Julietta didn't even look up. Emma and Nina gave her a look that said they knew exactly what she had done. Dropping into her chair, she barely picked up a French fry before the door opened again and into the restaurant rushed a tall young man with dark hair and an intense expression focused immediately and solely on Julietta.

Efan, Johanna mouthed. She was certain. Gratification warmed her through, though it could do nothing about the cold hamburger and fries on her plate. She picked up the burger and took a bite, trying to pretend she didn't notice Efan's ungraceful descent to one knee beside Julietta's chair. He took her hand, drawing her out of shutdown with a perfectly-Prince-Charmingly accented whisper, "Julietta?"

* * * *

Night two in her old bedroom, in the farmhouse on County Line Road. Night four since Gram's death. Night five since sleeping last in the room above the bakery, blissfully unencumbered by the memories and bonds so much easier to pretend did not exist. Johanna turned onto her side, pulled the locket free of the nightgown she took from Gram's drawer. She traced the engraved letters, clicked it open to run a fingertip over her mother's face she could not see for the darkness.

"I wish," she whispered. "I wish…"

Her throat tightened. So many wishes. How did one choose which regret to obliterate, and which were too familiar to let go?

Tucking the locket back into her nightgown, Johanna got out of bed and padded across the hall to Nina's room. She did not knock, but opened the door as quietly as she could, peeking around the edge to see her beautiful sister asleep on her pillow. Alabaster skin ethereal in the moonlight, her blond hair braided to keep it from tangling, Nina looked like a princess in a fairytale, deep in enchanted slumber.

"Come in and close the door, Jo."

She jumped but was able to stop herself from squealing. Darkness beckoned, and the familiar comfort of Nina. Johanna slipped into the room, closed the door softly behind her, and snuggled into the blankets beside her sister.

"How did you know it was me?"

"You've been sneaking into my bed since you were a baby. Who else would it be?"

"It's so cold in here. Why is your window open?"

"Because I like the fresh air. I don't get much of it in the City. Hush, now." Nina took her into her arms. "Go to sleep."

"Don't you want to know why I'm here?"

"Because you had a bad dream. Because there is a monster in your closet. Because you wet the bed. What does it matter? Come on. I'm tired."

"Okay."

Johanna cuddled in close. Even as teenagers, she and Nina sought one another's comfort, just as they had when they were very small, and frightened, and too often left alone. Days and days alone in the buttercream-yellow house, with only a bucket of water, a loaf of bread, and a jar of peanut butter to sustain them.

"It was really sweet, what you did for Julietta."

Johanna picked up her head. "He's adorable, isn't he? All that messy hair. And his accent is sexy as hell."

"He is apparently brilliant, too. They are perfect for one another. Julietta needs a man as intelligent as she is."

"And a man who understands what it is to be...different."

"That too."

Nina turned onto her side so they were face to face. For all her talk of going back to sleep, her sister's eyes were wide and glittering.

"And what about you, my little sister?"

"What about me?"

Nina waggled her eyebrows. "Charlie? He's still got it bad for you."

"Oh, stop." She tried to turn over but Nina pulled her back.

"Okay, we won't talk about Charlie. How about Emma and Mike?"

Johanna giggled like the girl she had once been. "This is so bad. Gossiping like old ladies at the laundromat."

"It's only bad if our intentions are mean-spirited, which they aren't. I'm worried about them."

"You think there's a danger of them splitting up?"

"That's been a danger for a while now."

"Really? Why? What's gone wrong?"

"This time?" Nina bit her lip. "Mike had a vasectomy without telling her. She's devastated."

"What? How do you know?"

"She told me when we were all here at Thanksgiving."

The twirling of Johanna's stomach hit a sudden stop. She lowered her gaze, unable to meet Nina's. "I should have come home. I wanted to, but it's such a busy time at the bakery and——"

"Jo." A finger under her chin, a slight tap. The familiarity of this gesture released the tears always too ready to fall. Johanna looked up and Nina smiled. "You couldn't have known it would be Gram's last."

"It has been eight years. I'm a horrible granddaughter, after all she did for me. For us."

"Gram understood, and so do I. Coming back here is a huge effort for me. If not for Gunner, I might not come home at all. It's why Emma stayed. Leaving means to risk never coming back."

"We had a happy life here." Johanna said. "Why is it so hard?"

"Because we had a happy life here without them."

Johanna was not as certain. Yes, it felt like betrayal, and happiness did not banish the ghosts that had followed them to Bitterly, but there were other factors, at least for her.

"What about Julietta then?" Johanna asked. "She seems content to stay here forever."

"Because for her, familiarity is necessary. Bitterly is what she knows."

"Do you think she remembers?"

"The accident?"

"That, and Mom and Dad."

"Do you?"

"Of course."

"Then why wouldn't she? You were younger when you last saw them."

"I guess you're right."

Johanna thought back. She had been almost four when the house in New Hampshire burned. Julietta had been just over when they cut her from the car wreck that killed their father. Johanna still remembered Gram leaving her and Nina with Poppy, returning to Bitterly with the little sisters she didn't know she had, and news none of them wanted. Johan was dead. Carolina had vanished again. Emmaline was six, skinny, and always scared of the government men coming to get her in the night. Their grandparents assured her again and again, it was Johan's illness that kept them always running from a non-existent government conspiracy. Their father had loved them, and so did their mother, even though...

After a time, Emma forgot about the government men, or at least came to believe they were indeed a figment of Johan's paranoia. Julietta had come to them a banged up, but mostly cheerful child. Johanna always hoped it meant she hadn't been scarred by the life she'd been living, or by the accident that changed everything.

"When she was little, I'd hear her crying in her sleep." Nina's trembling whisper broke.

Johanna resisted the urge to touch her sister's face, to wipe away the tears she would not let fall. "I never heard her."

"Her bed was, is still, right here." She tapped the wall above their heads. "It wasn't every night or anything, and it got less and less as the years went by, but over Thanksgiving, I heard her. Gunner did too."

"Really?"

"I used to go in and calm her. It usually worked. Once in a while, it didn't."

"You never told me."

"What is there to tell, really? Julietta had nightmares. We all did."

"Do."

"Still?" Nina asked.

"Don't you?"

Nina only stared at her a moment, those pale, unblinking eyes almost eerie in the moonlight. She had their father's eyes. *Johan.* Johanna got his name, but Nina had inherited his beauty, his striking eyes, his stature.

"It's usually of fire," Nina said at last.

Johanna tried not to react, but she felt her body tense, the tears sting, the apology form on her lips—the one she had never uttered. The one no one knew she owed.

"I wake up certain the apartment is on fire. That's pretty much it."

"Pretty much?" Johanna coughed as the words struggled to get around the truth.

A tear finally slipped free of her sister's eye. She nodded her lie. Now Johanna was the one gathering her sister into her arms. She held her close. "Remember," she whispered, "picking wildflowers with Mommy?"

"I do."

"And playing in the snow with Daddy?"

Another nod.

"He used to say the snowflakes were fairies?"

"Willies," Nina corrected. "Like in Les Sylphides."

"Sylphs."

Nina laughed softly. "Yes, sylphs."

Hush, Jo-Jo. Shhh. The sylphs are sleeping. If you wake them, they will make you dance until dawn.

She remembered the cold. She remembered hiccupping in the silence, and being held in strong, trusted arms. The clarity of that moment remained. Johanna never doubted the veracity. Eyes closed, she pulled his image out of baby memory. Daddy. Johanna was certain she remembered him bigger and more handsome than he actually was. "He loved us, Nina. He loved us so much."

"Of course he did. So did Mom. They couldn't help what they were. Even today, treating mental illness is such a crapshoot. Can you imagine what it was like for them?"

"Especially when they were separated. When they lost custody of us."

"And then again with Emma and Julietta." Nina sighed. "At least we didn't know we were desperately poor and squatting in an abandoned farmhouse. We ate. We were mostly warm."

"And we were constantly left all alone and unsupervised for days on end. Every child's dream."

"While they hunted, or picked through dumpsters. I believe nowadays they'd be called freegans."

Both sisters laughed. Gallows humor had its merits.

"At least we had a home," Nina said. "Jules and Emma didn't."

"Mom and Dad were pretty deep into the crazy by then."

"Jo, that's unkind."

"Oh, come on, it's true. I don't have to pretend with you, do I?"

"No. You don't." Nina settled. "How did we all escape it, whatever genes made them...you know..."

"Crazy?"

"Mentally ill."

"Same thing." Johanna answered. "Maybe just stupid luck."

"It does seem that way. I still worry a little about Julietta, but I don't think she's like they were. She's just Julietta."

Johanna stroked her sister's hair. None of them had ever doubted the extraordinary love affair between their parents. It was all in the letter Gram kept in her jewelry box. She told them the story as if it were a movie script, a dark comedy, or a tragedy of love blooming in a mental facility and culminating in a high-speed chase that left their father dead. But the story never included their mother dying too, only vanishing so completely, she might as well have.

"Do you think she's dead?"

Johanna opened her mouth to answer, and discovered it was she who had asked the question.

"I have no idea."

"Do you wonder? Or have you stopped?"

Nina turned onto her side again. Her brow furrowed. "It's like the nightmares," she said, "we all have them, and we all wonder. How can we not? She's our mother."

* * * *

My girls, look at them sleep. Like babies, in one another's arms. They whisper truths and hide them. They lay bare their souls and conceal them. They console and they hurt. Words are ever like that, never quite saying what is meant. Golden seraph. Wild sylph. Reasons one

*and two I wish for the locket, for the wish inside, and to
have back my painful life.*

Chapter 3

Ten Lords a'Leaping

More snow. Bitterly's record accumulation was already almost met, and it wasn't even Christmas. Johanna stood at the big front window, watching the snowflakes fall and doubting she would see New Jersey any time before the spring thaw. Though she hadn't told her sisters yet, she closed for the season after getting the call about Gram. Christmas would have helped line the coffers of her slow season—tourists loved Cape May during the holidays almost as much as they did during the summer—but business was always slow between New Year's and Valentine's Day, and didn't really get good again until Easter. She had been tempted, but never closed for the winter. It scared her a little, having no income, but Thanksgiving was profitable enough, if lonely. Watching the recorded Macy's Thanksgiving Day parade while eating holiday-in-a-container from the gourmet health-food shop wasn't as much fun without her sisters' snide commentary. Hosts whose hair never moved. Obviously lip-synched Broadway extravaganzas. This form of holiday-bashing was one of their favorite traditions of the season for as long as she could remember.

Her smile faded, but did not vanish. She had only just turned thirty their last Christmas together. Poppy died the summer prior and Gram could not face the holidays without all her girls. Even then, Johanna had been slacking on her visits home, but she returned to Bitterly and the melancholy-from-all-directions that permeated every visit. At least she had managed to avoid Charlie and his wife and kids and the newborns she had met briefly at Poppy's funeral.

And now he was finally free.

The thought came unbidden, warming her from tips to toes. Of all her reasons for avoiding Bitterly, he was no longer one of them.

He's still got it bad for you.

Nina's tease whispered between her ears. There was a time Johanna had been confident, even smug, about how bad he had it for her. A whole summer of just the two of them exploring the woods and one another. Over the years, she let herself daydream they hadn't stopped at exploring, that instead of prolonging the exquisite agony of waiting, they'd consumed one another in a teenage blaze of passionate glory. But those fantasies always ended up with her pregnant instead of Gina, of being stuck in Bitterly when every dream she ever had was to escape it, to become someone new, someone who was not even related to the little girl who'd set her life on fire, and been forced to watch it burn.

Johanna darted into the kitchen and grabbed the old, corded phone off the wall. Dialed. It rang once, twice. Emma picked up on the third ring.

"I want to do Christmas here," she said before her sister finished saying hello.

"Jo?"

"Yes, it's me. What do you think? You do the turkey. Nina and Jules will do the sides. I'll do all the baking. Your boys can help, if they want."

"So you're really staying?"

"Yes, I'm really staying. Say yes. Please?"

Emma sniffed. Her voice cracked. "On one condition."

"Name it."

"I want to make lasagna, too."

Johanna laughed, grateful her shaking hands did not show through the phone. "Done. Do you need to talk it over with Mike or anything? I know his parents are still nearby. His brother."

"We do Christmas Eve with them. I actually assumed we'd all be here at my house this Christmas. But Gram's is better, much bigger, and it will feel…right."

"Fabulous. I'll tell Nina and Julietta when they get back from shopping."

"Shopping? For…?"

"A new outfit. Julietta has a date with Efan…"

* * * *

Fifteen minutes later, Johanna hung up the phone, buoyed by the gossip and planning for Christmas dinner. The heights and depths of her emotions in a single morning exhausted her in the same way dancing all night would. She didn't know how much she could take before collapsing.

Already the idea of baking pies and breads and cakes and cookies flew through her head like recipes being born. Johanna would fill them all so full of dessert they wouldn't be able to look at another carb for a decade. She imagined Ian and Henry and Gio, flour on their faces and batter on their fingers, baking with her. She would teach them how to mix the dough for butter cookies, and how important it was to work on a cold surface. As she imagined her little nephews piping icing onto perfect star and Christmas tree shapes, the number of children gathered around the baking counter multiplied.

Johanna touched a hand to her clenching heart, felt the locket and took comfort from it. Like Nina, she had never wanted children of her own. They had beaten the genetic odds so far. She had no wish to tempt the fates. But these were not her imagined children. Not Emma's or Nina's or Julietta's.

The vibration of her cell phone ringing in her pocket startled the image from her head. Johanna fished it out.

"Hello?"

She looked at the screen. A dropped call from a number she did not recognize. One with the area code and call numbers for Bitterly. Johanna's scalp prickled. She hit the call button, listened to the ringing. Four. Five. Six times. He answered just as she was about to hang up.

"Hello? Hello? Jo, don't hang up."

"Hey, Charlie." Her heart hammered. "Did you just call me?"

"Me? No. Why?"

"My phone just..." Johanna closed her eyes. Behind her lids, those children reappeared around the kitchen counter. "Never mind. Doesn't matter. I was just wondering...what are you and the kids doing Christmas Eve?"

* * * *

"Daddy? Are you okay? Daddy?"

Charlie blinked at the phone in his hand. The screen showed Johanna had hung up, but the phone number he'd begged Mike for was still clearly illuminated. As he watched, the display went dark.

"Who's Joe?"

"Huh?"

Millie, his eight-year-old daughter, rolled her eyes, pointed to the phone in his hand.

"Oh. That was Johanna. You remember her from Henry's? We're going to bake cookies at her house on Christmas Eve."

"Yay!" Millie bounced. "But why did you call her Joe. Joe is a boy's name."

"It's just what I've always called her. Now turn around. Let me finish combing."

"But it's taking so long. I'm bored."

"Read your book."

"I'm tired of reading."

And I'm tired of combing lice eggs out of your hair. Charlie took a deep breath, resisted the urge to push potentially contaminated fingers through his hair.

"Come on, baby," he said gently. "Not too much longer."

"Okay, Daddy."

Charlie worked through his daughter's hair with the tiny comb—a feat in itself. Millie had his thick, copper hair. She squealed every time it snarled. Shortcuts would only result in having to do this all over again in a couple of weeks, so he took his tedious time. He thought about all he still had to do, even though Millie was the only one who actually had lice. It was a matter of days before they all did too unless he stripped every bed, vacuumed every surface and put the gazillion stuffed animals in Millie's bedroom into garbage bags. All the kids would have to be treated anyway, just to be safe. At least Millie was the only one who needed the comb-through.

"Can we still go to the carol-sing tonight?" Millie asked.

"Sure. Why not?"

"Because I got sent home from school. Doesn't that mean I'm sick?"

"No, baby." Charlie laughed softly. "Lice doesn't make you sick. It just makes you itchy."

"Why?"

"I really don't know. It just does."

The front door opened. Charlotte and Caleb. She had just picked him up from his guitar lesson. Will would still be at the hardware store, working. Caleb's footsteps pounded upstairs to the attic room he shared with his brothers, while Charlotte's slightly softer tread came towards the kitchen. She stopped in the doorway, both hands instantly going to her red, pixie-short hair.

"Not again."

"Again. You'd best stick to your room until I get the house vacuumed."

Charlotte started to back away, but stopped.

"Already shampooed?" she asked.

"Just combing it through."

"I'll finish. You go do the other stuff."

"You sure?"

"Come on, Daddy. I'm only around until the end of January. Take advantage of the help while you've got it."

"Thanks, Char." He handed the comb to his eldest daughter, kissed her cheek. "You're the best."

"I know."

Charlie got the vacuum out of the hall closet, for once grateful the house was small. He could hear his daughters in the kitchen, practicing Christmas carols for the evening's event—Millie's, high and sweet, Charlotte's lower and out of tune. His oldest daughter would come to the Green to help him with the twins, not because she wanted to, but because he needed her to. Halloween was more her thing. Not a single Hunter Moon passed without five pairs of shoes being set outside in hopes of being the lucky one to find theirs full of pebbles in the morning. After Gina left, his oldest daughter forgot to put the shoes outside on the full moon in October, but she did a lot of things she wouldn't have before— like comb lice eggs from her little sister's hair.

The vacuum's roar drowned out their voices. For the next hour, he cleaned. It took him only half that time to shower, wash his hair with the de-lousing solution, and get dressed again. Trotting down the steps, he smelled the sausage and peppers he had earlier prepared, already cooking.

"Thanks, baby."

His daughter barely looked up from the smartphone in her hand, her long and graceful fingers flying through a text. Charlie pulled the steaming pan from the oven and set it on top of the stove. Another ten minutes, to give it that crisp the kids expected. Gina had given him a few good tips before packing up her life and flying south. The secret to her sausage and peppers had been essential.

"Yours is better."

Charlie straightened and closed the oven door. "How so?"

"Mom always put too much garlic."

"She's Italian. I don't think there is any such thing as too much garlic for her."

Charlotte tried hard not to smile, but she cracked.

"You're a really good cook, Dad. And not because you don't just open a jar of sauce and splash it on boxed pasta. I'm really impressed with what you put on the table."

"It's because you're used to the cafeteria food at college."

"It's because you care. Anyone can put food on the table."

Another last lesson from Gina—there was food, and there was food. Taking the time to prepare something more than simply edible made people feel loved, cherished. Charlie had wanted the kids to keep that feeling after she was gone, even if they never consciously recognized it like his eldest had.

"I like to cook," he said. "But your mom is a tough act to follow."

Charlotte turned away, though not before rolling her eyes.

"Look, baby——"

Charlotte slammed the table. "Goddammit, Dad, look at me. I'm two years older than you were when you had me. I'm not a baby."

Charlie took a deep breath, tried to remember what the counselor said about kids over-reacting to one thing because it was really about another, one they didn't want to deal with.

"Charlotte," he said gently. "You will always be my baby. I'll never look at you that I don't, for a split second, see the infant in pink frills, the toddler I helped walk, or the little girl I taught to ride a bike. But I'll try."

She looked away, fiddled with her phone. "I'm sorry. I shouldn't have popped off like a stupid baby. It was dumb."

"I suppose I can forgive you, considering you combed lice out of your sister's hair."

Charlotte chuckled. "Why is it always Millie?"

"I have no idea. Call her and your brothers. Dinner's on the table in five."

His eldest left the kitchen, shouting for her siblings. Charlie took the hot pan out of the oven and started slicing bread. Worse than Tony and Millie, who he had worried about most, Charlotte's anger over her mother's leaving lingered the longest. Even Will, who vowed to never see her again, had mellowed. How would any of them feel if they knew, once his ego got over the sting of her affair, Charlie had been all for the divorce itself? It was the thought losing his kids he could not handle. To see them only every other weekend and two weeks a year? He couldn't do it. Gina had made a difficult decision, after more than half her life mothering, to follow love to Florida. Charlie didn't know how she did it, but he cried like a kid when she didn't contest his request for full custody, as long as he sent them to her over summer break, and every other Christmas. He had not done either, yet. The kids had refused. Gina let it slide, she said, to let them get used to things.

The real reason was that Gina and Bertie's house on the beach was way too small to house five kids. This summer would be different, though. His in-laws had finally forgiven Gina enough to see her. She was spending Christmas with them. If all went well, he'd put the kids on a plane as soon as school was out for the summer, and they'd spend it with their mother at their grandparents' house. She would see her children for the first time in over a year, and he would be alone in Bitterly for the first time in his life. A week ago, that thought had hollowed his stomach. Today, thoughts of Johanna Coco still popping up at random in his head, it brought an only-slightly-guilty smile to Charlie McCallan's lips.

* * * *

Luminaries lined the barely shoveled sidewalks. The street had not been plowed after the last snowfall to allow for the horse-drawn sleigh rides usually turned into hayrides for the lack of it. Strings of white lights lit up the trees erected along the length of the Green. The clomping of hooves and jingle of bells rang a constant harmony. Bitterly-town was a Christmas card, painted by Norman Rockwell, and already, groups were singing.

Charlie stood in line with Millie and Tony, gazing at the spectacular, drawn into the familiarity and the joy of this town he loved. He never understood the disdain his wife—ex-wife—had for Bitterly.

Probably reason one why we're not still married.

Charlie let his thought end there—it would lead to no place good—and instead hoped the twins got their turn before the caroling started. People came from several towns around for the annual sleigh-ride and carol-sing. There were more in attendance than in years previous. He and the kids had already been in line an hour.

"Here you go." Charlotte returned bearing hot chocolate, handing them around.

"Thanks," the twins chorused, using mittened fingers to flip the sip-lid that left brown stains behind.

"Do you mind if I go back to the coffee shop?" Charlotte leaned in to ask. "A few friends from high school are hanging out."

"Not at all. Go. You want me to come find you when we're done here?"

"Or you can use your cell."

Charlie laughed. "Right. I'll call you."

"Text. Dork."

He laughed. "Fine, I'll text you. Have fun."

Charlotte kissed her little brother and sister, cackling madly as they squealed and wiped their cheeks. She trotted across the street and back into the brightly lit coffee shop where she had worked during high school. Once inside, she pulled off her cap and mussed her hair into spikes.

Charlie sipped at whatever it was passing for hot chocolate in his cup just as the sleigh came whooshing by. The scent of chocolate, the phantom taste of Johanna's ambrosia a few mornings ago, and the sound of her laughter hit him all at once. He looked up in time to see her in the sleigh, arms raised over her head, whooping as if she were on a roller coaster.

Charlie's gaze followed her sleigh down the Green, and up again. He counted the people still ahead of him, the number of sleighs loading and unloading.

"You want to go ahead of us?" he said to the mother and her three kids behind him. "We have to finish our chocolate."

"You sure?"

"Go right ahead."

"Daddy," Tony whined as the family moved around them and into the next sleigh. "We could have gone. Everyone else has their hot chocolate on the sleigh."

"It's ok, Ton. We'll get the next one. Hey," Charlie pointed, "Isn't that your friend Henry?

"Where?"

"On the sleigh coming up, right there."

Tony and Millie craned their necks. His daughter scowled but his son waved a hand over his head. The sleigh carrying Henry, Gio, Ian, Julietta, some guy he didn't recognize, and Johanna slid to a stop. Tony ran to greet his friend, his booted feet clumsy and sliding out from underneath him.

"Ho, there, little man." The gentleman Charlie didn't recognize scooped Tony up just as he was about to slide under the sleigh. "Careful."

"That's my friend," Henry said. "Tony McCallan."

"Pleased to meet you, Tony. I'm Efan."

Efan offered his hand, man to man. Tony grasped it, pumping enthusiastically. "Thanks. I almost slid into horse poop."

"That would have been unfortunate." Efan let go of Tony's hand to turn back to the sleigh. He offered his hand to Julietta with a chivalrous bow. "My lady?"

"Why thank you, kind sir."

"'Tis my pleasure to assist a'wan so fair."

"Move it along, you two." Johanna nudged her sister from behind. Julietta stumbled forward and into Efan's arms. Charlie noted that he did not let go of her, but held her even closer.

"Our turn," Millie shouted, jumping up and down. Charlie offered his hand to Johanna. He, however, let go the moment her feet touched the ground.

"Thanks, Dan." She waved to the driver.

Charlie hadn't even noticed his friend sitting there. He murmured, "Hey, Dan."

"Nice night for this, eh, Charles?"

"I can't remember a better one."

"Because there has never been one. That's what we were just saying, weren't we Jo?"

"Hey"—Millie pointed—"he called her Joe too." Millie turned to Johanna. "Why does everyone call you a boy's name?"

"Only people I knew when I was little. Jo, like Johanna. See? Like people call you Millie, but your name is Camellia."

"How did you know my whole name? No one ever calls me it, unless I'm in trouble."

Johanna's eyes flicked to Charlie. "I've known your daddy and mommy a long time. I remember when you were born."

"You do?"

"Very, very well."

"Can Henry come with us?" Tony pushed between Charlie and Johanna. "Please?"

"He already had his turn," Johanna began, but Dan waved him back in—which naturally led to Gio and Ian both begging another turn.

"Climb on in, boys," Dan laughed. "I'll need at least one adult, though."

"We'll go." Julietta leapt back into the sleigh. Johanna opened her mouth as Efan climbed in behind her, but closed it again. After the sleigh pulled away with a whoosh and a jingle, she said, "I didn't have the heart to tell her to give you a turn."

"I wouldn't have had the heart to take it." He held up his now-cold cup of hot chocolate. "I can't drink this stuff anymore."

Johanna wrinkled her nose. Even in winter, she had a faint spattering of summer freckles across the bridge. "It's just so nasty."

"I never noticed before, until the other morning."

"I suppose I've ruined you for life." He laughed with her but Charlie's stomach flipped at the truth she unwittingly told. She took the cup from his hand and sniffed at it. "It doesn't even smell right."

She wore a red, fuzzy beret like a frame around her face. Stray curls peeked out there at her forehead, her left cheek. For all her wildness, Johanna Coco could have been an angel looking up at him through those heavy lashes, for the wide innocence of her eyes, the porcelain of her skin. Charlie tried to find words, any words to fill the prolonged silence.

"Who's the Brit?" he asked.

"Efan, Julietta's…friend. He's Welsh actually, but had to tone down the accent to teach here in the States."

"He teaches where?"

"The boarding school up in Great Barrington."

The familiar mischief in Johanna's smile, in her eyes, flipped Charlie's gut. He never had been able to guess what she was thinking, even when they knew one another so well they could sit for hours without saying a word. Johanna would grin that grin and anything could happen, and usually did.

"I'll be home for Christmas. You can plan on me. Please have snow and mistletoe, and presents on the tree…"

Johanna turned to the voices singing. Charlie heard them only as sound somewhere far, far away, in a place that might be Bitterly on a December night.

"I love this one." And she sang along, loudly. Sweetly. Swaying as if she waltzed. For a split moment, it was summer, and he was in the woods, his head on her tanned, flat belly, listening to her sing through the thrumming of her body.

"I'll be home for Christmas, if only in my dreams." Johanna clapped with everyone else.

Charlie did not.

"Aren't you going to sing?" she asked.

"I'd rather listen to you," came his automatic response, and Charlie blushed like the boy he had been. "I forgot what a beautiful voice you have."

"Ha! Never got me a part in the school play, though."

"Because you didn't play by the rules," he said. "The good parts always went to the kids in chorus."

"Chorus was boring."

"And Stacy Kinnigan didn't have anywhere near the voice you have."

"Stacy Kinnigan. Oh, wow. I haven't thought about her in years."

"She was here for the reunion," he told her. "She lives in Ohio now."

"Of course she does. Ohio has to be the most boring state in America."

"You've been there?"

"No." She smiled up at him. "The name is boring. Only four letters."

"What about Utah?"

"Fine. I see your point. So you're saying I should visit Ohio?"

"No. It's the most boring state in America."

"Charlie." Johanna shoved him playfully. Voices lifted in a rousing rendition of "Jingle Bells." She slid her hand through the crook of his elbow. "This is fun."

"It is." He covered her hand with his. Their joking, these gestures—it felt right. All around them, snow and song, sleigh bells and string-lights. All around them, Bitterly. Charlie saw only Johanna. "You want to have dinner with me tomorrow night?" he asked, and again the blush too many times creeping up on him this evening burned. He held her gaze and his breath. Johanna looked up at him. Her angelic face changed from girl to woman but otherwise, exactly the same. "I'd love to, Charlie. It's about time we caught up."

"Yeah, it is."

"What time?"

"How's seven? Too early? Too late?"

"Seven is perfect."

"Jingle Bells" had degenerated into "Batman Smells." The band switched songs. "Silent Night." Voices hushed and rose into the clear night. Johanna sang, softly this time, her head coming to rest against the arm she held.

Charlie fixed it all in his head, the perfection of this evening, like a snapshot lodged inside. If she vanished again for another eight years, he'd have it to pull out, to remember, to cherish. And if she didn't vanish— Charlie's throat constricted. His skin prickled and his body warmed—if she didn't, he would be able to look back on this moment as the beginning of the best part of his life.

Chapter 4

Nine Ladies Dancing

*Does she know her fingers travel? That they brush
unconsciously? Against that thing she hides? The thing
that belonged to Florentina—new-wife, on her way to
America? To Fiorenza—maiden aunt, teaching rich
young women in New York City? To Fia—dancer, dead
before her time? And to Fabrizzia—inventor, brought to
America to work with a famous man, his love for her
a secret he took to his grave? She doesn't, of course.
Always a creature of impulse, of emotion first and
thought when convenient. My wild girl. My Johanna.
The story changes, but the wish remains constant. A
secret kept. Unclaimed. And waiting.*

* * * *

Johanna rearranged all the ingredients on the counter. Again. She had
enough sugar, flour, chocolate chips, butter and brown sugar to fuel CC's
for a month. But did she have enough eggs? Reaching for her phone, the
locket still hidden under her shirt tickled against her skin. She pressed a
hand to it, to the fluttering there.

"Relax," she told herself. "It's just baking with your sister's kids."

And Charlie's.

She feared saying his name aloud, as if to do so would curse whatever
was happening between them. Their date—not dinner with a friend—
had been the kind of magical Johanna thought existed only in schmaltzy
movies. They were easy together. Natural. As if they'd been together all
those years yet still barely knew one another and had all the time in the
world to learn.

She dialed Emma's number, hung up again and hurried through the big house, to the front porch where her nephews were already stomping snow from their shoes. The six dozen eggs in a bowl on the counter would have to be enough.

"It smells like Christmas in here." Emma kissed both Johanna's cheeks.

"Did you start already?"

"Just a cinnamon bundt to nibble on while we wait for cookies. It's still warm."

"The same one you sent up last Easter?"

Johanna nodded.

"Move aside, boys. Mama wants some cake."

Johanna helped the boys off with their coats and hung them on the hooks behind the door. "Leave your shoes outside," she said. "Then the snow won't melt and make them all soggy."

"Can I have some cake, too, Aunt Jo?" Ian asked.

Johanna ruffled his dark hair. "As long as your mom says okay."

"Thanks."

And off he ran through the house he obviously felt at home in. Henry was right behind him, already calling for his mother's permission. Little Gio, only five and often left behind, was still trying to pull off his snow boots.

"Want some help?" she asked. He looked up and nodded, his lip trembling. Johanna consoled him. "Don't worry, there's plenty of cake. Your brothers won't eat it all."

Gio dissolved into tears. Johanna gathered him in and he buried his little face in her shoulder.

"Hey, buddy. What's wrong?"

"I miss Gram."

Johanna felt her own tears build. Since her dinner with Charlie, she'd barely thought about her grandmother, and the real reason she was in Bitterly. Gram had raised her, but the eight years being away took her out of Johanna's everyday. For Gio, his brothers, Emma and Julietta, her death was not just sorrowful, it was earth-shattering.

"I miss her too, buddy. We all do. But it's going to be okay. You have your mom and dad, your brothers, and your aunties who love you so much. And don't forget your dad's parents, and your Uncle Scott. Lots of little boys don't have so much family nearby."

Gio sniffed. He raised his head. "Mommy told me Gram was her gramma, too."

"That's right."

"Yours too?"

"Yep. Mine too. And Aunt Nina's and Aunt Julietta's. She was your great-grandmother."

He smiled then. "She was great."

"Yes, she was." Johanna hugged him closer. Gio, still young enough to enjoy shows of affection, snuggled into her.

"Aunt Jo?"

"Hmm?"

"If Gram was your gramma, who was your mommy?"

She tried not to stiffen, but failed for a split moment she could not take back. Her nephew didn't seem to notice. Johanna told him, "My mommy died a long time ago, buddy." *I think.* "But I have a picture of her. Would you like to see?"

He nodded. Johanna looked over her shoulder. She could hear Emma and Nina in the kitchen with the boys. Julietta was still in her office, working. Pulling the locket out of her shirt, Johanna clicked it open.

"See? That's her. Carolina. She's your mommy's mommy."

Gio picked up his head, looked closely. "She looks like you."

Johanna laughed. "I look like her," she said. "Your mom does too, a little. Don't you think?"

"My mom?" Gio scrunched up his face. "My mom looks like my mom."

"You're right. She does. You feeling better now?"

"A little."

"You want some cake?"

He smiled.

"Go on." She nudged him and he took off down the hallway to the kitchen. Johanna groaned to her feet. All these days keeping the locket to herself was about to be revealed, and she still wasn't ready to share it with them. Soon. Not yet. But when she reached the kitchen, Gio was face-deep in a piece of cake and her sisters barely acknowledged her arrival. More stomping on the porch sent Johanna back down the hall. Charlie's kids came barreling in, Charlotte bringing up the rear.

"Hey, Johanna." She slid her scarf from her neck. "Remember me?"

"Of course I do, Charlotte. You've grown a bit."

"Just a bit." She laughed. "You look exactly the same way I remember you."

"Do I?"

Charlotte nodded. "Dad's right. You're as pretty as a pixie."

"That's enough out of you, young lady." Charlie gently shoved Millie and Tony into Charlotte, who winked at Johanna and took them to the kitchen. Johanna pressed hands to her face. Pretty? Her eyes were too big and her chin, too small. At least her nose was properly proportioned even if it was perpetually freckled. She took Charlie's coat from him and hung it on a hook.

"Did you really say that to her or is she teasing me?"

"She's teasing me. But what if I did?"

"I'd say thank you."

"Then you're welcome," he said. "Will's still at work, but he's going to come by around four, if it's okay."

"Of course. If anyone can manage to eat later, we'll order from D'Angelo's. Cookies and pizza, Julietta will be in heaven."

She gestured him ahead of her, admiring the sway of his shoulders the way a man might a woman's hips, and those she admired as well. Johanna let the chills shiver along her skin instead of rubbing them away.

"The skinny kid sure did fill out nicely, didn't he?"

Johanna spun, hand to her chest. "Emma, I thought you were in the kitchen."

"Look at you blush."

"I'm not blushing."

"He does have a nice butt. Not as nice as Mike's though."

"Mike's ass is mighty fine." Johanna tweaked her sister's side. "I always thought so."

"Johanna!"

"Oh, now who's blushing?"

Emma poked her back, and then they were laughing instead of squealing, heading down the hallway to the warm and bright kitchen where all the children stood at the counter, just as Johanna imagined.

She stopped short. Her vision blurred. She blinked. A sensation like joy, like fear, wriggled through her. Already, Charlotte was inspecting little hands to make sure they were clean. Johanna remembered Charlie telling her his eldest was studying for a degree in early child development. She was tall and thin, just as her father had been at her age, but elfin in a way fair, redheaded girls made beautiful. Charlie had not been elfin. Even skinny, his features were bold. He'd grown into those features to make the handsome man standing in her kitchen, surrounded by children that were his and not hers, but for whom she already felt affection.

"Everyone ready to bake?"

"Yeah!" A chorus of small voices, and a few older ones. Caleb stood closer to his father, trying not to seem too eager.

"Charlotte, if you wouldn't mind starting the little ones measuring out the flour and sugar, I have a special task for Caleb."

"Sure, Johanna."

Johanna took Caleb's hand and led him to the oven. Already gathered on the counter were milk, butter, cocoa and sugar.

"What do you want me to do?" Caleb asked. Johanna put a big stockpot on the burner.

"Learn how to make real hot chocolate," Johanna answered, "so you never have to drink that crap out of an envelope again."

* * * *

By the time the second batch of chocolate chip cookies came out of the oven, Gunner had arrived, and Johanna had lost most of her help. Full bellies made for sleepy children. Emma took them into the family room to watch Christmas specials. Julietta came down, rolled a few cookies, ladled herself a mug of hot chocolate and went back up to her office to work. She had a deadline she was going to miss if she didn't get the research in to the agency by five o'clock. Julietta had never missed a deadline.

Nina and Gunner sat with Emma and Charlie at the dining room table, nibbling cookies and chatting. Soon, Mike would arrive just long enough to say hello and whisk his family to his parents' house for the traditional English Christmas dinner, complete with roast goose and a viewing of whatever incarnation of *A Christmas Carol* Emma deemed appropriate for the children.

Only Charlotte remained in the kitchen with her, which suited Johanna just fine. The dreamy-vision of baking with children hadn't quite lived up to expectations. Working with Charlotte was more like working with a colleague.

How young Charlie and Gina had been when their first child was born. How frightening it must have been.

The cookies were all done and waiting to be decorated. They had moved on to the pies for Christmas Day. Two apple already cooled on the counter. Two cherry baked in the oven. Two pecan awaited their turn.

"Did I see you put honey into the crust?" Johanna stood at Charlotte's elbow, watching her press the graham-cracker crust into another pie tin for the pumpkin that would come next.

"I did. It gives the crust a nice chew. Is that okay?"

"I don't know. I've never done it before, myself."

"It's how my mom taught me." Charlotte averted her eyes. "Whatever her faults, she is a really good cook."

"Must run in the family," Johanna said. "Even Gram had to admit your grandmother's meatballs were better than hers. I was sorry to hear your grandparents sold the pizzeria."

Charlotte shrugged. "They got old, and Mom had no interest. Neither did my uncles."

"Frankie and Aldo."

"You know them?"

"You forget I grew up in this town. You know how it is. Everyone knows everyone."

"True." Charlotte shrugged again. "They're all in Florida now. My uncles. My grandparents. My mom and her boyfriend. I fucking hate Florida."

Johanna's heart stitched. The need to hide the hurt behind anger was a familiar one. "Florida has some pretty places left."

"Not where they live. I wish they lived in Key West, or someplace actually cool. Then maybe I'd visit. It's not like my grandmother ever liked me much."

"Why would you say that?"

Yet another shrug. "I'm the thing that ruined her daughter's life," she said. "The child conceived out of wedlock. As if it matters anymore."

"It did back then, to some. But she's your grandmother. I remember how she showed you off to everyone when you were a baby."

"I stopped being a cute little baby and grew a mouth." Charlotte snickered. "Whatever. It doesn't matter."

Of course, it matters, Johanna wanted to say, but she handed Charlotte the measuring cup she was reaching for and told her, "You have a real flair for this."

"I love to bake," Charlotte said. "It's funny, I never did before, and I worked in the coffeehouse all through high school. Then I went away to college and suddenly, I'm constantly baking cookies and cupcakes. My dorm is the most popular on campus, mostly because it is now known as a free bakery."

"I bought CC's on a whim." Johanna's hesitation gave way to Charlotte's honesty. "It was the name, really, that sold me."

Charlotte looked up from pressing graham cracker crumbs. "Cape Confectionery?"

"CC's," Johanna said. "Carolina Coco. My mother's initials."

"Oh, I get it. How cool is that?"

Johanna's hammering heart eased. Perhaps it was obvious, and maybe her sisters had guessed long ago, but Charlotte was the first person she'd ever told her secret to, and she felt better for it. "I don't know how or why but as it turned out, I'm actually good at baking. Better than good, like you are."

"We make a good team."

Johanna gave her a quick squeeze. "We do. You know, if you're looking for a summer job, I can always use—"

"Yes!" Charlotte laughed when Johanna did. "Sorry. I got a little enthusiastic there. Do you mean it? Can I come work for you?"

A passing thought for Gina and the custody agreement Charlie told her about flitted in and back out of Johanna's mind. Charlotte was twenty, and no longer required to visit the mother she was obviously still angry with. "Consider yourself hired."

Charlotte hugged Johanna tight and quickly. "I can't believe it. I have to text Katie. Johanna, you're the best. I love you Coco women. You're all so cool." Charlotte blew past her father just coming through the doorway.

Charlie leapt out of the way, shaking his head. "What's got my daughter squealing like a teenager?"

"I just hired her for the summer."

Charlie's eyebrows shot up. "You did, huh?"

"It just sort of happened. You okay with it?"

He was silent for a moment. "She's a grown woman. She can do what she wants with her summer."

"Gina's not going to be happy."

Leaning over the counter, his elbows sending up puffs of flour, he said, "Charlotte wasn't going anyway. Even if she would have, it wouldn't be for the whole summer. Same with Will. He's already started hedging."

"But Gina can make him, no?"

"She can, but she won't. Gina made her choice. She knew what it meant when she made it. That's between her and her children."

"You're good, not to speak badly of her."

"Why would I? I'm sad for the kids, but I'm not sorry we divorced. Gina and I tried, but we just didn't work. Not from day one."

Johanna leaned back on the stove handle, her hands gripping it to keep from reaching for her locket. So many summers ago, she thought Charlie McCallan was the happily-ever-after she never wanted. Her own parents and their furious love ending so tragically convinced her she didn't want or need anything of the kind. Growing up, Johanna had few crushes that lasted more than a kiss, a fact she took pride in. Until the summer of her junior year. Until the skinny, ghost-pale kid whose parents took care of the local cemetery became the young man who made Johanna Coco's heart dance.

"I guess I should have seen something like this coming," Charlie was saying.

"Hmm…what?"

"Charlotte. I hoped by letting the kids out of Christmas in Florida would help Charlotte get over her anger. I guess it won't."

Johanna cleared her mind with a shake of her head. "She will, eventually. Gina is her mother. The only one she's got."

"That's what I keep telling her." Charlie straightened, dusted off his elbows. "I hope you know what you're getting yourself into. My daughter is…energetic."

"I prefer enthusiastic." Johanna looked past him to where the young woman still texted with her friend. "She really does have a gift for baking. It takes creativity, as well as a scientific mind. Baking is all about chemistry."

"Then how the hell did you become a baker." Charlie laughed. "You nearly blew up Mr. Ganatick's lab, remember?"

"Oh, wow. I do remember. The smell."

"Like rotten eggs and hair spray."

"Well,"—Johanna tossed her hair dramatically—"a woman can't be pretty as a pixie and brilliant."

"Sure she can." He moved to her side of the counter.

Backed up against the stove, Johanna had no place to go even if she wanted to. She looked up at him suddenly so close.

Charlie brushed flour or sugar from her face. "I've always known you were both."

"I—" She cleared her throat. "I never did well in school."

"That doesn't mean you're not brilliant."

"Not like Julietta."

"No, not like Julietta," he said. "Yours is a different kind of brilliance. The being able to light up a room just by walking into it kind. The charming a passing grade from a teacher who should have failed you kind. The buying a bakery on a whim and making it not just profitable, but a local treasure kind."

"How did you…"

"I know how the Internet works, Jo." He moved a little closer. "I looked it up. 'CC's in Cape May, New Jersey.'" Closer. "'Proprietress, Johanna Elsbet Coco.'" Charlie tipped her face up with one, thick finger. Johanna closed her eyes, closed off the world. Charlie whispered against her lips, "Best known for her chocolate mud cookies and—"

The door slammed, startling them apart. Johanna's heart hammered. Charlie was already lunging for the door. "Will," he shouted. "William James."

"Dad, what is it? What's wrong?" Charlotte stood in the doorway between dining room and kitchen, cell phone in hand and looking from her father to Johanna. "Oh," she said. "Maybe I should go after him."

"Let him go." Charlie pushed fingers through his hair. "We should probably head home anyway."

Johanna's racing heart stuttered, but she did not argue. He called his kids who groaned and complained but did as they were told. As he was helping them on with their snow clothes, Mike arrived to say, 'Merry Christmas,' swipe some cookies and hustle his wife and sons out the door. From joyful bliss to an almost-kiss to alone in fifteen minutes flat. Johanna leaned against the door.

"What happened?" Nina asked, coming down the hall.

"Charlie's son saw him about to kiss me and took off."

"Oh." Nina grimaced, and then she smiled. "Oh!"

"About to." Johanna sighed. "He didn't quite get there."

"It's only a matter of time."

"Maybe it's better if he doesn't."

Nina put her arm around her shoulders, jostled her. "I never thought you, of all people, would give up on something you want so badly."

"You might be laying it on a little thick, don't you think?"

"Are you honestly going to try to convince me you don't want Charlie McCallan?"

Johanna slumped, deflated and discovered. "It's only been a few days, Nina."

"Jo." Nina threw up her arms. "It has been twenty years. Do you really think we all don't know he broke your heart? That you stay away from Bitterly because of him?"

"Not only because of him." Johanna smiled despite herself. "I didn't think I was so obvious."

"Darling, there is nothing subtle about you and never has been."

Johanna leaned into her sister, whose arms came around her. Nina kissed the top of her head. "I know the other reasons you haven't come home. We all know about that too."

"They're like ghosts I can't escape here," Johanna said. "I think I brought them with me from New Hampshire."

"They didn't die in the fire, Jo. You know they didn't."

"They died for me. And for you. It's the last time we saw them."

"That's probably a good thing. At least we had weird but loving parents. They got so much worse after we got taken away."

"Poor Emma and Julietta. What do you think life was like for them?"

"We'll probably never know. They were both so small when Gram brought them home."

"When Gram brought who home?"

The sisters spun to see Julietta coming down the stairs, mug and cookie plate in hand.

"Those kittens we had," Nina said. "Remember them?"

"Sugar and Spice." Julietta made a face. "Why would you be talking about them?"

"I'm thinking of getting a pair of cats for the bakery," Johanna lied. "Did you make your deadline?"

"Of course. It's so quiet down here." Julietta looked beyond her sisters. "Where did everyone go?"

"Mike came for Emma and the boys," Nina answered. "And Charlie and his kids had to go."

Julietta grimaced. She looked at her watch. "Can we still get pizza?"

* * * *

His son still hadn't looked at him. Will spent his teenage years avoiding eye contact, but Charlie remembered when he was a little boy shy of strangers, yet with an intense curiosity that made asking questions a constant. Will never really liked cartoons, but would sit for hours watching a documentary about dinosaurs, or how telescopes were made. Sitting in the family room with his son now, knowing Charlotte was in the kitchen eavesdropping, Charlie missed the little boy he was and the simplicity of it all back then.

"I'm sorry, Dad." Words fell out of Will's mouth like water rushing down a mountain. "I don't know why I got so mad. I wasn't...it just didn't occur to me that you'd ever want..."

"Another woman?"

Will nodded.

"I'm only thirty-eight, son. Your mom didn't die. She left me for another man."

"She left us!" Another long exhale. "Sorry. This is just hard, you know?"

"Yeah."

"I ruined your big moment back there."

"A little bit." Charlie laughed. "I've done my share of ruining things with Johanna."

"She was your girlfriend before Mom, right?"

"Yup."

"Why'd you break up?"

Charlie's chest tightened. *Because I was an idiot. Because sometimes you make mistakes, son, and there's only doing what's right.* "Just a high school thing that didn't work out," he lied.

"I guess you can say the same about you and mom."

"I guess you can. We tried though. And we got you kids. No regrets, kiddo."

Will's eyebrow quirked, but he met Charlie's gaze and, slapping hands to his knees, got to his feet.

"Since I ruined pizza at the Coco's, I'll take care of dinner."

"That's not necessary, son."

"It's no big deal to call for takeout." He smiled and they laughed together as they hadn't in a long time. "Chinese okay? I'm kind of tired of pizza."

"Sounds good. Don't forget egg-drop soup for Millie."

He headed for the kitchen. "Hey, Dad?"

"Yeah?"

"Johanna gave me and Caleb twenty bucks each the other day for shoveling."

"I know. Caleb already told me."

"Snitch."

"You know he is. Thanks for telling me."

"Yeah, whatever."

Charlie sat in the quiet family room, listening to the distant noises in the rest of the house: Will on the phone with the Chinese take-out place, Caleb and Tony playing video games in their attic room, Millie singing to whatever dolls hadn't been wrapped up in plastic garbage bags and quarantined out in the garage. The boys never complained about sharing the big attic room. When Charlotte left for college and told Will he could borrow hers while she was gone, he hadn't taken her up on it.

Your room is too girlie.

But Charlie knew better. Since Gina left, his kids stuck together as ferociously as the Coco girls always had.

He knew little about their parents, only that Nina and Johanna arrived in Bitterly years before Emma and Julietta did. Something about a car crash and a psychiatric ward escape. He thought there was a fire in there someplace too. Or it could have all been gossip the small town thrived upon. Over the years, he did figure out that Adelina and Giovanni Coco must have adopted the girls officially. Though they all had the same parents, they bore their mother's last name. At least, it was what he decided during those years after Johanna left Bitterly, fantasizing about her when life as an eighteen-year-old father and husband got to be so hard.

"Hey, Daddy."

Charlotte's soft voice didn't startle him, but chased his thoughts away nonetheless. She sat down on the sofa beside him, put her head upon his shoulder.

"You okay?"

"Why wouldn't I be?"

"You looked so sad when I came in."

"I was just thinking."

"About Johanna?"

He nodded. "I really like her, Daddy."

"So do I."

"I don't think we like her in the same way." Charlotte nudged him. "You okay with me going to work for her this summer?"

"You don't need my permission."

"I wasn't asking it. I just asked if you were okay with it."

He put his arm around his daughter, kissed the top of her head. "You're going to have to see your mother sometime."

"No I don't."

"Char, she's your mother. And she loves you."

"But she loves Bertie more."

"It's not like that—"

Charlotte sat forward. She turned to face him. "I don't want to talk about mom. And why are you always defending her? But I don't want to talk about her. Okay? Let's just go back to talking about you and Jo and how you're going to go over there and make something magical happen for her on Christmas Eve."

Charlie sighed. "Is that what we were talking about?"

"We were getting there."

"What do you suggest I do?"

"I don't know. Sing outside her window?"

"You've heard me sing, Charlotte."

"True. How about...oh."

"Oh, what?"

"I have the perfect thing." Charlotte bounced on the sofa, clapping her hands like a little girl. "What's Dan Greene's phone number?"

* * * *

She had such different visions for the evening. After a day of baking cookies, and an evening of pizza, more cookies, and Christmas specials with the kids, Charlotte would have taken her siblings home, leaving Charlie to watch *It's a Wonderful Life* with her, her sisters, and their men. As it turned out, after yet more pizza and the beer Gunner brought with him, he and Nina curled up on one sofa, Julietta and Efan lounged on the floor, and Johanna sat with a pillow hugged to her chest, feeling like the fifth wheel on a hay-wagon.

She tried not to sulk. Until coming home for her grandmother's funeral, Johanna had spent years actively avoiding Charlie McCallan. He hadn't exactly ditched her this time. Will had gotten upset seeing his father about to kiss someone who wasn't his mother. He had to come first. She'd have been disappointed in Charlie if he brushed off his son's feelings for the sake of a kiss. Every rational bit of brain matter told her it was childish to pout, but Johanna found herself doing so anyway.

"Will you quit it?"

Johanna glanced down at her sister on the floor. She and Efan sat foot-to-foot, the only contact between them her plaid Christmas socks and his black ones.

"Me?"

"Yes, you."

"What did I do?"

Julietta threw herself back against the pillows stacked behind her, sighing dramatically.

"I am not doing that."

"You're not as loud," Gunner said. "But you are doing a lot of sighing over there. Sounds like a tire leaking."

Efan and Julietta snorted, then laughed at one another. On the screen, Donna Reed and Jimmy Stewart were dancing the Charleston.

"What is it about this house that turns otherwise mature adults into children?" Nina scolded, but snorted in her effort not to laugh. "You know, Jo, you could go over to his house. He's probably sighing like a leaky tire over there, too."

"Now who's being childish? I'm going to bed."

Tossing the pillow at Julietta, who caught it and put it behind her head, Johanna pushed out of the sofa and headed for the stairs. At the front door, she hesitated. Her boots sat on the rack. Her coat hung on a hook. The keys to Gram's old Explorer were still in the brass bowl on the breakfront. She picked them up. Gripped them in her hand. Her belly fluttered.

Johanna touched fingers to the place and found the locket beneath her shirt. Static sparked, nicking her fingers and coursing up to her scalp. For a split moment, she smelled summer. Hot air. The woods. The stream there. And it was gone.

She opened her eyes, only then realizing they'd been closed, and found herself outside beside the old Explorer, keys in hand. She looked to the house. Back to the SUV. When had she put on a coat, or stuffed her bare feet into fuzzy boots? She even wore mittens and a hat. A scarf wound 'round her neck.

"Damn..."

She leaned against the car door, staring at the keys. This was all too much. Being home, facing ghosts she'd been successfully avoiding for years, Gram's death, finding the locket. And Charlie. After so many years, Charlie McCallan. Johanna bowed her head and took deep breaths, wishing for something of summer to make her promises she was too afraid to ask for.

The jingling of bells picked up her head. The sound got louder, now accompanied by hoof beats on pavement. Johanna started towards the road. A carriage and two came to a stop at the foot of the driveway.

"Merry Christmas, Jo."

"Hey, Dan." She glanced to the passenger in the carriage bed. Bundled against the cold, there was still no mistaking him, or the summer scents suddenly rushing at her. "Hey, Charlie," she managed to say. "You gentlemen out for a night on the town, Colonial style?"

"My sister and her kids are home waiting for me to play Santa," Dan answered. He gestured over his shoulder. "He's the only one I'd do this for, on Christmas Eve, no less. But when Charlie McCallan says he needs a favor, there's not one person in this town who'd say no. Not even grouchy-me."

"When have you ever been grouchy, Daniel?"

"Daniel, huh? When my sister calls me Daniel, it means trouble."

"Am I going to get a word or two into my attempt to sweep her off her feet, Dan?"

"Oh, yeah. Sorry. Forget I'm here. I'm invisible. A deaf-mute. Honest."

"You're still talking."

Dan motioned a zipper across his lips, his eyes going skyward as if he would count the stars. Johanna leaned on the carriage door. "Are you here for me, then?"

"I thought a Christmas Eve carriage ride through Bitterly would be a romantic way of apologizing."

"You did, huh?"

"He's lying. It was Charlotte."

"I thought you were a deaf-mute."

"Sorry. Sorry." Another zip.

Johanna laughed softly, shaking her head. "Keep the heat in," she said as Charlie started lifting the mounds of blankets. "I can climb up myself."

"You sure?"

Johanna gripped the sides, tried to heave herself up into the carriage, but it was higher than it looked, she was very small, and her coat was too bulky. She heaved once, twice, on the third, she felt two hands pushing her up from behind.

"There you go."

"Just like in the movies," she laughed, flopping forward with the momentum of Dan's heave. "Such chivalry."

Charlie lifted the blankets and she got under them quickly. "This is not how I planned for it to go."

Johanna snuggled into him. "Nothing ever has with us, Charlie."

"True. You warm enough?"

"Mmm-hmm."

"I brought you this." He handed her a thermos as Dan slapped the reins, jerking the horses into motion. "Caleb made it. He says you taught him how."

Unscrewing the lid released chocolate-scented steam. She inhaled. "Heavenly." She poured some in the lid, sipped. "This is even better than mine."

"I imagine it's because we ran out of milk, so he used half-and-half."

"No wonder. I'll have to remember that."

The night was clear. The moon was bright and riding high. Warm as she was underneath the blankets, her face was soon near-frozen. Winding her scarf higher up on her face, she hunkered lower in the blankets. Charlie pulled her close, drew the blankets higher so only their eyes and noses peeked out.

"I guess the notion of a moonlight carriage ride on Christmas Eve is slightly more romantic in theory than it is in fact," he said, his voice muffled. "I'm sorry."

"Don't apologize. This is wonderful."

"Yeah?"

"Yeah."

His eyes were not quite green, not quite brown and staring intently into hers. Under the blanket, his warm hands worked their way under her coat to pull her closer.

"Is this okay?"

She nodded.

"Not just this." He gave her a squeeze. "But this. You and me, this. I'm not getting this out very well."

"I know what you mean," she said. "And yes, it's okay. It's better than okay."

"You have no idea how bad I want us to work out this time, Jo. Is it too soon to say that?"

"Maybe a little."

"I'm sorry."

"Please stop apologizing."

"Sorry."

"Charlie!"

They laughed softly, the sound mingling with the jingle. Johanna leaned her head against the back of the carriage seat. Her hand wormed free of the blankets. She moved the scarf from her face and pulled her mitten off with her teeth. Charlie had tugged the blanket off his face. His beard was so red, redder than his hair gone more to chestnut.

She drew him to her. Holding his face, she kissed him, not the passionate way that would lead them to bed, but the tender way of their past. Once, twice. For now, it was enough.

Charlie's eyes stayed closed. Under the blanket, his hand jerked, but he did not pull away.

"What's wrong?" she asked.

"I'm afraid to say the wrong thing, to act too fast or too slow. I don't want to scare you off again."

"Scare me off?" Again?

Charlie opened his eyes. "Like when we were kids," he said. "That Labor Day, at the beach down by the lake."

Johanna remembered. The beach, his sandy hands on her skin, their bodies sticky with sweat and the desire that led them back to their spot in the woods behind her house. Her groin twitched with the memory of almost, of should-have-been.

"I remember the day," she said. "You broke my heart."

"I didn't mean to push you. I was a kid, and crazy with wanting you."
Her hands fell slowly from his face. "You...you think you broke my
heart by wanting me?"

He shook his head. "By being like all the other boys you couldn't
stand, being the guy who just wanted in your pants."

"Didn't you?"

"Well, yeah. But our summer wasn't about playing a part until I got
sex, Jo. It was the best summer of my life. I should have told you that.
I should have told you a lot of things. Instead, I was like a stag in rut.
I didn't blame you for running away, not after the initial frustration of
it eased off. Then you wouldn't speak to me and the next thing I knew,
school started. The more you ignored me, the worse I felt. I practiced
a million different ways to apologize, to get you to like me again. By
Homecoming, I found enough courage to ask you to the school dance, but
then..." He blew out a long exhale. "You know what happened next. I got
roped into taking Gina to the dance instead. I don't think I ever forgave
Tim Grady for talking me into it. We got drunk, she got pregnant, and the
rest, as they say, is history."

Johanna could not get her mouth and brain to cooperate. She
remembered that Labor Day so clearly, right down to the intoxication of
fear mingling with desire. Charlie thought all these years that he'd been
a brute and scared her away, when in fact he'd been so tender. The way
he touched her, the way he kissed her, said all those words he believed he
should have. I love you. I want you. Forever and ever and ever. He made
her want to stay in Bitterly, to get married and have children and forget
all her plans to flee Bitterly and its ghosts. It was the wanting that made
her run.

"Oh, Charlie," she whispered at last, those tears always at her beck
and call freeing her voice. "You didn't push me away. I pushed you away.
What I felt for you frightened me, not that you wanted to make love. I
wanted to. I can't tell you how many cold showers I've had to take over
the years, remembering how much I wanted to."

"You...really?"

She nodded.

He touched his forehead to hers. "What a mess we made of things," he
said, and lifted his head. "But I wouldn't change it, Jo. Not to save either
of us heartache. I got five of the best kids who ever lived out of the deal."

"And I got the life I wanted, the life I ran away to have. Now here we
are."

"Now here we are." He lifted the blankets up higher, shielding her from the bitter air. "I should have told you then that I loved you, Johanna. I loved you so much. I love you still. I know it seems too soon, but really, it's over twenty years in the waiting. And if you don't love me yet, it's okay. I'll wait until you do."

Johanna snuggled closer. "You are so certain I will?"

"Pretty cert—"

She kissed the rest of his words from his mouth. Under the covers, she put her legs over his. He pulled her into his lap and even through all the snow-clothes, Johanna felt his desire. She wrapped her arms around his neck, kissed him until they were both breathless. The same ghosts that sent her running all those years ago whispered shivers up her spine. She lifted her head to look into his eyes, her heart flipping.

"You are not the only thing I was running from back then. You aren't the only reason I've stayed away from Bitterly."

"I know."

"There's a lot you don't know, Charlie."

"It doesn't matter."

"My parents were crazy."

"Mentally ill."

"No," she said. "Bat-shit crazy. They escaped from a mental institution not once but twice. We lived like little rats in New Hampshire. When the house burned and Gram came to—"

Charlie took her face in his hands and kissed her until she kissed him back. When she was calm, he pressed her head to his shoulder and whispered, "None of that matters. Only you matter. You and me. This night. This carriage. Dan pretending not to be listening to every word we say."

"I am not."

They laughed softly.

"I'm scared, Charlie," she said. "And I'm really tired of being scared."

"Then it's time to do something about it. For now…"

Charlie tipped her face up. He kissed her slow. He kissed her long. He kissed her until the carriage stopped in front of her grandmother's house on County Line Road. He helped her down from the carriage and walked her to the front door.

"Dan is never going to let me hear the end of this," Charlie told her.

"Then you can tell him I saw him wipe a tear or two away and he'll leave you be."

"I guess this is good-night then."

"Oh, you're not..." She blushed. "I guess you have to get home to the kids."

"Tomorrow is Christmas. Santa still has to put presents under the tree. Besides, I can't make Dan drive all the way back to town alone." He tucked a stray curl into her hat. "I'll take it as a good sign that you want me to stay."

"You didn't see me fighting you off back on the carriage, did you?"

"I kind of had you at my mercy."

"Oh, really?" Johanna tweaked his beard. "I thought I had you at mine."

"You did." He took her into his arms. "Always have. Always will."

Jingle bells interrupted another long, slow kiss. Charlie pulled away, stole another kiss, and headed back to the carriage.

"Merry Christmas," he called.

"Merry Christmas," Johanna whispered. She stood on the porch until the jingle and the clomp faded into the distance. Instead of going inside, she went to the wide expanse of snow-covered ground in front of the house. When they were kids, it would have been trampled by now. Snowmen and snow-forts would have dotted the yard. Tonight, it was pristine.

Johanna tilted her head back, gazed up at the moon, and the stars like salt sprinkled on black velvet. She turned slowly this way, then that. Humming, swaying, turning like a snowflake-sylph, a shiver raced itself through her body. And then phantom arms wrapped around her. She leaned into them, smiled, and wished.

* * * *

I see desire as snowflakes. They twirl about like a windstorm, like a breeze. It lets me remember; I was young once. I felt those stirrings, that love like no other. It kept me warm in the cold, and made the worst bearable. And the worst was so very unbearable.

She twirls in the moonlight, beneath the stars, in the snow. I twirl with her. She doesn't know. She sees no footprints mingling with hers. But she feels my arms hold her close, even if she imagines them to be his. It is me. It is me. Dancing with my girl.

Chapter 5

Eight Maids a'Milking

Christmas morning was a wind yawning across a painted sky. It was the sound of ice crystals whispering, the smell of cinnamon and butter lingering. The morning was the first of all her days ahead, and Johanna woke with a smile brought with her from dreaming.

And what dreams. Sexy dreams. Softly sensual. Sweet. Already fleeting. Johanna caught glimpses of Charlie, of summer long ago, of his kids gathered around the baking counter. She could still smell Christmas Eve's cold air, and the way her perfumed scarf tasted when she breathed through it. When the images faded completely, the feel of them left their imprint, a photo-negative pulsing behind her eyes.

Johanna dressed quickly, combed gently through her curls that would frizz wildly at the touch of a brush. Sounds of pots and pans and sisterly quarreling told her Nina and Julietta were already up and preparing their contributions to the feast. A smile twitched at Johanna's lips. She was not at all certain either of her sisters could cook. She recalled the one time Nina invited her to dinner at her apartment in Manhattan, a dinner that went from burned to take-out with a phone call. At least Julietta had proven competent at following a recipe when she came to help out in CC's a couple summers ago.

Johanna had walked into the bakery more than four years ago, in need of coffee and carbs after a day on the beach. The name hooked her, the for-sale sign attached to the front window reeled her in. The desperation to do something better than wander through her life nudged whimsy into action. Within a week, she had put in an offer. Before the month was out, Johanna Coco was elbows-deep in batter, and a resident of Cape

May, New Jersey. The boyfriend she'd been vacationing with got lost somewhere in the process. She couldn't even recall his name.

Johanna stared at herself in the mirror. Grimaced. She pulled the locket from its place under her clothes, clicked it open, and looked into the faded image of her mother's face. The curly hair. The tiny chin. The huge eyes. Even the curve of her smile. Johanna could have been looking at her own picture a decade-and-a-half-ago, but she would not see herself in her mother. If she did, she would never be able to look at herself again.

"Johanna," Julietta called up the stairs. "Where did you put the measuring cups?"

"Hang on, I'll be right down."

Johanna left the melancholy in her room, sailed down the steps and into the country kitchen. It was Christmas. She was in love. There was no room for ghosts no matter what Dickens had to say on the matter. Julietta had all her ingredients for the cranberry sauce, candied sweet potatoes, and peas with pearl onions lined up in gradient order on the counter. Every spoon she needed to stir, measure, or taste with, every bowl for mixing. The only things missing were the measuring cups that would go into the spot Julietta had left open for them.

"They're right here." Johanna pulled them out of a drawer and handed them to her sister.

"That's not where Gram kept them."

"Sorry."

"Did you use all the butter yesterday?"

"No. It's there in the bowl, on the counter."

"You didn't put it in the fridge?"

"Of course not. I always keep my butter on the counter. It's butter."

"That's disgusting."

"Come on, Jules. I run a bakery. If there was something wrong with room-temperature butter, I'd know by now."

"Well, I can't use it."

"Of course you can."

"No, I can't. Can you take me to the store?"

"On Christmas Day? Nothing's open."

Julietta looked from her ingredients, to the bowl of butter, to her sister. "Leave everything the way it is. I'm going to look it up."

"You can't take my word for it?"

"No," Julietta said, and took her laptop to the dining room table. The fury of her fingers on the keys had Johanna and Nina exchanging worried glances.

Johanna moved closer to her oldest sister. "This is odd, even for Julietta."

"Not really." Nina resumed slicing the *sopressata* Gunner had brought from Queens. "You know she's very particular."

"But this?" She pointed to the perfectly aligned ingredients and cooking utensils. "And since when is she some kind of germophobe?"

"It's not germs. It's something not being the way it always is. Gram didn't keep butter on the counter. It's as simple as it gets."

"Or measuring cups in the drawer by the sink." Johanna sighed. "I worry about her, Nina. What is she going to do without Gram? With all the changes? How will she cope?"

"Fine." Julietta returned, her laptop tucked under her arm. "I'll use the butter. But from now on, it goes back in the fridge."

"Sure thing, commandant."

While Julietta began assembling the sides and Nina sliced and arranged the antipasto, Johanna poured herself a glass of milk and grabbed some cookies from the massive pile on the counter.

So many cookies. So many pies. And Charlie had left without taking anything home. There was no way she and her sisters would eat it all, not even if all three of Emma and Mike's boys ate nothing but sweets all day. Johanna wished she'd thought to send something home with Dan last night after the carriage ride...

"Well, why not?"

"Why not what?" Nina asked.

"I'm going to bring some of the baked stuff over to Charlie and the kids. I want to drop something off to Dan Greene, too, to say thanks for the carriage ride."

"Just make sure you save a cherry pie. I've been trying not to dive into it since yesterday."

Johanna rummaged around in the mudroom for the grocery boxes her grandmother preferred to bags. She loaded up with four of the eight pies, and half the cookies, she left them in the mudroom and went back inside for her coat and the keys to the Explorer.

Nina glanced up from her finished platter just as Johanna came back through the kitchen. Her sister's eyes narrowed, focused on...

"Is that Gram's locket?"

Oh, shit.

Both sisters were on her before she could zip up her coat.

"Where did you get it?" Nina asked. "I haven't seen it in ages."

Johanna considered lying, telling them Gram gave it to her years ago, but Julietta would know better.

"I found it in her box the other night when I couldn't sleep." Zipping her coat, she scooted around her hovering sisters. "I'm just wearing it," she lied. "I missed the funeral. It makes me feel better."

"But Gram—"

"You better not have—"

"We'll talk when I get home." Johanna darted into the mudroom, grabbed the box for Charlie's family and dashed out the door. Dan would have to wait for his goodies. There was no way she was going back in where her sisters could corner her again.

The SUV didn't turn over right away, but neither of her sisters came after her. While she let it warm up, Johanna thought about Julietta's assembly of ingredients and hoped taking the locket from Gram's box didn't set her off. Her youngest sister had always been odd. Whether her particularities stemmed from a chaotic childhood, the accident, or some gene in her pool, no one could say. They made her Julietta, best-loved and strange. Johanna wouldn't change her for anything in the world, though she often wondered if Julietta felt the same.

Johanna breathed in through her nose, out through her mouth. On the seat beside her was a box full of Christmas cheer for Charlie and his kids. She breathed in their sleigh ride, breathed out her sisters' discovery, breathed in the first kiss, breathed out Julietta's future, breathed in all the kisses thereafter, and, smiling, backed out of the driveway.

* * * *

Pulling to a stop in front of Charlie's house just outside of town, Johanna tried to quell the fluttering in her belly. She had no real idea how Will felt about her and his father and their almost-kiss that had, since then, multiplied. Maybe he was still upset. She hadn't even thought to ask. At least Charlotte would be happy to see her.

And Charlie.

A thrill shuddered through her. If Will was still upset, she'd leave the goodies and head home, happy enough to have delivered what they didn't get on Christmas Eve.

She got out of the car, reached back in to pull out the box of cookies and pies. Balancing it, she closed the car door with her butt. Shouting stopped her before she got to the front door. Charlotte, and another woman. Johanna's heart sank.

The door flew open and Charlotte came barreling down the steps, nearly bowling Johanna over in the process.

"Charlotte Rose, come back here!"

"You had no right coming. Dad paid you for the house. You're trespassing."

Charlie came down the steps. The kids piled in the doorway behind him. His eyes found Johanna's. He mouthed an, *I'm sorry.* She didn't know what to do, and thus did nothing but stand like a statue.

"I have every right to see my kids." Gina kept her voice down. "It's Christmas. You are all supposed to be with me."

"Yeah, right. You couldn't even bribe Millie and Tony down with the promise of Harry Potter World. Get it into your head, Mom—no one wants you here."

"Charlotte, enough," Charlie told his daughter. Caleb had his arms around Millie and Tony, who were crying. Will stood stone-faced, his arms crossed over his chest like a shield. Gina's face was a mask but for the tears rolling down her cheeks. Then her eyes moved from one child to the next, and with each glance, she thawed just a little.

"This was a mistake," she said. "I didn't think it would be this way. I thought you'd be happy to see me."

"You thought wrong."

"I said enough, Charlotte Rose. Gina, come back inside. This is not the place to—"

Gina's shoulders went back. "I want my kids. The divorce decree says I get them every other Christmas. It's my Christmas. I can't force Charlotte but Tony, Millie, Caleb, Will, get some things. We're going to your cousin Tracy's."

Millie wailed and clung to Caleb, who held her closer to him.

"Gina," Charlie moved closer to his ex-wife. "Do you really want to do this?"

"I miss my kids," Gina wailed like her daughter and threw herself into Charlie's arms. "You have no idea what it's like to be without them. Over a year, Charlie. Millie and Tony don't even look the same."

Charlie's stricken, confused gaze met Johanna's again. She smiled wanly, and nodded, backing towards the car. An arm around his ex-wife's heaving shoulders, he led her back into the house. The kids in the doorway parted to let her in.

Charlotte remained in the driveway, her breath coming in foggy bursts, her face rage-red. "Can I come home with you?"

Johanna struggled for words, and found only, "I came to deliver these."

"Will," Charlotte called to her brother still standing in the doorway. "Can you take this?"

Will trundled down the steps. He took the box from Johanna's arms. "Merry Fucking Christmas, huh?"

Johanna tried to find some quippy answer but the tears too-near brimming stopped her cold. "You want to come too?" she asked.

"Nah," he answered. "But thanks."

"He has no choice," Charlotte said. "But I do, and I don't want to be here. Do you mind, Jo?"

"I—"

"Tell dad I went to the Coco's," Charlotte called to her brother and hauled Johanna in her wake. Though younger, she was bigger by several inches and a few pounds. Johanna was no match for her strength or her barely contained fury. Charlotte climbed into the passenger seat of the Explorer, pulled out her cell and started texting.

"You sure you want to leave?" Johanna turned over the ignition, flicked on the heat. She felt a little sorry for Gina, but she was a grown woman and had made her choices. Millie and Tony, Caleb and Will—Johanna's heart broke for them. She could only imagine their confusion. They had to miss their mother, no matter how loyal they were to Charlie. Charlotte's fury only made it worse. What would she have done if Nina hadn't been there for her when they were taken from their parents? What would have happened to Emmaline and Julietta had their two older sisters not comforted them after the crash? Johanna found herself tearing up, but quelled it before Charlotte looked up from her text.

"Dad says it's fine, see?" She turned the screen to Johanna.

There was more to the text, but Charlotte hadn't lied. Johanna gave her credit for making sure he was all right with her leaving. Pulling away from the curb, she spotted Gina at the window in the house that had been hers, the house she raised her children in. A hollow opened in Johanna's belly, but she drove away.

The further they got from her house, the more Charlotte relaxed. "Crapola."

"What's wrong?"

Charlotte held up her foot, and the hideous pink-piggy slipper she wore. Laughter erupted, easing Charlotte's fury a little more, enough to have her sigh.

"I can't believe she just showed up," Charlotte said. "Like, surprise! Mommy's here! What was she thinking?"

"That it's Christmas and she misses all of you," Johanna said before thinking better. Thankfully, Charlotte's explosive temper seemed reserved for her mother.

"I guess. It was still wrong, ruining Christmas for the kids."

"How did Millie and Tony react?"

Charlotte shrugged. "They were happy, at first. Then she said she was taking us to her cousin Tracy's for the rest of the school break and Millie freaked out. That's when I lost it. How dare she, Johanna? How fucking dare she?"

"I don't know what to say, Charlotte."

"There's really nothing to say. Don't worry about it. So—" She put her cell phone in the pocket of her flannel shirt. "It was nice of you, bringing over the goodies we didn't get to take home yesterday."

"There was no way we were going to eat it all." Johanna grinned. "And I wanted to see your dad."

"Score another one for Mom." But Charlotte laughed this time.

Talk turned to summer, and Cape May, and how great it was going to be. Johanna was mostly happy to let the conversation turn, though she was slightly uncomfortable with the assumptions Charlotte made. She and Charlie only just rekindled a romance twenty-years cooled. It was new. Fragile, and not the done-deal Charlotte seemed to believe it was. The morning's troubles slapped Johanna in the face with the fact that being with Charlie meant an instant family of kids who would look to her as a stepmother, not just someone fun to bake cookies with. It meant dealing with Gina and the scars she'd created with her leaving. And because he had five children who needed the stability of the home they knew, it meant living far apart from him.

Or moving back to Bitterly.

Johanna listened to Charlotte chatter on, her already hollow belly emptying further. To make a sour morning completely unpalatable, as she pulled into the driveway on County Line Road, Johanna remembered the locket and her sisters and the scolding she was in for. She tucked it under her sweater in the hopes they'd forgotten. Emma hadn't arrived yet, but they called her, she was certain. Thankfully, Efan's Audi was in the driveway. His presence, and Charlotte's, would probably buy her some time.

"Are your sisters going to be pissed?" Charlotte slid along the icy spots in her pig slippers. "I don't want to spoil Christmas Day for anyone."

"What's one more?" Johanna assured her, though that's not what Charlotte had actually been worried about. They tromped together into the house already redolent with yummy things cooking. Charlotte took off her pig slippers and left them near the heating vent to dry. Before Johanna had her boots off, Nina and Julietta were standing in the mudroom doorway, arms crossed...until they saw Charlotte.

"Charlotte's going to spend the day with us," Johanna told them quickly. "Gina showed up at the house and there was a...thing. Charlie knows she's here."

"I hope it's okay," Charlotte murmured.

Nina held out her arm, a mama-bird taking her under a wing. "Of course it's okay. There's plenty."

She passed Johanna, eyes meeting hers over Charlotte's head. If there was any doubt of the meaning there, Julietta dispelled it.

"You are not off the hook with the locket," she whispered, glancing towards the kitchen. "Nina thinks it's rightfully hers, but Gram promised it to me, Jo."

Johanna felt the blood rush to her head.

When I am gone, I give this to you. The wish will be yours to make.

"That...that can't be." Grasping Julietta's arm a little more tightly than she meant to, she pulled her farther into the mudroom. "Did Nina say why she thinks it's hers?"

Julietta shook her head slowly back and forth. "She said Gram told her. But I know what Gram told me."

"And so do I. Jules. Gram promised it to me, too. And if she promised it to me, you and Nina, then you can bet she told Emma it was going to her."

Her sister paled. "Why would she do that?"

"I have no idea."

"Hey, ladies." Efan poked his head through the door, smiling his toothy smile. "I think there might be something burning in here."

"My sweet potatoes," Julietta groaned. She grasped Johanna's wrist. "We'll talk about this later." And ran into the kitchen where the first acrid tinge of burning brown sugar filmed the air.

Emma arrived and, after putting food in to warm and settling her kids, wanted to see the locket.

"I know," Johanna whispered, "Gram promised it to you too, right?"

"Why?" Emma traced their mother's face. "Why would she do this?"

"I don't know, but now's not the time. Let's just enjoy the day. I promise I'm not going to vanish with it." Before they were out of her mouth, Johanna regretted her choice of words.

Emma met her flustered gaze, clicked the locket closed and let it fall against her sister's chest.

She kissed Johanna's cheek. "Of course you won't."

* * * *

Bellies full, kitchen cleaned, locket temporarily forgotten, the adults sat around the dining-room table playing Naughty Scrabble while the kids took advantage of the pristine snowdrifts out back, and the last of the day's sunshine.

"Lovebite," Gunner called out. "I get a bingo. And on a triple-word score."

"No way," Emma said. "Love bite is two words."

"Who says?"

"Let's vote," Charlotte said. "Two words?"

Everyone but Gunner raised their hands.

"No fair."

"Of course it is," Nina took his tiles off the board. "It's basic grammar, darling."

"Oh, and boink is grammatically correct."

"It's on the approved list, so it's a word."

"Look up lovebite."

"I just did." Emma showed him the screen of her tablet. "Two words. Don't be a baby, Gunner."

"It's useless arguing." Mike leaned closer to Gunner. "Once a Coco woman has her mind made up, there's no changing it. Take a lesson from us, Efan, and save yourself some headaches."

"Michael," Emma scolded. "That's not very nice."

"But it's true, isn't it?"

"Oh." Glancing at his crotch, Emma pursed her lips. "Is it?"

Mike's face turned an instant, painful shade of red. He glared at his wife, pushed away from the table, knocking several tiles from their places in the process.

"Guess that's the end of the game." Efan rubbed his hands together. "And it looks like I've won."

"No one wins when the game gets ruined," Julietta murmured.

Efan got to his feet, and pulled Julietta to hers. "Then let's go play out in the snow before it gets dark."

"Efan!" She laughed, but Julietta did not protest. She let him tug her into the mudroom. They were soon outside, calling to the boys still out there having snow battles.

Emma broke the silence with a long sigh. "Whatever," she murmured, and went after Mike, their arguing hushed but obvious.

While Nina and Gunner put the game away, Charlotte cleared coffee cups and pie plates. A buzzing in Johanna's pocket stopped her short of gaining her feet. She pulled out her phone. Charlie's number flashed on her screen. "Hey, she said softly. "How'd it go?"

"Bad, then worse, but then okay. How's Charlotte?"

"She's fine. You know how kids are."

"I know how my kid is." He laughed. "That's why I asked."

"How are you?"

"Me? Fine. A little drained. Gina's gone. The kids are all here, but I think Millie, Tony, and probably Caleb will go with her to her cousin's for a few days."

"Does it bother you?"

"Should it?"

"I have no idea."

Charlie let go a deep breath. "I let it go on too long. They should have gone to her last summer. It wasn't fair, what I did."

"You didn't—"

"Yeah, Jo. I did. I let them be angry for me."

Johanna doubted he saw himself clearly. Charlotte was always accusing him of defending her mother. He'd also thought himself to blame for the misunderstanding between them all those years ago. Some people were good at laying blame. Others were good at taking it.

"So what now?" she asked.

"I guess we wait for tomorrow and see. If the kids go, do you want—"

"Is that my dad?"

Johanna spun, heart hammering as if she'd been caught gossiping. "Yup. Want to talk to him?"

Charlotte held out her hand. She curled herself around Johanna's phone and spoke softly to her father, then, "Do you mind bringing me home, Jo? Will and Caleb went to the movies, and dad doesn't want to drag the little ones out. They're pretty beat."

"No problem."

Charlotte put the phone back to her ear. She smiled. "He says do you want to watch a movie?"

Johanna opened her mouth, a ready smile and 'yes' on her lips. Her mind zipped through the evening. Watching a movie cozied up on the couch. Kissing. Moving to the bedroom…and Gina showing up in the morning to pick up her children. She held out her hand for the phone.

"How about a raincheck on the movie?" she asked him. "Just until things are settled with Gina and the kids."

Charlie laughed softly, a sound reverberating through her body. "Tomorrow then?"

"Tomorrow."

"I'm going to hold you to that."

As long as you hold me tight. Johanna shuddered, the feeling like flight. "Charlie?"

"Yes, Johanna?"

"Don't come outside when I drop Charlotte off."

"Why not?"

"Because if you come outside, I'm going to kiss you. And if I kiss you, I am not going to be able to stop."

"Promises, promises."

"I mean it."

"Okay, okay. I'll wave from the door."

Johanna hung up, turned to face a grinning Charlotte.

"Not a word, you."

"I didn't say anything."

"Get your hideous slippers. I'll warm up the car."

Pulling on her coat, her boots, dipping into the pocket for the Explorer keys, Johanna tried to soothe the heat rising from her body. After running away from Charlie that summer day, Johanna had waited a long time to take a lover. Since her first, a sweet college student who spoke little English, she had never lacked for intimate company. Neither had she felt this overwhelming desire for any one of them. Just the notion of kissing Charlie was enough to make her burn from cheeks to groin. Face pressed to the cold windowpane, she fogged it up waiting for Charlotte.

"Where are you going?" Emma asked from the doorway.

"Taking Charlotte home. Why? You're not going yet, are you?"

"No. I'll wait. We have to have a talk. The four of us."

"Oh." The locket hung like a weight around Johanna's neck. "Right."

"I'd love to know what Gram was thinking, promising it to all of us like we'd never find out."

"Me too."

Emma leaned on the jamb, fiddled with the ends of her hair. "Did she...? Did she ever mention...? Oh, this just sounds silly, but did Gram ever mention a wish?"

Johanna pressed palms to her burning cheeks. She nodded.

Emma blew out a deep breath. "This family just gets stranger and stranger."

"It's our curse."

"No matter how we've all fought it." Emma sighed, and then she smiled. "Except Julietta."

Johanna laughed softly. "Efan's great, isn't he?"

"Seems so."

"You don't sound sure."

Emma shrugged. "I can't tell if he's being chivalrous or paternal."

"Does it really matter, if she's happy?"

"She needs a man, not a dad."

"She needs someone to love her," Johanna said. "Someone who's going to make her feel safe now that Gram's gone."

"She always has us."

"Would it be enough for you?"

Emma's lip trembled. She bit it, but a pair of tears rolled anyway.

"Hey." Johanna put an arm around her. "What's wrong?"

"Everything." Emma whispered, her shoulders slumping. "Mike, the boys. I love them. I love my life. It's everything Mom and Dad never got to have but I feel this...this piece missing. I thought I wanted another baby."

"But you don't?"

"Well, I can't now, can I?" Emma ground out, then took a deep breath. "I'd have liked to have a little girl, but I adore my boys. I can't imagine not having my trio. But it's not even that, Jo. I don't know what it is. Do you ever feel it?"

Warm metal tingled against her skin, under her sweater, like a second heartbeat.

"I do." she said. "I have been running away from that hollow space my whole——"

"My slippers are still wet so I borrowed the sneakers from the rack." Charlotte stopped short. "Oh, sorry. I'm interrupting something."

"Nothing that can't wait until Johanna gets back." Emma kissed Charlotte's cheek. "Those are Gram's sneakers. If you want them, you can keep them."

"Won't Julietta freak out if they're not on the rack?" she asked. Johanna did not know whether to be impressed by her insight or offended by it.

"If she notices, I'll tell her I took them." Emma answered. "It was very nice having you with us today, Charlotte."

"I like being here. I felt like a little sister for a change, instead of the oldest."

"I can imagine it's a welcome switch once in a while."

"You ready, Char?" Johanna asked. "Your dad's going to be waiting."

"Sure. Thanks again, Emma. I said good-bye to Nina, but could you hit Julietta up when she comes in? I don't want to pull her from Efan and the boys."

They all looked out the window to the two adults and three little boys rolling a colossal snowman. In the gloaming, magenta clouds scuttled. The perfect Christmas card, right there on the lawn, but it wasn't anything near the truth.

Holiday images, like those made-for-TV movies, were shallow. Lifelong sorrows fixed in two hours, complete with uplifting music and images like the one out the window right now. They never showed the next day, when the outcast girl melted down, scaring off her perfect new boyfriend, because her grandmother's sneakers weren't in the place they've always been. Those movies didn't show the troubled marriage rolling into oblivion, or the successful power-couple silently filling the holes left by things money could not buy. Or the prodigal daughter coming home to realize being with the love of her life meant making sacrifices she wasn't sure she could make.

Johanna caught her breath, held it. She waved to her sister, hurried outside, unable to let go that breath until she was in the car, fumbling with the key in the ignition.

Thankfully, Charlotte was young and oblivious. She chattered about the marvelous day she had, of Naughty Scrabble that she was definitely playing with her suite-mates, and how ridiculously gorgeous Gunner and Nina were.

"Whew. She really isn't here."

They sat in the driveway, engine idling. The source of Charlotte's chatter wormed its way to clarity.

"Who? Your mom?"

Charlotte nodded. "I thought they were trying to trick me, to get me home."

"Would your dad really do that?"

"I guess not. I just...I mean, it's not like I don't love her. She's my mom, you know? I just can't stop being..."

"Being?" Johanna prodded.

Charlotte's mouth chewed on thoughts she did not wish to become words. Her cheeks reddened. Tears brimmed but did not fall. She turned so they were face to face, even if she only looked at Johanna through her lashes.

"Dad has always loved you, Jo. I don't think I realized it until recently, but I'm all growed up now." She laughed softly, her eyes flicking to

Johanna's. "He and Mom would fight whenever you came to town. I didn't realize it either until I started thinking about it, but it's true. I don't know the whole story, why you two split or if you'd have lived happily-ever-after if it hadn't been for…" Again the furtive glance. "…for me. Over the years, listening to them fight, I got enough of it to know that my parents had never been a couple of crazy-in-love kids."

"They tried," Johanna said, but Charlotte shook her head.

"They just kept having kids, hoping one of them would make them love one another."

"If you know all this, why are you so angry with your mom?"

Charlotte looked up, those brimming tears hanging on thick lashes. "I'm not angry. She fell in love with someone who's not my dad. It happens." She sniffed. "I want her to be happy, just like I want dad to be. It's not about them."

"Then what is it?"

Another sniff. Charlotte wiped her eyes. "I've known, all my life, that if my dad had the chance to go back and start over, he'd do it all again. And I've always known that my mom wouldn't."

Johanna's heart lurched. Her brain buzzed with heartfelt words she could not know the validity of. Would Gina choose differently? Johanna simply did not know.

"I didn't mean to make you cry."

"I cry a lot." Johanna laughed, wiping her face with her fingertips. "I seriously do. I cry over schmaltzy commercials."

"You must be a mess every Christmas then." Charlotte sniffed. "Did you see the beer one this year? The colt and the dog?"

"Ugh! They grow up together and get separated—"

"And then are reunited years later when the horse returns in full regalia. I feel like an idiot but it makes me tear up every time."

"I do too."

Silence fell, this time, a more comfortable one. Charlotte started taking off the sneakers.

"You don't have to give them back," Johanna told her. "You heard Emma. Just keep them."

"Better if I don't," she answered. Stuffing the piggy slippers on, Charlotte grimaced. "Thanks again, Jo. I had a great day."

"You're welcome."

"I'll see you tomorrow?"

"Probably."

"Probably?"

Johanna tried to smile. "Let's take this a day at a time, okay?"

"Okay. But I'll see you tomorrow."

And out the door she flew. Johanna took several deep breaths, drained yet somehow, uplifted. She could almost hear the sappy TV holiday movie soundtrack playing in the back of her brain.

She watched Charlotte go up the driveway. The door opened for her, and there Charlie stood, silhouetted by the lights behind him. He waved, just as she'd asked him to. Johanna imagined his smile, sad and tired but glad to see her. Her heart thumped. Being this close, it was silly not to at least say a proper hello. She opened her window to wave him closer.

"I thought you didn't want me to come out," he said, leaning on her car door.

Johanna pulled him gently to her. She breathed him in, kissed him deeply, and let him go.

"Now you can go inside."

"Sure you don't want to come in?"

"It's what I want more than anything. But I have to get home. My sisters are waiting."

He did not back away and wave as a small part of her wished he would. Charlie reached in, pushed his fingers through her hair and kissed her as the bigger part of her wished for.

"You made today bearable," he said against her lips. "Knowing if I got through without my head exploding, you'd be here at the end of it is all that kept me together."

"Charlie, it wasn't m—"

He kissed her again, this time longer, deeper. Johanna was breathless when he pulled away. "Not my kids, Jo. Not my nice-guy nature. You. Whenever I wanted to scream at her, whenever my kids were crying, I thought of you. I thought of this. It calmed me down enough to keep my cool. Wherever this goes from here, I wanted you to know that."

"Where is this going?" she asked, her face burning for doing so, but she met his gaze and did not let it fall.

"Where do you want it to go?"

"I don't know, Charlie. All I do know is I'm…I'm happy."

"I am too. For now, that's all it has to be."

This time when they kissed, it was no one pulling anyone in, but mutual and soft and sweet. Johanna took her foot off the brake, let the car roll them apart. Charlie sidestepped along a moment, then jumped back laughing. She watched him in the rear-view. He stood in the road, hands in his pockets and shoulders hunched against the cold. She thought the words she could not say. Not yet. And drove home to her sisters waiting.

* * * *

It is so fragile, so fleeting. No one understands this truth until it's gone. Eternal emblem, confounder of time, effacer of all memory of beginning, all fear of an end! Take it in your hands, little sylph. Hold it tight and never, ever let go.

Chapter 6

Seven Swans a'Swimming

Johanna entered the house through the front door, leaving Gram's sneakers on the rack where they belonged. But for the soft discussion coming from the kitchen, there was no sound. No television. No little boys. No men. Just her sisters, waiting.

She stripped off her coat, kicked off her boots, and walked slowly down the hall to the kitchen. Before stepping through the doorway, she pulled the locket out from underneath her sweater.

"Where are all the boys?" she asked, sliding onto the empty seat at the table.

"We sent them to the movies," Nina answered. "The theater in town is playing four different versions of *A Christmas Carol*."

"Didn't they just watch one with Mike's family last night?"

"Not the Muppet one."

Emma's smile faded into the silence falling. The locket Johanna clutched seemed to pulsate. She lifted the chain from around her neck, and opened her hand.

"When I took it out," she said, "I thought it was mine. I wouldn't have taken it had I known Gram promised it to all of us."

"I just don't get it." Nina took it from Johanna's palm, clicked it open. "Of course she would know we'd all want it. Could it be she just couldn't bear to disappoint any of us?"

"Gram?" Julietta snorted. "Are you kidding? You can't be talking about the woman who told me to suck it up when I cried over the tooth-fairy not being real."

They all laughed softly.

"She had a reason for what she did," Emma insisted. "We just have to figure it out."

"But how?"

They looked at one another, waiting for someone else to start. Finally, Johanna asked, "Emma and I already talked about this, but did Gram ever mention a wish to either of you?"

"One no one has had the courage to make yet," Julietta said solemnly.

Nina's cheeks were suddenly pink. "You're not saying you believe it, are you?"

"I'm just asking if she ever mentioned it."

Nina nodded.

"Then we know two things. One, Gram promised it to each of us, and two, she told us all there was a wish inside, waiting to be made. Agreed?"

"Agreed."

"Now let's see if she told us all the same story of where it came from, too…"

* * * *

To Nina, Gram told the story of Fiorenza, the maiden aunt who taught etiquette to the fine young women of New York City. Her young man hadn't the money for a ring, but they made their promises on the locket her *nona* had given to her before leaving the old country. One evening, he left her on her doorstep after their nightly stroll, and was never seen again.

The story Gram told Emma was even more tragic—the locket belonged to Fia, a dancer with a small ballet company touring America. She met a man, married him, and contracted tuberculosis by the tender age of seventeen. She left behind the locket—again, a gift from her *nona* before leaving Italy—and a baby daughter when she died at twenty.

And to Julietta, the most adventurous tale—the locket first belonged to Fabrizzia, an Italian inventor hand-selected by Nikola Tesla to assist him in his work. Her *nona* gave her the locket, but warned her not to go to America. Fabrizzia didn't listen. Tesla fell madly for her, she did not love him in return, and was erased from history.

"Tesla?" Nina gaped at Julietta. "And you believed her?"

"Why wouldn't I? This is Gram we're talking about. She doesn't make stuff up, and we all got our mouths washed out with soap more than once for lying."

"Why do you think she told us such sad stories?" Emma asked, turning the locket over and over in her hand. "Why did you get the only happy story, Jo?"

Johanna turned the details of the story Gram told her, of Florentina leaving for America as a newly made bride. A story of hope and new horizons that ended with a life well lived.

"I wish I knew," she said at last. "Could it be there is no reason?"

"We've already established that Gram didn't do anything without a reason," Nina said. "She made us all the same promise, knowing we'd find out one day. She also made sure each story had one common element."

"The wish," Julietta said.

"The wish," Nina repeated. "She knew this would happen, after she was gone, we'd share all the stories, we'd all want the locket."

"Then there's a reason my story ended with a dead mother, and your story with love unrequited, Julietta's, a woman erased, and Jo's, happily-ever-after."

"Maybe she just liked Jo best?" Nina asked, and they all laughed. Johanna did as well, though the hollow-belly feeling was beginning to creep up on her. There was something they were missing, something trying to make itself clear to her.

Vanished. Dead. Erased. Happy. *Oh, Adelina Coco, you've really done it this time.*

"There is one more common factor," she said. "In each story, the girl's grandmother gave her the locket before leaving Italy."

"That's right," Emma said.

"And she is giving it to us," Nina added. "That's something, right?"

"It must be."

"Or we are over-thinking this whole thing. She was rather old."

"But she wasn't when she told us the stories," Johanna said, "and promised us each the locket."

"Another piece to the puzzle," Emma sighed and stretched. "We're not going to figure this out now, if ever."

"So, what do we do about the locket in the meantime?" Nina asked. "Take turns?"

"Starting with you, of course."

"I'm the oldest."

"But that's not what Gram wanted," Julietta cut in. "Whatever her reason, she wants us to figure it out."

"But…how?"

Again, the silence. Johanna could almost hear their minds whirring through possibilities. The crunch of tires in the driveway signaled the boys' return, and the end of their conversation. Whether or not any of them believed in the stories or the wish, there was an unspoken agreement to keep it to themselves. The women rose from the table as if pulled by the same cord.

"Gunner and I are going to stay through New Year's Day," Nina said. "We'll head back to the city on the second. Let's see what happens between now and then. Jo? Can you stay until then?"

"I was planning on it. Actually..." She took a deep breath. Once she said the words, she could not unsay them. "I closed CC's for the season. I'm staying in Bitterly until the spring, if it's all right with Julietta."

"Are you kidding me?" her youngest sister grabbed her hands and started twirling. "You're staying! You're staying!"

"Is this because of Charlie?" Emma teased.

"I closed the bakery before I left Cape May." Johanna extricated herself from Julietta's grasp. "But I won't lie. It's a definite perk to the decision."

"I don't care why you're staying, just that you are." Julietta hugged herself, swayed back and forth. "I say Johanna is the one who started all this, she should hold onto the locket until we figure it all out."

"Fine by me." Nina yawned.

"I suppose it is by me, too," Emma said, then wagged a playful finger in her face. "But no making any unauthorized wishes."

"I won't." Johanna made an X over her chest. "Cross my heart, that's no lie, stick a booger in my eye."

Her sisters laughed, Julietta the hardest. "You remember that? Where did we get it from?"

"Probably Gram," she lied. It wasn't Gram. Johanna remembered quite clearly.

Gunner, Mike, and Efan each carried one of the sleeping little boys. Hushing them all, Emma gestured upstairs where the boys were stripped, and tucked into the trundle-beds set up in what had once been their mother's room.

"We can sleep in Gram's room," Emma said when they all came back down again, but Nina halted her.

"Or you and Mike can go home and have a nice night just the two of you."

"Light a fire," Gunner added, "turn on some music, have a glass of wine..."

"Or two," Johanna added.

Mike slipped his arm around his wife's waist, whispered in her ear. Emma shoved him gently, but smiled and kissed him before asking, "You sure you don't mind?"

They left moments later, laden with Christmas gifts and dinner leftovers, half a pie and a plate of cookies. Emma would come back in the morning to get her sons.

"A glass of wine by the fire does sound nice." Nina curled into her husband, a smile on her lips and a sparkle in her eye. He kissed her nose. "You crack the bottle, I'll stoke the fire." He turned to the parlor, nearly bowling Efan over. "Oh, sorry. Would you guys like to join us?"

"No thanks," Johanna said quickly. "I'm heading to bed."

"And I have an early day tomorrow," Efan said. "No rest for the wicked."

"Isn't it supposed to be weary?" Julietta asked. He took her hand, kissed it floridly.

"It is an alternate to the old saying, *cariad*. A play on words. Now if you will escort me to the foyer, I shall depart this warm and wonderful place to brave the elements and my lonely carriage house anon."

"You're so weird."

"Which is why we get along famously." He offered his arm. Julietta took it and fell into step beside him. Johanna watched them, their heads close and voices low, her heart doing little flips. Her youngest sister had liked boys just as any other teen. When she reached her twenties and the quirks of childhood became problematic for an adult, she seemed to retreat from the world that included men in a romantic capacity. Efan's quirks made him a bit dorky, but that was all he was—not like Julietta, for whom a missing pair of sneakers could be a traumatic event.

Caught in the kitchen by Efan and Julietta at the front door and Gunner and Nina in the parlor, Johanna tidied up. She washed the teacups in the sink and set them on the rack to dry, piled cookies into plastic containers, put the butter in the fridge. Johanna hummed Christmas songs, sad the holiday was mostly over. The days leading up to New Year's Eve seemed more like a deep breath after a long run, and then came the lead up to Little Christmas, once a grand event in the Coco household, now mostly forgotten, and Johanna wondered why that was so.

The front door closed softly. A moment later, Julietta was tiptoeing into the kitchen. "Oh, Jo. I thought you went upstairs. I was sneaking in for a cookie or two."

"Help yourself." She slid a container her way. The fair skin of her sister's face flushed the fresh-pink of kissing. Her lips were bright red.

"You know," Johanna hedged, "I think he was hinting he'd like to spend the night."

"Of course he was. I'm not an idiot, Jo."

"I didn't mean to imply you are."

"It's just not me."

"Ok, honey. I didn't mean—"

"You all think I'm a baby. The little sister. I wish you'd all stop treating me like a perpetual child. I have three degrees and a Masters in linguistics."

"Hey." Johanna moved closer. "What's this all about? You know I didn't mean anything like that."

Julietta slumped, took an angry bite of a cookie and several deep breaths.

"Sorry," she said. "I didn't mean it either. It's just…I really like him, enough to care what he thinks of me, of…how I am."

"How you are is why he likes you."

"But doesn't that make it, I don't know…gross?"

"Gross?"

"Like he's into freaks or something."

"Julietta, don't say that. You are not a freak."

"We're all freaks, Jo." She smiled a little sadly. "All four of us, in our own ways. I just happen to be the freakiest."

Johanna did not quibble. She knew exactly what her sister was saying. Their reputation as the crazy Coco sisters had been well-earned, once-upon-a-time. No dare untaken, no adventure refused, no slight unaddressed, the moniker had become a badge of honor that nevertheless hurt to hear spoken aloud.

"Who wants to be normal, anyway?" Johanna asked. "Normal is boring. When do you think people stopped understanding that normal just means average?"

"Probably when it started making all those boring people feel better about themselves."

Julietta ate her cookie. Johanna finished tidying up the kitchen. Folding the dishtowel, she opened her mouth to say goodnight.

"What would your wish be?" Julietta asked.

Johanna thought about it a lot when she was a kid. Frivolous wishes, like a pony or to go on a date with Justin Timberlake, to more serious wishes about never being parted from her sisters all gave way to one wish, the one that first came to her head when Gram told her she had it to make.

"I don't know," she lied to her sister a second time. "What would you?"

"It…it would be hard to pick just one."

"True."

"Do you think there could really be a wish in the locket? Like, for real?"

With Emma or Nina, Johanna would laugh and tell them to be serious. With Julietta, she could say, "Yeah, I do."

"So do I." Julietta hugged her then, tightly.

The locket, tucked back under her clothes, pressed against Johanna's skin, warm, then cool, then warm, its rhythm again like a heartbeat. Her sister let her go. "Don't forget your promise."

"I crossed my heart and stuck a booger in my eye, didn't I?"

A tear rolled down Julietta's cheek. "It wasn't Gram who said that."

"I know."

"He was weird too."

"A freak, like the rest of us."

"I miss him every day."

"I do, too."

"Not more than I do. I…" Julietta took a deep breath. "I'm going to bed. Night, Jo."

"Night, Jules."

Johanna waited until her sister's door closed upstairs to tiptoe past the parlor where Nina and Gunner were crawling all over one another beside the fire, and trudge up the stairs. She checked on her sleeping nephews. Behind her own closed door, she stripped down to nothing but the locket, climbed into bed, and fell instantly to sleep.

* * * *

Little girls should never speak of dying, or sticking needles in their eyes. They are sugar and spice and everything nice, with heaven in their eyes, and star dust glistening on fairies' wings. They are my joy and heart's delight. They walk in beauty like the night. Little girls should never be hungry or scared or cold. They should never know such horrors. They should never see such things.

Chapter 7

Six Geese a'Laying

In the attic room, the boys were arguing. Charlie listened to them, making sure it did not escalate. Tony and Caleb were packed for the few days they would spend with their mother. Will still insisted he wasn't going. He had to work. He had plans. He didn't want to spend a week sleeping on the floor in Tracy's house when he could have the whole attic to himself. Charlie was torn. As much as he loved his kids, he wouldn't lie and pretend it wouldn't be nice to have a few days completely to himself. He hadn't had one of those since he was eighteen.

The knock at the front door took him by surprise, not the sound, but that she knocked at all. Gina stood on the porch, framed by the window, her back to him. Small and slim, slightly wider in the hips, she had let her hair grow in the year since she left. "Short and sassy" had been the pervading style during their marriage. Easier to deal with. She turned when he opened the storm door, a wary smile on her full lips.

"Hey," she said. "The kids ready?"

"Mommy!"

Millie came running down the stairs, her purple pony duffle dragging behind her. Gina bent to catch her in a hug. Charlie's heart squirmed a little. He quelled it before he could decide if it was a happy sensation, or a frightened one.

"*Stellina.*" Gina held her close. "How I've missed my little star."

"The boys aren't ready yet," Charlie said when she put Millie down. "You want coffee? We still have a ton of cookies here."

His ex-wife eyed him skeptically, but she nodded. "Go hurry your brothers along. We have an hour drive to Tracy's, and your cousins want to have a snowball fight before lunch."

Millie clapped her hands and pounded back up the steps. "Will, Caleb, Tony! Mommy's here!"

At the counter in the kitchen, Charlie poured coffee, slid the container of cookies Johanna had brought over. Gina picked up a star-shaped one. "Johanna Coco, huh? Finally?" She took a bite. "Wow. This is better than I was expecting."

Again that squirmy feeling. In the year and some since she left him, he'd mostly stopped being angry. Johanna's return to Bitterly banished the anger completely. Much as he hated how it all happened, Charlie could not be sorry it had.

"Will is still insisting he's not coming with you," he said. "We could make him. I just didn't want to push it until we discussed it first."

Gina finished her cookie and dug out a chocolate and toffee chip. She closed her eyes in only slightly exaggerated bliss as she ate it. "Really good. I'm going to take some of these with me. If that's okay."

"Sure."

She wiped her hands on her jeans. "If William comes down ready to go with me, great. If he doesn't, I don't want to force him. That's not going to do anything good."

"You're probably right."

Gina leaned on the counter. She sipped her coffee out of a mug, Charlie realized, Charlotte had given her for Mother's Day, years ago. If she noticed, she didn't say anything. After a moment, she set the mug down.

"In all the chaos yesterday, we never got a chance to talk."

"Do we have anything to talk about?"

She smiled a little sadly. He'd forgotten how perfect her teeth were. Her olive skin, Florida-tanned, made them seem even whiter. "How have you been, Charlie?"

"Okay, I guess. I haven't had much time to think about it."

"Is that good?"

He laughed. "I suppose it is. Kind of. You?"

"I've had way too much time to think." Gina plucked another cookie from the container. "All these years, life has been so…noisy. Soccer and school and summer camp and homework and squabbles and who gets to watch what on television. Now, life is so quiet, just me and—" She glanced at him. "Just my own voice in my head most of the time. It's been good, and really awful."

Charlie let go a deep breath. He sipped his own coffee. "I can't imagine being without them," he said, "but I wouldn't mind some quiet."

"You'll have it this summer."

His gut seized, but Charlie nodded.

"Look forward to it, Charlie. You're a good dad. You always have been. But you need time to be Charlie McCallan, too." She bit into the cookie still in her hand—a snowball. Again the slightly exaggerated bliss. "Damn, these are really good. So...Johanna Coco, huh?"

"I heard and ignored you the first time." Charlie laughed. "Does it bother you?"

"Why would it?"

"Because we used to fight whenever she came to town."

"That was envy," Gina admitted. "She had what I never would."

"What you never wanted."

"Only a little true. I wanted us to work, Charlie. Not just for the kids, for us. You deserved better than a spouse going through the motions. And so did I."

Anger battled compassion. Truth battled pretense. He pushed fingers through his hair, rubbed at the beard that needed a trim, both grown out since she left because he could, and Charlie McCallan could not find it in him to disagree. "You really have done a lot of thinking."

She nodded. "I hate all the hurt I caused you, Charlie. I really do."

"You didn't just hurt me, Gina. You humiliated me."

"How many times can I say I'm sorry?" The question trembled from her lips. It had taken a lot of courage to return to Bitterly, to face the children still so hurt they had refused to see her, the man she humiliated, and the town that had rallied around him. She was a villain. And still Gina came back. For her kids.

Several pairs of feet pounding down the steps had Charlie stepping away and Gina wiping her eyes. By the time the kids got to the kitchen, they were both smiling.

"All ready?" she asked, arms outstretched. Tony and Millie took a hand each. Caleb's eyes strayed to his father, his smile unsteady. And though Will's stony expression had not changed since the day prior and his earbuds were in his ears, his backpack hung from his shoulder.

"Say bye to Daddy, kids. He gets a few days of peace and quiet."

"No, he doesn't," Millie chirped. "Charlotte's staying and she's the noisiest."

"No, you are." Tony shoved his twin.

"No, you are." Millie shoved him back. Caleb grabbed his little brother by the backpack and hauled him to their father.

"See you in a few days, Dad," he said, then leaned closer. "You sure this is all right?"

Charlie kissed his son's cheek. "It's fine. Have fun."

* * * *

"You have everything you need?" Charlotte fussed over the groceries on the counter. Charlie took the potatoes she was inspecting out of her hands, reminding himself this was her way of avoiding the otherwise empty house, and her mother's hand in that.

"Everything. Now stop—"

"You remembered she likes merlot?"

"Yes, Charlotte. I remembered she likes merlot. Will you relax? I'm the one cooking for Johanna."

"I just want it to be perfect for you."

"Honey." Charlie took her shoulders in his hands. "Thank you, but I got this. Okay?"

Charlotte bit her lip. "I want you to be happy, Daddy."

"I am. I have been. Getting to know Johanna again is a bonus, not the only key to my life's happiness."

"You don't...I thought you wanted to, you know, marry her or something."

Charlie let go of his daughter, took a step back. "It's a little soon to start thinking that way. There's twenty years between the kids we were and the adults we are. For now, we're getting to know one another again."

"If you say so." Charlotte kissed his cheek. "I might be home late. Katie is not letting me go back to school until I hit up a karaoke night with her."

"Katie has heard you sing, right?"

"Funny, Dad." She smacked at his arm. "Don't wait up."

"I won't."

She took her coat from the rack. Pulling her hat onto her head, she grinned at him. "And if Johanna's here for breakfast, I promise not to torture you too much."

"Get going." He laughed.

"I'm just saying."

"Go."

Charlie pushed closed the door that never shut on the first try. The house wasn't just small, it was old. Windows and doors didn't open or close without a struggle. One window in the front room hadn't opened in all the years they lived there. The floorboards in the kitchen didn't always meet up in the winter, and buckled in the summer. He and Gina bought it with a down-payment loan from her folks. It was all they could afford. He remembered their excitement, their plans.

Charlie smiled sadly. Whatever their beginning or their end, there had been happiness. Family vacations, birthday parties, back-to-school nights and end-of-the-year picnics. What he and Gina had in common were their children, no more, and no less. They loved them, even if they hadn't been in love themselves. And now he was making dinner for another woman in the house they had shared.

Cooking Italian seemed wrong, somehow. Johanna was the granddaughter of Adelina Coco, arguably the best cook in Bitterly. Her lasagna never made it through five minutes at a potluck. Instead, he dug out an old recipe from his Irish grandmother. Shepherd's pie. All the ingredients lined the counter, checked and double-checked. Charlotte's claim that he was a good cook did little for his confidence. Everything he knew how to make, Gina taught him. He'd never made anything this elaborate on his own.

He floured and browned the beef, added the stout, onions and thyme, and let it cook low and slow. The house was soon abundant with the aroma conjuring his grandparents so clearly he could almost see the stone cottage, the ivy-covered trellis, the mossy roof—their home created to mimic what they left behind in Ireland. Granddad even had a peat-burning stove installed. Charlie could still close his eyes and recall the scorched-earth scent.

Cork popped, he set the wine out to breathe. He stirred the vegetables into the pot, gave the mashed potatoes one last whip, smooth and creamy. He layered them thick on top. Brushing it with butter, he afforded himself a small swell of pride before he slid the pie into the oven to crisp. Charlie was setting the table when she knocked on the door. He looked at his clothes smeared with his cooking. No shower either. Where had the time gone?

Johanna stood on the porch much as Gina had earlier—her back to him, hair curling down her back. She was looking streetward, waving to someone walking a dog. Charlie took a moment to brush off his shirt, smooth his hair, and stopped. This was the girl he'd spent a summer exploring the woods with. She'd seen him sweaty and dirty and covered in worse than a bit of mashed potato, when he was skinny and next-to-hairless, when he was little more than a boy. Opening the door, he pulled her inside and into a kiss before she could even say hello.

"Well," she breathed when he released her. "That was some greeting."

"I missed you."

"We saw one another last night."

"Only for a minute." He let her go. "Let me take your things."

Johanna handed him her coat, stuffing her hat into the sleeve. Her static-charged hair stuck straight up. She didn't seem to notice. "It smells amazing in here."

"Shepherd's pie." He smoothed her hair, kissed her lips. "I hope you like it."

"I don't think I've ever had it."

He led her to the kitchen and poured them both wine. She asked how the morning had gone with Gina and the kids. Charlie answered as casually as he could. They ate and they talked and they reminisced, all talk grazing the surface of things and safe. Pleasant, easy, comfortable. As they washed dishes side by side, Johanna telling him about how crowded Cape May got starting Memorial Day, Charlie felt as if the years between that teenage-summer and now had been otherwise spent. Without the kids in the house, he could almost convince himself it were true.

They took their wine glasses into the family room and sat together on the couch. The video game console, a bin of toys in the corner, the blanket Millie always wrapped up in when she watched television, shoved Charlie from behind, making him feel as if his earlier thought betrayed the kids somehow. Johanna curled into his side, her head resting on his shoulder. He tried to regain the easy feeling, and failed.

"You want to watch a movie?" he asked.

"As long as it's not scary. I hate scary movies."

"Let's see what's available." He clicked through the movie channels. Johanna's hand shot out to stop him.

"Go back."

"*Shaun of the Dead*? Sounds scary to me."

"Have you ever seen it?"

"No."

"It's hilarious." She took the remote from him. "*Hot Fuzz* and *The World's End* are on too. We could do a Cornetto trilogy marathon."

"What's a Cornetto?"

"Are you kidding me?" Johanna shifted so she was facing him. "Don't tell me it's been nothing but Disney movies for you."

"There were a few others in there."

"But not *Shaun of the Dead*."

"No, no *Shaun of the Dead*. What's it about?"

"Zombies."

"A funny zombie movie. Sounds fantastic. Queue it up."

Johanna snuggled back into him, clicked the remote. It took a few minutes for his pulse to ease and his body to relax with her so soft in his arms, but he managed. Halfway through the movie, Charlotte came home. Early. They paused the movie to hear about her abysmal experience at the karaoke bar with Katie, who she would never forgive for dragging her there.

"I'm just not a bar person," she said. "Does that make me weird?"

"What would you rather be doing?" Johanna asked.

"Playing board games with my friends in the dorm."

"You'll be able to soon enough," Charlie said. "Break is almost over."

Too long a pause, then, "Yeah."

Charlie and Johanna exchanged glances.

"That sounded like more than a yeah. What's up, Char?"

His daughter picked at the already-chipped polish on her thumbnail. "I've been thinking."

"About?"

She looked up. "School."

"I should go." Johanna started to rise, but Charlotte shook her head.

"No, you're kind of the straw that broke the camel's back. Stay."

"Uh-oh."

"No, it's good." Charlotte's laughter trembled. "I've been thinking about it for a while now. I don't think early childhood education is for me. I...I want to go to culinary school."

"You've got two years into this degree—" Charlie began, but she cut him off.

"I know, Dad. It's a lot of money spent, but most of it was on scholarship, and I'll pay off the rest. This is my gig. I'll cover it. Spending two more years working and paying for a degree I don't want seems like even more of a waste, don't you think?"

"It's a degree that will always get you a job."

"And that's really the only reason I went for it to begin with. It's not the reason to become a teacher, Dad. It should be my passion, and it's not. Baking is."

Charlie rose from the couch. Part-time caretaking at the cemetery was not lucrative, especially in a small town like Bitterly. He'd always worked as a handyman to compensate. It had been enough to support his family. Period. Scholarships and loans were the only way his kids were going to college, and now Charlotte spoke of tossing two years aside to start over again.

"It's not as bad as you think, Daddy," Charlotte told him gently. "I already looked into the CIA in Hyde Park. It's in New York—state, not city. A lot of my credits will transfer, so instead of getting an Associate degree in baking and pastry arts. I can get a Bachelor's. And there are grants and scholarships I can apply for."

"Isn't it a bit late to do that now?"

"For the spring semester, yes," Charlotte said. "But my classes in New Paltz haven't been paid for yet. That's money I won't have to put out. I'll apply to the CIA for the fall."

"So you're not going back to school after break."

"Just to get my stuff. Say good-bye to some friends."

"You've already made your decision, then."

"I want you to be okay with it."

"And if I'm not?"

Charlotte's chin went up in that way she had since earliest toddlerhood. "This isn't a whim, Dad. I've really thought it out. It's what I want more than anything."

Charlie blew a breath through his lips. Paused on the screen, Simon Pegg and Nick Frost battled zombies frozen mid-shamble.

"I know it's not a whim," he said. "I trust your judgment, baby."

Charlotte launched into him from her perch on the couch. "Thank you, Daddy."

Holding his daughter, Charlie was overwhelmed by the sensation of time spinning away from him. She didn't need his approval, or his consent. Charlotte was a woman grown, one who knew her mind. He trusted her completely and always had. It wasn't the change in schools or money lost, it was acknowledging she no longer needed him that grabbed his gut in a fist and squeezed.

* * * *

Johanna tried to imagine the thoughts racing through Charlie's head as he held his daughter tight. Parenthood was an alien thing, one she had never aspired to or understood. Her own parents had known nothing about children, about the care they required. No matter how much they loved their girls, in the end, it had not been enough. Wonky genes aside, the notion of loving so much only to lose it one day had helped to quell any inkling she ever had when she held a baby in her arms and thought, *maybe.*

Until now.

Cool heat rose to her cheeks. All the years denying herself any real and binding love had not been able to withstand Charlie McCallan's freedom, his smile, the place she'd been holding for him in her life. Was it the same with children?

"I hope you really do want me to work with you, Jo." Charlotte bounced onto the couch beside her. "It's a prerequisite to attending the CIA, working in the food industry. I mean, I worked in the coffeehouse for three years, so that counts too, but an actual bakery is going to look great on my application."

"Of course I want you to work with me." The cool heat altered, making her belly a little queasy. Summer, Cape May, leaving Bitterly and Charlie and her sisters. "It'll be great."

"Oh, I just realized, I could—" Charlotte's fair cheeks pinked. "Crap. Now I'm being presumptuous."

"What do you mean?"

Charlotte pressed palms to her cheeks. "I was going to say I could go back with you when you go and help from now. But you probably don't need help this time of year, and I can get some hours with the coffeehouse, and I didn't mean to…and you and my dad and…" She bit her lip. "And I'm rambling. Sorry, Jo."

"Don't be silly. I can definitely use your help when I reopen, only…"

"Only?" Charlie asked.

Johanna gathered her courage along with a deep breath. She met Charlie's eyes, held them, and let the words fall. "It's really slow this time of year. When I came north, I closed for the season. I figured on opening again in the spring."

Charlie's smile was sunrise breaking the horizon. He moved closer, took her hands one at a time, studying each of them before lacing his fingers through hers. Johanna's heart hammered something like fear, like joy. Charlotte muttered something that might have been goodnight, and beat a hasty retreat.

Charlie asked, "Does this mean I have a date for New Year's Eve?"

Johanna nodded.

"And Valentine's Day?"

Those blasted tears stung, blurring his image. A lump formed in her throat. His hand came up, fingers caressing her neck, under her chin, along her cheekbone. "Johanna," he whispered her name like a wish before kissing her tenderly, releasing the tightness in her body. The fear that kept her from letting go with other men she might have loved did not stand a chance against Charlie. What she felt for him was too old, too strong, what she wanted too intense to crush. The choices of her youth had not saved her grief, only changed its guise. Maybe it wasn't too late to make it right.

Charlie pulled her back into the couch only recently vacated by Charlotte. A passing thought to her self-conscious retreat was all Johanna spared her. Kissing Charlie was the only thought in her head, and it was not so much thought as carnal, euphoric instinct.

Arms wound about his neck, fingers caught in his thick hair, Johanna gloried in the feel of his weight pressing her into the cushions, of his hands on her face, her shoulders, her breasts. He shifted only long enough to push his hands up under her sweater, his mouth finding the pulse in her throat. Johanna's back arched to him. It was easy, so easy, to lose herself. In this. In him. At last. She pulled at his shirt. He yanked it off. Muscle and hair and sweat-slicked skin. Charlie straddled her hips, breathing heavily, waiting.

Johanna's heart swelled. Desire and need mingled with the overwhelming love his hesitation inspired. She wiggled underneath him, freed her sweater and lifted it over her head.

He smiled. "You still don't wear a bra."

"You remember that?"

"It's not something a guy forgets." He ran his hands up her ribs. "You are so beautiful."

Johanna reached for him and he fell gently to her, their lips meeting before bare skin touched bare skin.

"Ouch! Oh!" Charlie pulled away, rubbing at his chest.

"What is it? What's wrong? Are you having a heart attack?"

"No." He laughed. Leaning over her, he picked up the chain to her locket in his teeth. "You shtabbed me."

Watching the locket swing, Johanna tried to breathe without gasping. A sensation like cold water dripped all over her skin. She reached up, took the locket from his clenched teeth. He lowered himself on top of her again, but the euphoria of his weight pressing her into the cushions had ebbed to comfort.

"What's wrong?" he asked.

Johanna dragged her gaze from the locket in her hand, to the concern in Charlie's eyes. She brushed the hair from his face. He caught her fingers with a kiss. It would have been easy enough to lose herself in him again, to forget the fear of the past that never left her, but it would rise up again. And again. Until she told him. Until he knew.

"Charlie." She stopped the trail of his kisses moving from her wrist and along the inside of her arm. "What do you know about my parents? About my childhood?"

"I don't know anything." He shifted his weight so he was bearing most of it, without moving off her. "Why?"

"Because you should know, before you get in too deep."

"Johanna." He brushed her lips with a kiss. "Too late for that. Twenty years too late. It doesn't matter."

"It does. Charlie, listen to me. Please."

"All right. I'm listening."

She thought about moving out from under him, thought about facing him with clothes on and at a safe distance, but Johanna stayed in the comfort of his weight, of his skin on her skin.

"They were cra...mentally ill," she began. "As far as I can tell, my mom was bi-polar, Daddy was schizophrenic. I honestly don't know for certain. They met in a psychiatric hospital in the early 1970s. I don't know if they were ever legally married but they called themselves husband and wife. When my mom got pregnant with Nina, they ran away. I don't know where my sister was born, but by the time I came along, we lived in a condemned farmhouse somewhere in the back-of-beyond in New Hampshire. They weren't abusive or anything. They loved us. I know they did. They just weren't capable of taking care of little girls. Neither of us had birth certificates when Gram and Poppy came to get us at the home in Massachusetts."

"After the fire," he said. Johanna's heart lurched. She felt as if she would vomit, but Charlie pushed her hair back from her face just then, and she eased.

"They left us alone a lot," she said. "Sometimes it was to go hunting or foraging, or garbage picking. I remember being cold, and hungry, and scared. Nina's not much older than I am, but she always took care of me. I remember that too. The day of the fire, I only wanted..."

She fell silent then, closed her eyes. Her little hands. The burning stick she threw when Nina came home with more wood. The pile of dry leaves and debris that caught instantly. There, in those memories, behind her lids, that fire burned. Charlie did not press. He simply waited, caressing a spot just below her ear. Johanna took slow breaths until she could speak without weeping.

"The firemen came and found Nina and me outside, watching our house burn. I remember crying and crying, so afraid Mom and Dad would be angry with me. The next days are kind of a blur. I was so scared. I didn't know it then, but when my parents finally showed up to claim us, there was trouble and they both ended up being taken into custody. Mom must have given them her parents' information, because Gram came to get me and Nina. She told us who she was and that we'd be living with her until our parents were able to come get us. Eight years later, Gram and Poppy got a call in the middle of the night. She was gone when we got up the next morning, and didn't come home for days. When she did, she had Emma and Julietta with her."

"I remember when they came to Bitterly," Charlie told her. "We were eleven."

"We were. I can't believe you remember."

"I was pretty much obsessed with you, Johanna."

"Even then?"

"From first grade, the day you kicked me in the shin because you thought I purposely stepped on your foot."

She could almost laugh. Almost. But she wasn't finished with her story, and he needed to hear it. She needed him to hear it.

"Apparently, my parents escaped again or were released at some point in those eight years, but if they ever came for me and Nina, I don't know about it. They had two more daughters. Nina and I had it good compared to Emma and Jules. From the little I've been able to get out of Gram over the years, my dad got much worse and mom just wasn't right enough to understand. He was convinced the government was after him, trying to take his family and lock him up. He died in a car crash that left my mom severely injured. Julietta was pretty banged up, but Emma had hardly a scratch. The authorities called Gram and Pop again, and you can figure out the rest."

"What about your mom?"

The big question, one Johanna had been asking and hiding from most of her life. She lifted the locket from her chest, clicked it open and showed him inside. "This is her," she said. "Carolina Coco."

"You look like her."

"And it has always scared the shit out of me."

"Why?"

"Because I thought it made me like her. I was afraid I'd be crazy too. It could still happen."

"I'm pretty sure you're safe at this point."

"No one is ever safe from mental illness, Charlie. You never know when it's going to hit. When the person you thought you were becomes someone you can never know. I'm terrified. I've always been."

"And you're telling me all this now because you are warning me of what might come, or because you're going to vanish before it can?"

Johanna swallowed hard. "Which do you want it to be?"

Charlie looked at her a long time, too long, his expression unreadable. Tears rolled down the sides of her face. He caught them, wiped them away. "Johanna." He breathed her name against her lips. "You have always been a little nutty, but you are not bi-polar. You're not schizophrenic. You are dazzling and wild and my life will never be boring, but I can't imagine not having you in it. Not now, after all this time. I'm sorry for your past, for your parents. I wish I could take it all from you and hide it away where you never have to be afraid of it again. I can't. All I can do is swear to you that it doesn't matter. I can't not love you, and I tried for a very long time."

Johanna's sob popped like a cork. She wrapped her arms around his neck. All his weight came to bear on her, squeezing the breath from her lungs. She held him there, held the sensation. Something burst inside her. It rushed through her like blood, like relief, like freedom after years in a cage. It was horrible and wonderful all at once, the vulnerability, and the power.

"Hey." Charlie gently pried her arms from around his neck. He pulled her onto his lap, cradled her head against his shoulder. She stayed there for a long time, bare-chested and matching her breaths to his until she could remember the rhythm of breathing again. On the television, a screen-saver blip of frozen zombies, glided about the screen.

"Not how either of us imagined this evening going," she said at last, her voice trembling just a little. "I didn't mean to spoil everything."

"You didn't." He lifted her chin, caught her gaze. "You didn't, Jo."

She turned in his arms, her naked breasts too near his face for him to avoid. "Where did you come from, Charlie McCallan?"

"I guess you wouldn't buy the stork bit, eh?"

They laughed softly together, the rumbling of their bodies stirring what the locket had interrupted. Charlie's hands moved up her sides. Face to face, smiles fading, Johanna leaned in to kiss him.

"I think it'd be best if we call it a night."

Johanna startled upright. "Now?"

"Now," he said. "Before this happens."

"You don't want to…"

"I think you know I do."

Johanna grinned. She ground against him. "I might have some inkling."

"Then you know how hard it is for me to say that." He kissed her nose. "Pun totally intended."

"Very witty."

"Thank you. I try." He held her tighter, a moment longer, then rose from the couch, taking Johanna with him and setting her on her feet. "I can wait," he said. "I don't want you to have any reason to run, and taking you to bed after you just spilled your heart out doesn't seem the best way to go about preventing that."

Johanna opened her mouth to speak, but closed it again. He was right. Making love to him now would be too much about losing herself in him, in sex, and reburying the past. He picked her sweater up off the floor, slipped it over her head. His hands moved the material down her sides, lingered in places that made her sigh. Pulling the neck over her head, his mouth was on hers before she could move the hair from her eyes.

"Go home," he said. "Before I can't let you."

He put his shirt back on as he walked her to the door. Johanna put on her fuzzy boots. Charlie helped her with her coat. He did not kiss her good night, but touched her lips with his fingertips.

"See you tomorrow?"

Johanna closed her eyes, resisted the urge to kiss those fingertips. It was more than sexual desire prickling her skin and making her body ache. Wave after wave of love for this man who had been the boy that crushed her heart had washed over her since the moment she realized it was he who pulled her into his car at the cemetery. The biggest one broke over her now, standing at his front door, wanting him and knowing he wanted her, but would wait. Had been waiting. For twenty years.

Johanna opened her eyes. She caught his hand in hers. "Charlie, I—"

Still, he waited.

Say it. Tell him. "I…will see you tomorrow."

He seemed to deflate a little, but he smiled. "Tomorrow."

* * * *

Johanna undressed in the dark, trying to remember the ride home. She stood naked in front of the mirror. Charlie had called her beautiful, and he wasn't the first. She looked pretty good for thirty-eight, though a little wider in the hips than she'd been in her twenties. Her belly was no longer flat and taut, but she was one of those lucky people who could eat whatever she pleased—a very good thing for a baker. Bouncing on the balls of her feet, she was gratified to see her breasts jiggled more than they flopped. She chuckled at herself, started to turn away from the mirror, and stopped.

A *click* and the little light on her dresser illuminated what she had spotted by moonlight. There, just above her heart, was a smear of what looked like blood. It was blood. Charlie's. It had to be. When the locket bit him.

Johanna clicked off the light. Licking her finger, she snatched a tissue from the box. She wiped away the smear too much like an omen and slipped in between the cold sheets, telling herself they were the cause of her shivering. The pops and creaks of the old farmhouse usually soothed and now unsettled. Johanna felt eyes watching her, was certain she heard words whispering. Only when she stopped trying did she fall into a fitful slumber devoid of dreams.

* * * *

These halls are so quiet. They once screamed with laughter, with little-girl games. Now the house groans like an old man trying to stand, in a night no longer holding dreams of ponies and boys and flying like fairies. Rising now are those dreams of women. Dark dreams. Memories masquerading. Hopeful longings finding form. They are dreams of desire churning and turning the sheets. Sweat beaded on brows, across breasts. They ignite a different kind of light, one that flames, then burns low, but never goes out. It is there in a child, waiting to become more. Waiting to be allowed. Waiting and waiting and waiting...

Chapter 8

Five Golden Rings

Johanna did not see Charlie the next day. He had to go pick up Will, who demanded to come home through the choked-on tears of a seventeen-year-old boy. Sending Charlotte would have been a mistake, and Johanna did not even offer to drive out with him.

"Your son needs you," Johanna had said on the phone when he told her, "not you and your girlfriend."

Silence. She checked her phone. "Charlie?"

"Yeah, I'm here."

"I thought I lost you."

"No chance," he said. It wasn't until she hung up the phone that she realized her own choice of words, and though she blushed, it was from happiness, not chagrin.

Nina and Gunner invited her to join them on the ski slopes, but Johanna declined, instead asking Emma if she and the boys wanted to go to the wildlife sanctuary in the next town over, like they used to when they were girls. Just as Johanna was leaving, Julietta emerged from her office upstairs, declaring her latest deadline met and the rest of the year—a whole two days—off, and that she was tagging along on their outing.

"This place hasn't changed even a little bit," Johanna said as they sat at a rickety table, sipping watery coffee. "I think even all the animals are the same as when we were kids."

"Can't be," Julietta said. "Well, maybe the turtles, but not the deer and raccoons."

"Ian found a baby bird once," Emma said. "We brought it here, and visited it until it was big enough to fly off on its own."

Ian, Henry, and Gio played in the maze, dug "fossils" in the sandbox, tapped on glass tanks and begged to feed the animals despite the signs saying they couldn't. Johanna's genuine affection for them was tempered only by the opinion that Emma spoiled them to the point of being annoying, but she kept her mouth shut when her sister slipped Henry a crumble of her cookie to drop into the koi pond when no one was looking. Julietta did not.

"Emma."

"What? It's just a piece of a cookie."

"The sign says not to feed the animals."

"They're fish."

"Don't pretend to be dumb."

"Come on, Jules." Emma laughed, looking sidelong at the attendant behind the desk. "He didn't hurt anything."

"How do you know? Are you an expert on the digestive tracts of koi? You can't teach your boys to obey the rules only when it suits them. Rules are created to keep people from doing stupid things."

Emma and Johanna exchanged glances. Their sister was not looking at either of them, but rather to some random point beyond the koi pond.

"You're right," Emma said gently. "You're absolutely right. I'm sorry."

Julietta blinked, scowled, nodded. Emma called her sons away from the koi pond, diverting their attention to the guess-what's-in-the-box game still hiding away the glued-down piece of deer antler, turtle shell, trilobite, and squirrel skull in it the first time Johanna ever put her hand inside.

"She spoils them." Julietta grumbled.

"They're good boys."

"They won't be if she lets them break the rules."

"I broke the rules all the time and look at me," Johanna joked.

"Gram never let you, though."

"But Poppy did." Johanna nudged her. "Remember he let us have donuts for breakfast whenever Gram worked on Saturday mornings?"

It took a moment, but Julietta thawed. She grinned. "Donuts in front of Saturday morning cartoons. She'd have flipped."

"And see? We're all fine."

"Are we?"

"Aren't we?"

Julietta shrugged. Her attention strayed to their nephews now climbing the kiddie-rock-wall. Johanna sipped her coffee, disgusting as it was. She was ready to go home, make a good pot of coffee, and wait for Charlie to call.

"What's it like, Jo?"

She blinked. "Sorry, what was that?"

Julietta grimaced. "Being in love. What's it like?"

"Scary," she said the first word that popped into her head. "And amazing. Why? Do you think you might be falling for Efan?"

"I'm not sure what it is I'm doing," she said. "Sometimes my emotions get confused. Sometimes I wonder if I actually feel anything, or if simply react to my surroundings. Like a starfish or something."

"I have no idea what that means, Jules."

"Starfish just react," she said. "To food. To light. To other starfish. There's no thought, no plan. Just reaction. It's how I feel sometimes. Most of the time, really. But—"

"But?"

"I've never reacted to anyone the way I do Efan. He makes me... happy. I think about him when he's not around, and when he is, I just want to touch him, to know he's real and not...not..."

Julietta's eyes welled. Johanna moved to the seat beside her, put an arm about her shoulders. "Oh, honey. Of course he's real."

"But would you tell me if he wasn't? Or would you let me believe in him because it makes me happy? Because it's safer than telling me the truth?"

Heart churning, eyes stinging, Johanna could not speak through the constriction of her throat. She could only hold her sister's hand, caressing the spot between forefinger and thumb, trying to find the right words to assuage the fears they shared.

"You're not like Daddy," she managed at last.

"But would I be, without all the medication I take?"

"The medication is for anxiety, not schizophrenia."

"I'm afraid you are all keeping the truth from me. That's paranoia."

"Being afraid doesn't make you like Daddy any more than me nearly freezing myself in a cemetery makes me like Mom."

Julietta fell silent, then she startled and reached into her jeans pocket for her phone. Tears gave way to a watery smile. "It's him."

"Well, answer it."

Julietta tapped the screen, put the phone to her ear and rose to her feet. "I was just talking about you."

Johanna tried to focus on Emma and the boys now looking intently at the winter cluster of bees keeping warm their queen, through the

plexiglass panel of their hive. Her ears strained to hear her youngest
sister's conversation, or at least the tone in her voice. Julietta started back
to the rickety table.

"Great," she was saying. "I'll ask them. It sounds like fun."

"Who will you ask what?" Johanna asked once she sat down again.
Julietta smiled, all remnants of their earlier conversation banished with a
single phone call.

"First Night. Ever been to one?"

"I don't know. What is it?"

"When a whole town celebrates New Year's Eve together. Great
Barrington is doing it this year. Entertainment, food, games, contests,
music. It sounds like a lot of fun. Efan wants me to come, and he asked if
you, Nina and Emma want to come too—with the guys, of course."

"I'm up for it. I'll see if Charlie is."

Johanna gratefully steered the conversation to the catamaran Nina
and Gunner were thinking about buying, and the trip around the world
they would take in it. Her brother-in-law was already talking about
the curiosities shop they could open with all the odd things they found
exploring. As Nina predicted, Gunner was not content to live the life of
the idle rich.

It had been much the same since Christmas Day, and their discovery
of Gram's secret. The sisters skirted about the bigger issues they faced,
like what was going to happen with the house, and Julietta, once Nina and
Johanna went back to their own lives. Emma had no interest in moving
into the farmhouse. She liked her neighborhood and the abundance of
children there. Suggesting she move in with her sister insinuated Julietta
was incapable of taking care of herself—the truth of which Johanna could
not quite grasp. It had simply been easier to let it all slide. There was
time. Johanna was staying on until spring, but time passed quickly, even
in winter. Even in Bitterly.

* * * *

It was decided—they were all going to First Night. Charlotte had
happily offered to watch Emma's boys through the night, considering she
had no plans that did not involve Katie and yet more karaoke.

Johanna stood before the mirror in her room, inspecting the thick
sweater, black jeans, and the white goat-hair boots she had splurged on
when it became apparent that a slinky, sequined dress was not suitable for
traipsing about Great Barrington in the cold. She tugged at the cowl of the
sweater, itchy in the warmth of the house.

"You'll be happy for it later," she told her reflection. Pulling the locket out from under her clothes, she decided to wear it openly. It looked lovely against the grey sweater. Perfect, in fact—even if it bit Charlie.

"They're here," Julietta called up the stairs. "Come on, Jo!"

Johanna blinked away the image of Charlie's blood on her skin, stuck her tongue out at herself in the mirror and turned away. She trotted down the steps, her furry boots like excited little dogs underfoot. Nina and Gunner were already putting their coats on. Her oldest sister pulled the long, blond braid from the neck of her ski jacket. Flushed and smiling, she looked up at Gunner, laughing at whatever he had said before Johanna came down the stairs.

"What's so funny?" she asked, slipping her own coat on.

"Going out in a minivan on New Year's Eve," Gunner answered. "I don't know that I've ever been in one."

"Oh, come on. There are a lot of minivan cabs in the city."

"Yeah, but those are cabs." Gunner tugged her braid. "I like your boots, Jo. What are they? Endangered albino gorilla?"

"They're goat hair, smart ass, and a by-product of the meat industry, so unless you've gone vegetarian, I don't want to hear it."

"What? I said I liked them."

"Stop teasing my sister." Nina slapped his arm. "I've been known to go postal on anyone who does."

"Like when I was in seventh grade and that girl, Ivy, was terrorizing me?" Johanna asked.

"Oh, wow. Yeah, Ivy. I forgot about her."

"You can be sure she never forgot you. Or your right hook."

"She deserved it."

"We're just lucky her parents didn't sue."

"Things were different then."

"Johanna, Nina," Julietta called from the kitchen. "Let's go."

They piled into Emma and Mike's seven-seater, the only vehicle they could all get into. Emma volunteered to be designated driver, though warned her husband, on pain of torture and death, she would not be sympathetic with a hangover on New Year's Day. Gunner and Nina, the tallest of them all, took the captain's chairs in the middle. Johanna climbed into the back to sit between Julietta and Charlie. He put his arm around her.

"You squished?" he asked.

"A good kind of squished. It's a short ride. How's Will?"

Charlie grimaced. "He's fine. I'm calling shenanigans. Seems as if there's a big New Year's party at his friend Brian's house, and a certain young lady was hoping he'd be there."

"So it wasn't that he couldn't stand being with his mom."

"Highly doubtful. So, did I kiss you hello yet?"

Topic changed, just like that. Johanna smiled. "No, you're neglecting me horribly."

Charlie pulled her in closer, his kiss uninhibited by the crowded car. Johanna let what little sense of decorum she had slide away.

"Fer cryin' out loud, you two." Emma laughed from the driver's seat. Johanna looked up to see her smiling in the rearview. Emma winked and Johanna blew her a kiss, but she didn't dive back into Charlie the way she wanted to. Instead, she hooked her arm through Julietta's.

"You have enough room?"

"I'm small. It's fine."

"Where are we meeting Efan?" Emma called back.

"He said to park at the school, lot A," Julietta answered. "He'll be waiting for us there. It's not open to the public, but he got us a pass."

"Awesome," Mike hooted. "Preferred parking, no kids, just a bunch of friends having fun. This is great, isn't it Emma?"

She leveled a glance her husband's way, and backed out of the driveway. Nina swung her head around the side of her seat, eyebrows raised. Johanna grimaced and shook her head. The harder Mike tried to make her happy, the tighter Emma held on to her anger.

"You should talk to her," Nina whispered.

"Me? Why me?"

"Because she thinks I'm perfect and can't possibly understand what she's going through."

"I'm not sure how to take that."

"The way it was meant."

"What are you two whispering about," Emma asked.

Talk to her, Nina mouthed, and turned back in her seat. "We're talking about you, obviously," she said. "We think you should go blond again."

All the girls laughed.

"My hair was like straw."

"You had to practically shave your head." Julietta snorted. "That was funny."

"Funny for you guys," Emma said. "It took forever to grow out again."

* * * *

The fifteen-minute drive over the border into Massachusetts flew by on funny memories, laughter, and good-natured teasing. Even Emma joined in, her self-righteous anger, for now, set back to simmer. As they pulled into the parking lot of the school where Efan worked, Julietta tugged on Johanna's arm.

"I'm going to ask Efan to drive me home," she whispered.

"Oh, honey, you should have told me you were squooshed."

"I'm not. I mean, I am, but—jeez, Johanna. You're kind of dense."

"I'm...oh." She nudged her sister. "I gotcha."

"Tell Nina and Emma, but don't make it obvious."

"Will do."

"And when we get home, don't tease me or I won't be able to go through with it."

"Jules." Johanna jiggled her. "We're not adolescents. And if you're uncomfortable, why not just spend the night here with him?"

"He lives on campus. No overnight girlfriend stays allowed."

"Ah, I see. That does put a damper on things. I'll tell you what, you and Efan leave a little before us. Then you can get home and upstairs before anyone else gets home."

"Okay." Julietta hugged her tightly. Fiercely. "Thanks, Jo."

"Hello, hello, my fine friends," Efan called as he slid open the door. "And where is my bewitching lady?"

"I'm here!" Julietta darted forward, through the narrow aisle between captain's chairs, and nearly fell face-first into the center console. Efan caught her, pulled her out of the car and into his arms.

"It's good to know you are as anxious to see me as I am to see you."

Julietta only buried her face in his shoulder. Efan reached into his pocket and pulled out a parking pass, handing it to Mike to put on the dash.

"Is everything all right, Julietta?"

"Fine. Wonderful. I'm fine."

Johanna loved the way he always used her little sister's full name, and the way he stressed the *tt*. It made her name sophisticated instead of diminutive, another plus in the Efan-column.

Charlie offered his hand, and Johanna stepped into the night as if she were stepping into a ballroom wearing glass slippers instead of goat-hair boots. The sky was the perfect midnight blue from a box of crayons, awash with the wealth of stars visible in the Berkshire Mountains. Already, music drifted from somewhere beyond the walls of the school. The distinct aroma of fried dough reached her nostrils. New Year's Eve.

With her sisters. With Charlie. Johanna could not remember spending a single New Year's Eve with anyone but herself for company. Erstwhile relationships never lasted through Christmas, leaving her unwilling to try again until the spring, with yet another man who would not make it through the end of the year. It had never struck her as odd. She had never considered it at all.

She took Charlie's hand in her mittened one and squeezed it. He looked down at her with the smile that had been turning her heart upside down for many years, for many reasons. Though not always for good reasons, they'd always been born in love.

"Where to first?" Nina was already tugging her husband towards the gate. "I'm hungry. Can we eat?"

"There are a few places to choose from," Efan said. "The restaurants, of course, but there are also all kinds of street vendors, a spaghetti dinner in the church hall at St. Mark's, and authentic Greek over at the VFW."

"Greek," they all shouted at once. Efan led them through the festively crowded town decked in lights and garlands. They stopped for a mulled cider, then again to watch a pair of jugglers in drag, tossing dolls dressed in motley. It took a good hour to reach the VFW, and another half hour before they made it to the front of the line to get their food.

"Worth every second standing in line," Gunner said, his mouth full of moussaka. "This is the best I've ever tasted, and I've eaten a lot of Greek food."

"See the little woman serving roasted chicken?" Efan pointed to an elderly woman who looked just like every cafeteria lady Johanna had ever known. "She does it all."

"All?" Charlie asked. "I have a hard time cooking for just me and my kids."

"I imagine she gets some help," Efan told them, "but you can be absolutely certain she has her hand in all of it other than slipping something into the oven, or stirring a pot."

"Does she have a restaurant?" Emma asked.

"No. Once a year is all we get." He leaned in. "But if I ask her nicely, she makes me something now and again."

They ate and they talked and they made room for others still waiting for a seat. Out in the cold, fresh air after the heat of the VFW, Johanna tugged at the itchy cowl of her sweater, wishing she'd worn something underneath. Staying together was nearly impossible. Emma and Mike wanted to go to the music pavilion where a country band was twanging. Julietta and Efan headed to the poetry reading outside the bookstore.

Charlie suggested the Gauntlet Thrown Shakespearean Insult Contest. Gunner and Nina joined them, but the couples got separated trying to worm through the crowd.

Charlie held tight to her hand, shielded her from elbows and hips with his body. Somehow, they made it near to the front, close enough to see the contestants battling with verse.

"You blocks, you stones, you worse than senseless things," shouted a portly man dressed like Friar Tuck, complete with tonsure. An equally portly woman, dressed sensibly for the cold, shouted back, "Thou whoreson zed! Thou unnecessary letter!"

Back and forth they raged. Johanna could not have said if their insults were genuine, but there were two men and a woman judging, tablets in hand, so she assumed they were. After a few hurled insults, Friar Tuck stammered, "I shall laugh myself to death on this...this...aw, damn, on this foul-footed monstrosity?"

"Wrong." The woman judging tapped her tablet. "Sorry, Fred. Anyone know the insult? Not you, Sandra," she pointed to his competitor. "It goes to the crowd, first. I'll give you a hint. It's from *The Tempest*. Can anyone pick up the gauntlet?"

"I shall laugh myself to death at this puppy-headed monster."

Johanna glanced up at Charlie, his hand raised in the air.

"Correct! Come on up, sir. Let's see if you can beat Sandra."

"Charlie?" Johanna asked as he started forward.

"What? I have a mug at home."

* * * *

For every insult Sandra flung, Charlie had one to fling back. Johanna's heart raced. The insults got bawdier. She oohed and aahed with the crowd, pride and surprise alternating in her heart. Sandra's drawled, *Thou misshapen dick*, had nearly made her spit mulled cider out her nose, but Charlie's answering, *Dissembling harlot, thou art false in all*, had made her cheer.

"They have to be running out," Gunner leaned in to murmur. He and Nina had made their way to her after Charlie went up on-stage.

"I don't know," Nina leaned close to say, "the Bard was fond of his insults. This could go on for hours."

Sandra clapped loudly, arms raised over her head. "I have one that will end this. Ready for it?"

"Throw it at me, Sandy." Charlie laughed. He crouched a little, motioning her in like a little boy getting ready to brawl. The woman straightened her coat dramatically, tugging at each glove before clearing her throat.

"A knave," she said. "A rascal; an eater of broken meats; base, proud, shallow, beggarly, three suited, hundred-pound, filthy, worsted-stocking knave; a lily-livered..." Sandra's brow furrowed. She cleared her throat again. "A lily-livered, action-taking knave, a whoreson, glass-looking—no, gazing. Glass-gazing..."

"Come on Sandra," onlookers called. "You got this."

The woman's jaw worked back and forth. She shook her head slowly. Finally, she threw up her hands. "Sorry, folks. I just can't remember the rest. That's what I get for showing off."

"No!"

"Come on!"

"Try again!"

But the judges were raising their hands for silence. The female judge called, "Anyone in the audience want to take a shot at it?" Everyone hushed. No one stepped forward. "All right then, Mr. McCallan. It's yours. Can you pick up the gauntlet?"

Johanna held her breath.

Charlie stood on the little raised platform. He found her eyes and smiled. "A knave; a rascal; an eater of broken meats; base, proud, shallow, beggarly, three-suited, hundred-pound, filthy, worsted-stocking knave; a lily-livered, action-taking knave, a whoreson, glass-gazing, super-serviceable finical rogue; one-trunk-inheriting slave; one that wouldst be a bawd, in way of good service, and art nothing but the composition of a knave, beggar, coward, pander, and the son and heir of a mongrel bitch: one whom I will beat into clamorous whining, if thou deniest the least syllable of thy addition." He bowed. "King Lear."

The gathering erupted in a riotous cheer. Charlie was swarmed from all sides, congratulated and clapped. Johanna could not hope to push her way through the crowd but neither did she lose sight of him, his auburn hair like a beacon burning there on the platform. A few moments of chaos and the judges called order, shooing people off the platform.

"Let's give a hand to Sandra Doubleday for a great effort," one of the male judges called, and again the cheering pounded. He handed her a second-place ribbon, holding an envelope up in the air. "Two tickets to any performance of The Shakespeare Company's upcoming season and a backstage tour."

More cheering, this time, polite. Sandra clutched the tickets to her breast, her face beaming. A gentleman helped her down from the platform, hugged her close, and led her into the crowd.

"And to Mr. Charles McCallan..." The other gentleman on the platform placed a blue ribbon into Charlie's hand. "First prize, a gift certificate for Valentine's Dinner for two at Blue Pearl, two season passes to all performances of the Company's upcoming season." Hands raised, he waited for the cheering to stop. "And a back-stage tour."

Johanna whooped with the rest, pushing her way to Charlie on the platform. As she neared, he reached for her hand and pulled her up beside him.

"I had no idea you were so well-read," she shouted over the noise.

"I'm not. I told you, I have a mug. I'll show you when we get home."

Tucked under his arm while he was congratulated again and again, Johanna simply basked in the moment of being where she was, with Charlie. Home, he had said, and the momentary tremor became a small but steady warmth burrowing into her chest.

"The fireworks are about to start." Nina was suddenly there, a golden goddess with her blond braid and her white coat, white jeans and blue boots. Gunner had her hand, tugging her in the opposite direction. "Come on, Jo! Charlie!"

Like children running from a rainstorm, they all grasped hands and started through the crowd. Johanna spotted Emma and Mike eating fried dough on a corner.

"Emma, Mike, this way!"

Her sister grabbed Charlie's free hand and they joined in the chase, dodging and shrieking their way through town. Johanna had no idea where they were going, or why they were running to get there. It just felt good. She felt free. She wanted to run like this forever.

"Here." Gunner led them behind a brick building, to a fire escape. "We can get up on the roof."

"Are you crazy?" Emma panted. "We'll get in trouble."

"We're adults." Gunner laughed, pulling the ladder down. "Not a bunch of kids the cops'll hassle. Come on, Emma. Where's your sense of adventure?"

"What about Julietta and Efan?" Johanna looked over her shoulder, as if they'd appear.

"Up first." Nina was already climbing behind her husband. "We'll call her from the roof."

The first whistled rocket lit the sky as Johanna legged-up over the ledge. Charlie was next, catching her from behind and holding her against his chest. They gazed skyward together, watching the sparkles and laughing when the boom hit the pit of their stomachs.

"She's not picking up," Emma said during a lull. "Does anyone have Efan's number?"

"I do." Gunner pulled out his phone. "Hey, Efan. We're up on the roof of the brick building—yeah, that's the one. I know," he laughed, "but we'll be careful. Guess you won't be joining us up here then, eh, you dawg?" Another laugh. Gunner hung up the phone, waggled his eyebrows. "He says he and Julietta are heading back to Bitterly as soon as the clock strikes midnight. They'll stay on the ground."

Ten minutes until midnight. Another round of fireworks lit up the sky. Johanna rested back against Charlie's chest, warm and comfortable in his arms and so happy she could not stop smiling. Five minutes to midnight. A band struck up Auld Lang Syne. People started singing. Nina and Gunner, Emma and Mike did too.

Johanna turned in Charlie's arms and kissed his mouth, opened to sing. He gathered her to him. The world fell away. Only they existed, only this kiss no longer enough. Anticipation was sweet, but Johanna's was more than twenty years waiting. She wanted more. She wanted it always.

Somewhere, far away in some other world, a thousand booms crackled into being. Another sky over another town lit up in sparkled, explosive light.

Ten.

Nine.

Eight.

Seven.

Six.

Five.

Four.

Three.

Two.

One!

"Happy New Year!"

The chorus on the roof brought Johanna back to Great Barrington, Massachusetts. Charlie still held her in his arms, his eyes holding hers. Johanna pulled her mitten off with her teeth, reached up to touch his face. His beard was soft but thick. She rubbed warm fingers through it. Words, three of them, tried to get past the emotion, the fear, the joy. Words he waited to hear. Words she wanted to say. Johanna opened her mouth, but they did not escape. Charlie kissed her again and she imagined he could taste them on her tongue.

"Hey, There's Julietta." Nina leaned over the roof wall, waving an arm over her head and calling to their sister. Emma, Mike and Gunner joined her. Johanna tugged at Charlie's beard, took his hand and hauled him to the edge. Below, Julietta and Efan were looking up, waving furiously.

* * * *

Piled into the car again, this time minus Julietta, they all stayed contentedly quiet. Johanna tucked herself into the crook of Charlie's shoulder, her head resting there. Nina and Gunner held hands across the narrow aisle between captain's chairs. Mike's hand rested on Emma's shoulder, the two of them more at ease with one another than Johanna had seen them since her arrival before Christmas.

It took a while to get out of the parking lot, out of town. Though First Night festivities would continue for several hours yet, most seemed to have the same idea they did—go home. Go to bed. Though Johanna had no intention of sleeping. Charlotte watched the kids at Emma's house. Will was sleeping at his friend's. When Emma dropped Charlie off at his place, she would simply get out of the car and go with him inside. The notion set her skin to tingling, her body to aching.

Battling slumber, Johanna found her seventeen-year -old self behind her lids. Charlie, and the woods, and the old quilted blanket they used to make out on. His face was so clear, and with the benefit of hindsight, the fear mingled into the desire was clear too. Then, it had frightened her. He had frightened her. Then, she had run away. Then, she had been a child.

"What's going on up there?"

Emma's voice sounded out of place in the contented silence. Johanna blinked back to awake to see a long, dark stretch of road ahead, and a pair of hazards blinking red flashes in the snow.

"Looks like a car went off the road," Mike said. "I'll call 911. Aw, crap."

"What?" Gunner asked.

"No coverage. You?"

They all checked their phones. Dead zone. Not uncommon in the mountains, even for smartphones. Emma pulled over to the shoulder, the tires spinning, the van sliding precariously.

"Black ice," she said. "Thank goodness there are no trees around."

Johanna leaned forward. Mike was saying "I'll go. You guys stay here," as realization dawned, as Mike opened his door, as the silence in the van became screaming from the Audi that had slid off the road, as the voice screaming became Julietta's.

"Oh, my God." All three women spoke at once, leapt from the van as one entity homed in on a target. Nina pounded on the driver's side door while Johanna and Emma tried to open the passengers'.

"Unlock it," Nina yelled. The locks clicked. Johanna yanked open the door.

"Daddy, Daddy. Daddy, Daddy," Julietta screamed, her voice raw and raspy.

"Jules," Johanna gathered her sister into her arms, pulled her from the car and onto the cold and icy pavement. "Julietta, it's me. Johanna."

Julietta screamed on. Emma and Nina pulled both sisters into a clutch, like oyster shells around a pearl.

"I don't know what happened," Efan was saying. "We hit a patch of ice and went off the road, but that's all. She started screaming. I didn't know what to do. My phone wouldn't work."

"Mike," Gunner said. "Take Efan in the van and go back until you get cell coverage. Get an ambulance."

"I swear, I didn't hurt her!"

"Tell him," was all Johanna heard Gunner say, and then car doors slamming, tires spinning, and the men driving away. Julietta's screams had become whispers. The same word over and over again—Daddy. Wrapped around her little sister, wrapped up by her other two, Johanna was comforted and heartbroken at once. Emma and Nina let up on their grip. Cold air made Johanna gasp.

"Let's get her off the ground and into——" she began.

Julietta clutched at her, her whispered cries for her father now a mewling sound.

"Here, sit on this."

Parka. Hand. Arm. Face. Charlie's face.

"But you'll be cold."

"Gunner and I are going to change the tire. The front one blew. I'll be fine."

"The guys will be back in a minute," Nina said. "It'll be okay."

Johanna let go of her sister long enough to get Charlie's coat underneath her. When she took Julietta back into her arms, she was limp as a rag doll, and silent. She trembled slightly, a hiccup of nerves firing intermittent spasms through her body. Johanna looked up at her other sisters, their worried expressions mirroring the one tensing the muscles in her own face.

A flash of blue and red lights turned all their heads. Nina put her hand on Johanna's shoulder, standing over her like a sentry. Emma walked towards the police officers getting out of their car. Gunner and Charlie joined them. A moment later, one officer, a young man hardly older than Charlotte came to squat on his haunches beside the clutch of sisters.

"Is she injured?"

"Not that we can see," Johanna told him. "The driver of the car said they only went off the road. They had seatbelts on."

"Who was driving?"

"He's not here," Nina said. "He and my sister's husband went up the road to make the 911 call. They should be...here they are now."

The minivan pulled over beside the police car. Efan started towards them, but was stopped by the other, older officer.

"An ambulance will be here in a few minutes," their officer said. "We'll get her taken care of."

"They're going to take her away," Nina said when he was gone.

"Don't say it. Don't."

"You know what's happening."

"She's had a shock. That's all."

"It's what we've all feared, Jo. You can pretend all you like, but now it's happened. Be prepared for what's coming."

A silent ambulance pulled up, red lights flashing. EMTs scrambled out of the back, took a limp and unresponsive Julietta from Johanna's arms. *She was in an accident as a child. She saw our father die.*

But words would not come out of her mouth. Gunner was already talking to one of the EMTs, a young woman with her hair pulled into a ponytail that bounced when she nodded to whatever he was saying, what Johanna knew he was saying.

"Jo?" Charlie was suddenly beside her. Johanna turned into him, buried her face in the front of his shirt and there stayed, his arms holding her close, until there were no more flashing lights in her periphery.

"What will happen to her?" she asked at last.

"They are taking her to the hospital in Great Barrington. Once they know there are no physical injuries—"

"We know there aren't."

"Sweetheart." He drew her close. "They just have to make sure."

"And then?"

"They'll make her comfortable until they can get someone to check her out psychiatrically. The EMTs said to go home. The hospital will call if there's any change. We can see her in the morning."

Johanna sniffed. She wiped her eyes. Efan leaned against the Audi, head bowed and Gunner's hands on his shoulders. He nodded, but he did not look up to whatever Gunner said to him. Emma and Mike sat in the open door of the minivan, her head on his shoulder. Nina stood in front of Efan's car, watching tail lights no longer visible in the distance.

"We should go," Charlie said. Johanna nodded. He went to the van, she to the Audi.

"I can't go home," Efan was saying. "I'm going to the hospital. I'll sit at her bedside."

"Will they let you?" Gunner asked. "You're not next of kin."

"She isn't dying!" Efan put a hand over his mouth. "I'm sorry. So sorry. It's just…I didn't realize how deeply I love her. It's so fast, but… there you have it. I love her. I have to be there when she wakes. If they won't let me in her room, I will wait outside of it."

Gunner gently clapped his shoulders. "If you're sure."

"Will you call us if she wakes?" Nina asked. "Or if they give you a hard time."

"No one gives me a hard time." Efan smiled a shaky smile. "Would you refuse this face?"

He hugged Nina, then Johanna. They waited while he got into the car and headed back north. The silence in the minivan was anything but contented. Johanna leaned against Charlie, eyes closed and wishing.

How did the most perfect night of her life turn so quickly?

The food, the contest, the music and fireworks and laughter. The plan for the rest of her night, the rest of her life. All gone. Every happy spark in her soul doused for a patch of black ice on a country road.

Her head snapped up when the car stopped. Johanna blinked awake, lifted her head from Charlie's shoulder. "Stay with me." Johanna barely felt her mouth move, though she heard her own words clearly. "Please, Charlie. Stay with me."

Charlie took her face in his hands, kissed her brow.

"I wouldn't leave you now for anything in the world, Jo. I already called Charlotte."

* * * *

This man lies beside you, and only holds you gentle against the fearsome night. He was the boy you used to sneak in here, when you were just a girl. I see him in this man's sleeping face. Naughty sylph. Such abandon. My highest hopes were for you. Of all, you were the wildest, most free. Sorrow slid from you like water from a selkie.

*Now it holds you close. Banish it, and they all will—my
Valkyrie, my Madonna, my precious sprite. Wild women
caught and sang the sun in flight! You are who they look
to. You cannot let them go gentle into that good night,
lest they learn too late, and grieve.*

*Banish we burdens from these halls! Life is joy! Not
madness and secrets and headless ghouls. Rage, my
sylph. The light cannot die if you rage against it.*

Chapter 9

Four Calling Birds

Efan stood in the hallway with a woman in a white coat, their heads close together and voices low. He lifted his head, motioning Johanna, Emma, and Nina closer, held out his hand as they drew near.

"Then she must be moved," he was saying, and gestured to the sisters. "These are the ladies Coco. If some sort of permission is required, they can give it."

"What's going on?" Nina asked. "Julietta needs to be moved where?"

"Ladies?" The woman in the white coat gestured them into a conference room and closed the door behind them. "I am Dr. Faust, currently your sister's physician. May I speak frankly?"

"Please do," Emma said.

"There is nothing physically wrong with Julietta," she began. "Not even a bruise from the seat belt. There is nothing we can do for her here. This hospital has no psychiatric ward, and I have no expertise with psychiatric matters. From what Mr. Bowen has given me concerning your sister's past—"

"Mr. Bowen?" Johanna asked.

"That would be me." Efan raised his hand. "I have only repeated what Michael told me last night in the car, about Julietta's parents being untreated psychiatric patients who died in a car crash when she was a toddler, and that she nearly died as well."

"That's not exactly how it went," Emma said.

"Forgive me. It is what Michael told me."

Emma turned to Dr. Faust. "I was in the crash too, and I was older."

"Can you tell me what happened?"

"I hardly remember. I doubt Julietta does either. We were both knocked out."

Dr. Faust and Efan exchanged glances.

"What?" Nina asked. "Tell us."

"Perhaps we should sit." Dr. Faust gestured to the conference table and chairs. "Mr. Bowen, would you get the ladies some coffee?"

"Of course."

Efan put pods into the coffeemaker and pressed the necessary buttons. Johanna focused on him, on every move he made.

It's worse than we feared. Oh, Jules.

"Your sister woke crying," Dr. Faust began. "She was calling for her father."

* * * *

Johanna put her head in her arms, closing off the hospital conference room, her sisters, Efan and Dr. Faust still discussing their best options. She wanted it to be yesterday, wanted last night to have never happened.

If not last night, it would have been another time.

Johanna's own voice in her head sounded callous, however truthful. Julietta's breakdown had been building since she was a tiny girl strapped into a car seat, bleeding and in pain, while the emergency crews cut her free, while she screamed for her father.

"She is fine staying for today," Dr. Faust was saying. Johanna picked up her head. "But other than keeping her comfortable, there is nothing we can do for her here."

"I'm not putting my sister in a ward." Nina said. "That is absolutely out of the question."

"She has reverted," the doctor continued. "At the moment, she is a little girl who just suffered a terrible tragedy. She needs the proper care, doctors who know how to bring her back without causing more harm."

"No wards. I will not have her subjected to what goes on there. There must be private facilities available."

"Of course there are, but insurance rarely..."

"Fuck the insurance," Nina raged. "I've got money. Show me where to sign."

"Nina." Efan rose from his seat, his hands raised in supplication. "There is a better option. Will you listen?"

"We're listening," Johanna answered for her. "Nina, come on. Sit."

"There is a small hospital at the academy," Efan began. "A private one. A colleague of mine, the school psychiatrist, has technical rights to practice there. If I can pull the proper strings, we can get her in a bed, and he will treat her himself, at least for the time being."

"There is a good chance she will come out of this on her own," Dr. Faust said. "Follow-up care will be necessary, but there is no reason to believe this event is in any way indicative of the sort of mental illness your parents suffered from. PTSD is vastly different from——"

"PTSD?" Emma asked.

"Post traumatic stress disorder," Efan answered.

"Isn't that a veteran thing?"

"Common misconception," Dr. Faust said. "Traumatic events embed themselves in our brains, so to speak. In many cases, the person suffering has no idea what is causing the seemingly random anxiety that, when you really dig into it, isn't random at all. A time of day can trigger it, or a sound. It could be any number of things. Then there are episodes like Julietta is experiencing—a full-blown reversion to the moment of trauma, brought back by the car going off the road."

"I thought psychiatry wasn't your area of expertise," Nina grumbled.

"It isn't. That's about all I know, which is why I feel your sister needs to be with someone who knows more."

"What do you think?" Efan asked them all, but looked at Nina. "She will be close by, and in a private room that will not bankrupt you should her insurance refuse."

"Who is this colleague of yours?" she asked. "Not some crusty old Freud-devotee, is it?"

"He is neither old nor a great admirer of Freud, I assure you. He's a good man. Dr. Sam Chowdary. A good friend. I called him last night and he is very happy to be of assistance."

Nina folded her arms over her chest. Johanna held her breath.

I didn't realize how deeply I love her.

Efan's words echoed back from the night prior, earnest and bewildered. Johanna's heart swelled, pulled him into her family as swiftly and completely as it had Charlie's children.

"All right," Nina said. "Jo? Emma?"

"For now," Emma answered. "But if she doesn't come out of it——"

"She will." Johanna rested a hand on her sister's arm. "She will, Emma."

"Whether she does or doesn't, it's a first step." Efan stood up. "It's all we can take. Doctor? Can we see her now?"

"I will go look in on her. Wait here."

* * * *

Whether for the sedatives administered or shock, Julietta did not respond to any of them. Her unfocused eyes moved from face to face, lingering only on Johanna's, and only for a moment. Efan spoke quietly to her. Nina held her hand. Emma kissed her cheek. When it became too obvious to ignore her lack of any reaction, the sisters filed out one by one, leaving Efan at her bedside.

"This is bad," Emma whispered outside the door. "Thank goodness Gram isn't here to see."

"I'm certainly glad she's dead," Nina drawled. "What a thing to say, Emma."

"You know what I mean. She…" Emma averted her gaze. "She must have gone through stuff like this with Mom."

"Dr. Faust said this is completely different—" Johanna began, but Emma cut her off.

"I heard what she said. I also know what I remember."

Nina grasped her sister's hand, and for the first time, Johanna understood why she and Julietta had always been closer when it was Nina she had grown up with, Nina who had cared for her in the house in New Hampshire.

"You both remember more than Jules and I do," she said. "We've never talked about it."

"What is there to talk about?" Nina let go Emma's hand and turned away. "Why share that kind of pain when it isn't necessary?"

"Well she obviously remembers," Johanna insisted. "Something, anyway."

Emma flopped into a chair that hissed air from the cushion as she sank into it. They all waited for it to go silent, collected whatever thoughts whirred overhead.

"Hindsight is a cruel, cruel thing." Nina shook her head slowly. "All these years, the anxiety, the need for order and control. It's all there, like a roadmap to be followed. Dammit."

"We couldn't have known," Johanna said.

"I should have. I was too wrapped up in my own life to notice."

"Don't do that to yourself, Nina. Don't do it to us."

"I was in the accident too," Emma said quickly. "Why does Julietta have PTSD and I don't?"

"Maybe because she was injured?" Johanna answered. "Maybe she's just wired different."

"Maybe."

"Ladies?" Efan entered the conference room smiling. "The ambulance is here. They are going to move her now."

"Ambulance?" Emma asked. "Why?"

"Policy. They can't discharge her in her state, but they can move her."

"I thought they were keeping her through tomorrow."

"I got everyone to cooperate." He grinned. "It is my gift."

"You sure it's safe?" Nina asked.

"Absolutely. And it's for the best. Sam will better know how to handle whatever state she wakes from sedation to, and she'll be closer. To all of us."

The sisters and Efan waited in the hall while Julietta was transferred to a stretcher and strapped securely in. An IV in her arm, Julietta stared straight ahead. Efan lifted her hand to his lips and kissed it.

"I'll be right behind you, *cariad*," he said, and placed her hand gently down again, but it didn't stay down. Julietta's unfocused stare shifted as her hand came up again, reached out at first unsteadily, then most definitely for Johanna.

"I'm here, Jules." Johanna rushed to her sister's side. "I'll go with you in—"

"Mommy..." Words trembled. Hands grasped, pulled Johanna in close. "Mommy. I didn't mean to. I didn't."

Johanna leaned closer. "You didn't mean to what, sweetie?"

"I pushed him and it fell off," Julietta whispered. "I was scared."

Julietta wailed, a sound like a teakettle coming to a boil. Her wail became keening and thrashing that had Dr. Faust injecting something into the IV port. Another moment and Julietta was staring placidly again, but her eyes were locked on Johanna. As they wheeled her out of the ward. As they wheeled her through the hallways. As they loaded her into the waiting ambulance and closed the double doors.

"What did she say to you?" Nina asked.

"I—I'm not sure," Johanna lied. "She thought I was Mom."

"Someone should go with her," Emma said. "If she thinks you're Mom, you should."

"Bad, bad idea." Nina shook her head. "You saw what just happened. I'll go."

"It's probably better than none of you do." Dr. Faust put the matter to rest. "Who knows what memories will be triggered, and why. It's best to keep the stimuli down to a minimum."

"What about me?" Efan asked. "Could I ride with her? I know she's not herself, but there might be a small part of her that will know me. I have no connection to her past further back than a few weeks. Perhaps I will be a comfort to her."

Dr. Faust nodded. Efan pounded on the ambulance door, dug into his pocket and pulled out his keys. "Will one of you take my car back to Great Barrington?"

"Is it automatic?" Johanna asked.

"Stick."

"Then I'm out. Nina?"

"I got it. Where are you parked?"

* * * *

Julietta spoke no more, not even when she saw Johanna again. Dr. Sam Chowdary had been waiting when the ambulance arrived. Johanna breathed an immediate and relieved sigh. Young and handsome in the way of a Bollywood actor, he took charge immediately, focused all his attention on Julietta. He spoke to her as if she would respond, wrote notes even though she did not. Most comforting was he greeted Efan with a warm and concerned embrace that made no excuses for itself.

"I will need some background information," he said once Julietta was settled into a private room in the tiny, but well-funded Great Barrington Academy Hospital. "A private interview with each of you would be best. Ms. Coco-Allen, I understand you have pressing matters to attend to back in New York."

"Nothing that can't happen without me," Nina answered.

"Nevertheless, we will start with you. If you wish, I can interview you today, your sisters tomorrow. Mrs. Chambers? Ms. Coco? Will that be all right?"

"Sure."

"Yes, it's fine."

"Excellent. Ms. Coco-Allen, if you would give me a few moments to prepare, I will be with you shortly."

Dr. Chowdary acknowledged each of them with a slight bow, and left them outside of Julietta's room.

"Does he meet with approval, ladies?" Efan asked, his face wide and wanting as a child's.

"He's great." Johanna assured him. "I feel better with her here. With him."

"How did he know our names," Nina asked, "down to the form of address we each prefer?"

"I informed him," Efan answered. "Was I incorrect?"

"No, not at all. It was just…odd. And odd that you know, come to think of it."

"Not when you were mostly raised by my mamgee." He laughed. "Very forward thinking for a woman from a certain time. She despised the fact that a woman's marital status was announced in her name and, from what my Mum tells me, was quite pleased to adopt Ms. when it first came about. She always told me, '*Cariad*, names are important. They have power.' I didn't think it was fair, women getting to choose from three titles when men only got one. Do you know what her response was?"

"I couldn't guess," Johanna said.

"She told me that went to making up for the years upon years they got no choice at all."

"I like your mamgee. Does it mean grandmother?"

Efan nodded. "I lived with her during my childhood and teen years so I could go to the boys' school in her district. When one is the fifth son and seventh child, funds do grow meager. Mamgee was as happy to have me as I was to be free of my older siblings."

"Ms. Coco-Allen?" A nurse stepped out into the hall. He waved her to follow.

Nina turned to her sisters. "I don't know how long I'll be. Why don't you two go home and send Gunner to get me?"

"No need," Efan said. "I will stay with Julietta for a while, then take you home."

"Are you sure?" Emma asked. "I don't mind waiting."

"I am positive. Go home. Rest. It has been a wearying twenty-four hours."

"Is that all it's been?" Johanna asked as she and Emma sat in her car, waiting for the heat to kick in.

"Not even," Emma answered. "This time yesterday, we were all just waiting for night to come. I can't believe this."

"Me either."

Emma turned sideways. "Do you have the locket on?"

"Always." She pulled it out from under her clothes. "Why?"

Lifting it from her sister's hand, Emma clicked it open, brought it close to her face. "You really do look exactly like her."

"Not exactly."

Emma's gaze shot up. She pursed her lips. "You do. It doesn't mean—"

"I know." Johanna pushed out a long breath. "I know. Habit. I do look like her."

Emma closed the locket, rubbed circles on the etched surface with her thumb. "Where do you think this really came from?"

"I have no idea. Maybe Gram just bought it and put all those stories to it, for us."

"You don't believe that."

"How do you know?"

"Because you believe in the wish. No, don't deny it." Emma let the locket drop. She turned in her seat, facing front and putting the car in gear. "I know you don't think so, but I do too."

* * * *

Charlie had been trying to shake the jittery feeling in his gut all morning. It wasn't until Johanna called just after noon to tell him she was on her way home that it eased. Though he chastised himself for thinking of his own heart when Julietta was in the hospital, he allowed himself the joy.

Johanna was coming home.

"I'm heading to work, Dad." Will bounced down the stairs. "I'll be late for dinner."

"You have to go in now?" Charlie checked his watch. "Your mother will be here to drop the kids off soon."

"I know. I gotta go. Keep something warm for me?"

"All right, son. Have a good day."

Despite the crocodile tears Charlie suspected when his son called sobbing, his avoidance said there was more to it. While Charlotte spouted her feelings, Will buried them. The result was the same. He was glad, at least, that Caleb, Tony, and Millie seemed to be having a good time with their cousins. With their mother. Perhaps they were just young enough to be freer with their forgiveness.

His eldest had also absented herself from the house, necessitating Charlie's presence there instead of letting him head out to finish building shelves for the new owners of the trendy restoration of the old dime store in town.

Cleaning up lunch dishes, as always, left in the sink instead of put into the dishwasher, Charlie itched to get back to work. Once Gina returned the kids, he would leave them with Caleb, call Charlotte home, and put in a couple of hours before Johanna got back.

Kitchen cleaned, Charlie checked his watch. Gina said she'd be there by one o'clock. It was almost two. So much for getting to work. He blew an exasperated breath through his lips. Until Gina left him with sole custody of his children, he never realized how much freedom he had formerly enjoyed. Going to the cemetery, or a client's place, was his job. A given. Every morning. Doctor appointments and school conferences were arranged around it. Now the kids were his job that work got rearranged for, and it was more difficult than he ever imagined.

Two o'clock came, and went. He made himself a cup of tea in the Shakespearean insults mug he got as a gag gift many years ago, the one that sparked his interest, and got him reading the plays he dreaded in high school, that then sparked his determination to read and understand every one good ol' Billy Shakes ever wrote. Then it was three o'clock, his second mug of tea finished, and his interest no longer in the insults book he bought when he found out about the contest. Johanna was due to arrive soon, and though there were no issues between the women, he would have preferred to keep his ex-wife very separate from the re-budding of his relationship with Johanna.

Calls to Gina's cell were not answered. Texts weren't either. He cursed his firm decision about unemployed children not needing cell phones. Where could they be? Why hadn't she called? Unthinkable thoughts first trickled then careened through Charlie's head. They'd already been gone for days. For all he knew, they were in Florida. Gina was enrolling them in school there. She was telling them he wasn't able to take care of them all on his own, that they were better off with her and Bertie, that he had Johanna now and didn't want them anymore, that—

Feet pounded up the front steps. His racing heart eased enough to keep him from bolting for the door and yanking it open. Charlie dropped into the couch, his head back and eyes staring at the ceiling. He collected himself in time for Millie to come bounding into the room and dive onto his lap.

"Daddy, I missed you."

"Oh," he groaned. "Careful there, Mills. Did you have a good time?"

"Lots and lots. Tony was mean to me though."

"How was he mean to you?"

"He told me I couldn't play blocks because I'm a girl."

"Well, that isn't very nice. You want me to talk to him?"

"It's ok, Daddy. Mommy did."

Tony and Caleb entered the room just ahead of Gina, who had Millie's pony duffle slung over her shoulder.

"Hey, Dad," Caleb called and headed up to the attic. Tony, at least, gave him a hug.

"Sorry we're so late." Gina slid the duffle from her shoulder. "You know how Tracy is. I tried to tell her you'd be waiting."

"Why didn't you call?"

"We took the kids to the...what was it called, Ton?"

"Discovery Dipstick."

Gina laughed. "Discovery District. In Torrington. You know how bad coverage is there. Were you worried?"

"No."

"You were."

Charlie shifted the twins on his lap. "Why don't you go put your stuff away," he said. "Johanna's coming over. We're going to bake cupcakes to take to her sister."

"Do we get to keep any?" Tony asked.

"I'm sure we can."

The twins leapt off his lap and ran from the room. Charlie listened to Tony's footsteps until they reached the attic.

"Something wrong?" Gina asked, sitting beside him.

"Things have been a little intense here."

"Is it ever any different with the Coco girls...women? What happened?"

Charlie told her, and found he felt a whole lot better afterwards. The jittery feeling in his gut wasn't just fear of Johanna bolting in the face of this adversity, but a genuine concern for Julietta.

"That's rough," Gina said when he finished. "I didn't know about the accident. I always thought their parents were involved in drugs or something."

"I don't think so. I guess nothing would surprise me at this point."

"And on top of all this, I'm three hours late getting the kids home. No wonder you were thinking I took off with them."

"I didn't—"

"Charlie, please. We were married for sixteen years. Give me the benefit of knowing you better than just about anyone."

He managed to smile. "It wasn't real worry."

"Good. I would never. The kids belong here, with you. I know that, even if after these few days, it's killing me to leave them."

"I'll get them to you this summer. Even Will."

"Not Charlotte, though."

Charlie picked at the throw pillow beside him on the couch. "She says she's going to work for Johanna in Cape May this summer."

"You okay with her going?"

"She's all grown up. She can do what she wants."

"I meant Johanna."

Charlie startled silent. "I hadn't really thought about that part of it, to be honest."

"You think she'll move back to Bitterly?"

"I really don't know."

"What will you do?"

Leave Bitterly? The revitalized town center, the schools, his kids' lives so rooted to this town that Gina had not fought him for custody. Would she fight him if he pulled their roots to follow Johanna to Cape May? Taking things with her a day at a time, a moment at a time was suddenly not the best idea he ever had, even if it had been necessary until now.

"I'd better get going." Gina patted his knee as she rose from the couch. "I got myself a room near the airport. My flight out is at butt-crack o'thirty tomorrow morning."

Charlie laughed softly. "Call when you get home. The kids will want to hear from you."

Gina shouted up the stairs for the kids to come say good-bye, a scene Charlie had been dreading but that went over just fine. Millie and Tony cried a little, but Gina promised them Harry Potter World—at last!—when they came to Florida for the summer and tears were banished. Caleb hugged his mother tight, but didn't shed a tear. The cordless in his other hand, finger over the mouthpiece, he whispered, "Love you, Ma," and hurried back up to the attic, hunched and muttering into the phone.

Charlie walked Gina to the front door

"Looks like our son might have his first girlfriend," she said. "He spent most of the time on the phone. My phone. Maybe we ought to reconsider the cell phone thing. It's kind of a necessity these days."

"You're probably right. I'll take him over to Torrington this weekend."

Gina cocked her head, smiled sheepishly. "I was hoping you'd say that." She dug into her bag and pulled out a box. "I got this for him, but I didn't tell him. I swear. I wanted to talk to you about it first."

Charlie took the phone. Thin, sleek, the newest and the best. Gina did not make much money. He wasn't even sure where she was working these days. "I'll pay for the plan."

"I got it," she said. "I put him in on mine."

"What would you have done with it if I wouldn't let up?"

Again the sheepish grin. "I had a pretty good feeling you would." Her hand came up to rub at his hairy chin. "You're a good dad, Charlie. A good man. I always did like you."

"We've always been good friends," he said.

"I hope we can be again."

"Aren't we?"

"Not yet." She smiled. "But we will be."

Gina trotted down the steps. Charlie closed the door against the cold coming in, but stopped when he heard, "Oh, hey, Johanna."

Caught between pulling the door open and closing it firmly against eavesdropping, he did neither.

"Hi, Gina. How was your time with the kids?"

"Really great. Thanks. I hate leaving them."

"It must be hard. You okay?"

"I will be, once I get home. Tonight's going to be a little rough, but I'll live." She continued down the steps. "Have fun baking cupcakes."

"Thanks."

Charlie opened the door as Johanna came the rest of the way up the steps. She handed him the bag of ingredients. "Everything okay here?"

"It's fine. Will and Charlotte will be back later, but Tony and Millie are looking forward to baking cupcakes. Caleb's just looking forward to eating them."

He carried the groceries to the kitchen. Johanna followed. "Hey!" She held up the tea-stained mug he had set into the sink. "You really do have a mug."

"I told you I did."

She inspected it. "I don't see most of the insults you hurled."

"I might have studied a little, when I found out about it."

"You learned it all in two days?"

"Well, I already knew a few on my own." He took her into his arms. "I wanted to impress you. Did it work?"

"Maybe a little."

Charlie kissed her softly, quickly. They were both on edge, and the kids were home. Anything more than an affectionate peck might have proved too much for him. He let her go. "How's Julietta?"

"Not good." Johanna put the mug back into the sink and started taking groceries from the bag. "We moved her to a smaller hospital at the academy where Efan works. Her doctor wants to interview me in the morning…"

* * * *

Nina told Dr. Sam, as he preferred to Chowdary, about living in New Hampshire, the abandoned farmhouse they called home, being left alone to fend for themselves as toddlers, and the fire that landed them in Bitterly. What she recalled of life with her parents was being loved, if not well cared-for. Kooky and well intentioned, they did their best. She held nothing against them.

Emma's interview went much differently. She had been frightened of her father most of the time, frightened of the people he insisted were in every hallway, around every corner, waiting to snatch her away. But there were times he was the best of playmates, telling stories in his accented voice, making them puppets and dolls out of things he found. She learned how to tell which Daddy he was, day by day, and when to avoid the one who scared her. What Emma remembered of Carolina were the bouts of depression, followed by bursts of crazed energy Emma had learned to fear almost as much as her father's shadowy government men. Carolina did whatever her husband told her to, without question, not out of fear but for absolute faith. Of the accident, Emma remembered nothing.

"My interview went much the same as Nina's," Johanna told her sisters as they shared stories over lunch. "Our Carolina and Johan were not the same people as yours, Emma."

"Lucky you." She sipped her iced tea. "I loved them. I loved them so much, but I was afraid all the time. I hate to say it, but if all that didn't happen, if I'd been left with them to reach adulthood, I would have been a goner."

"We all would have been," Nina muttered. She raised her glass. "To Adelina and Giovanni Coco, our saviors."

Johanna raised her glass to toast their grandparents, even if she was suddenly nauseous. For the first time in her life, she had to acknowledge her life had been better for losing her parents. Had they lived—she shuddered, and that shuddering made her feel even worse, because what she did not share with her sisters, what she had never shared with them, was her own role in her parents' descent into the madness.

"You cannot possibly blame yourself," Dr. Sam had said when she confessed her accidental arson to him. "You were a baby, Johanna. You'd been left unattended but for your sister who was barely older than you."

"I knew better than to play with the fire," she said.

"That is what you told yourself as you got older, as you remembered it. I can assure you, absolutely, a child of three has no real sense of such dire consequence. You must let all such notions go."

"But all that happened to them after, being separated from one another, from their kids, committed into whatever psychiatric wards the state put them in had to have tipped their already unbalanced minds beyond the breaking point. It must have, don't you think?"

Dr. Sam had tapped his pen to his teeth, his intense eyes on her. "I would need access to the records to know for certain," he said, "But mental illness, left untreated, usually gets worse with age, Johanna. I don't know their experiences in the hospitals they went to, but given their ages, and the apparent severity of their illnesses, I can say with confidence that, with or without events transpiring as they did, they would indeed have become more and more unstable as time went on. " He had leaned forward then, touched her hand. "You cannot carry the blame for their actions. It was their job to protect you, to guide you, to take care of you. Perhaps they were incapable, but that does not make them inculpable. You were a baby. It was not your fault."

"He asked if I knew what happened to her." Emma swiped a potato chip off Johanna's tray. "To Mom."

"Me too," Nina said.

"And me." Johanna bit into her turkey sandwich, swallowed her prior thoughts along with it. "He thought it was odd we didn't know. That we hadn't heard from her at all."

"I got the feeling he believes Gram and Pop did," Nina said. "I've always thought so myself, actually."

"You think they'd have kept her from us?" Emma asked. "Even as adults?"

"I wish I knew."

"What? If they knew? Or where Mom is…was…whatever."

"Both," Nina answered, her eyes suddenly downcast. "I gave Dr. Sam permission to get whatever records are still available. It's been a really long time. The records for the accident, and anything that might have happened after could well have been destroyed by now, or impossible to locate." She looked to Emma. "You don't have to read them, if you don't want to. I know all this is way more painful to you than to me and Jo."

"I still want to know what happened to her." Emma closed her eyes, inhaled deeply. "It's my wish. The one I always told myself I would make when I got the locket." She opened her eyes to wag a finger at Nina. "And don't you start on me about believing in wishes. It's not like it would have hurt any."

"I didn't say anything, Emma." She reached across the table. "It's my wish too."

Johanna's heart pounded so hard she could barely hear for the rush in her ears. All the silly wishes through her life had always been eclipsed by the same one. The wish she feared making. Feared being granted. The one her sisters shared.

She took another bite of her sandwich—*I wish, I wish*—and swallowed down more thoughts she could not put into words.

* * * *

Johanna lived the next days in a sort of limbo. Julietta did not come successfully back to them. Moments of true awareness turned almost instantly to agitation. Dr. Sam treated her acute anxiety with medication, and rest. One time, he assured them, she would awaken and be more herself. It was only a matter of time.

Still they visited her daily, taking turns sitting at her bedside. Efan was there all hours of the day and night, and vowed he would be until the academy was back in session. Emma's kids and Charlie's went back to school. Gunner returned to New York to complete the sale of the gallery.

Charlotte had already pulled out of SUNY, New Paltz and applied to the Culinary Institute of America. Financial aid forms were being filled out, she resumed her position at the coffeehouse in town, and in another week, she would head out to New Paltz to collect her belongings and say good-bye to friends. It astounded Johanna, her ability to transition between such huge changes in her life so seamlessly. And yet seamless was an act Charlotte played almost as well as Johanna did herself.

When they were not running back and forth to the hospital, Emma and Nina spent most of their time with Johanna at the house on County Line Road. They went through Gram's things to donate, to save. They found boxes of Poppy's clothes Gram had been unable to part with. Photo albums, old tax returns, bank statements, boxes of canceled checks—the accumulation of a life lived united, and then apart. They carefully considered every item. Except the locket. It, as well as all talk of what they would do with the house, was firmly, and most defiantly, avoided.

The sisters cooked together and ate together. Mike only joined them once, when Charlie and his kids did as well. Even then he took the kids home early. Emma stayed overnight, left when it was time to get her boys ready for school in the morning only to show up at the door at nine the next night, a bottle of wine and a deck of tarot cards in hand.

Nina had given Johanna her arched-brow look and popped open the bottle. And when Emma went to her old room to sleep the night, Nina stopped Johanna at her door.

"You have to talk to her."

"What am I supposed to say?"

"Tell her to knock it the hell off, she has three beautiful boys and needs to get over it."

"That's not what it's about, Nina. He betrayed her trust."

"Well, she betrayed his first when she got pregnant with Gio, so she has nothing to say about it."

"What?" Johanna hauled her sister into the bedroom and closed the door. "Are you saying what I think you're saying?"

"If you think I'm saying Mike didn't want to have another baby and she lied to him about her birth control to get pregnant, yes, that's what I'm saying."

"Oh, wow." Johanna pressed cool hands to her burning cheeks. "Are you sure?"

"Positive. She told me herself. Mike doesn't say anything about it now. He adores his little guy. But he was furious at the time."

"So he can't be angry about that without seeming like an asshole," Johanna said. "And Emma gets to be all self-righteous."

"Yup."

"This is way out of my league."

"No it's not. Just talk to her. I'll end up screaming at her."

She didn't. Not that night or the next morning. Johanna could not swear to it, but she was close to certain Nina chose to head up to the hospital at the precise moment Johanna could not accompany her, which happened to coincide with Emma's arrival after getting Gio off to afternoon kindergarten. Having lunch with her younger sister, Johanna fumbled with the right way to open the subject, and ended up blurting, "If I don't talk to you about Mike, Nina is going to do awful things to me."

Emma paused mid-chew. "It's none of your business, and Nina's bark is way worse than her bite."

"Come on, Emma. Your marriage is in the crapper. Do you really want a baby this bad?"

"He had no right to take the choice from me."

"And you have no right making it for him."

Emma narrowed her eyes. "What has Nina told you? That I got pregnant with Gio on purpose?"

"Well…"

"Damn it all—that's not how it was. I legitimately forgot to take my pill, but then later, I forgot and…things happen. Mike is…anyway. I didn't even think about it until I skipped a period."

"It seems highly unlikely skipping one pill would—"

"Exactly! That's what the doc said too. Sometimes, for whatever reason, birth control fails. My husband doesn't believe me, or the doctor. Getting a vasectomy was retaliation, plain and simple."

"Emma." Johanna shook her head. "That doesn't sound like Mike at all."

"I would have thought so too, once."

"He adores his little boy. You can't think…"

If dad were given the choice of going back and starting over, he'd do it all again. My mom wouldn't.

Charlotte's tearful words on Christmas day hit Johanna full in the face. She couldn't imagine a parent feeling that way, but neither could she presume to know what Gina truly felt. Still…

"Do you think," she asked Emma. "if Mike could go back and make it so you never got pregnant with Giovanni. he would?"

"Of course not."

"Then how can you believe he did what he did to somehow get back at you for giving him a son he adores. You said it yourself—your birth control failed. He just doesn't want another child he has to feel guilty for not actually wanting at the outset. "

Emma was silent a moment. "You know nothing Jon Snow."

"What?"

"Sorry. Game of Thrones reference. Don't you read? Or watch television?"

"Whatever. Emmaline, talk to your husband. He's a good guy. He loves you and your boys. Don't fuck it up."

Emma smiled. "You kiss your mother with that mouth?"

"I would if I could." Johanna laughed, but it fell short, and the two fell deeply silent.

"Just sort of hits every now and then, doesn't it?" Emma let go a deep breath. "First Gram dying, now all this with Julietta, is really hitting me hard, bringing up the past and things I haven't thought about, haven't wanted to think about in forever."

Johanna pulled the locket from underneath her shirt. She clicked it open, stared at her mother's face. Gathering her thoughts swallowed the day before, she chose her words carefully. "Yesterday, you said if the wish was yours to make, it would be about Mom."

"That I could know what happened to her. Why?"

"Because it's Nina's wish too." Johanna clicked the locket closed, just in case. "And it's always been mine. It made me think—what if it's Julietta's too?"

"It's a good possibility. What are you getting at?"

What was she getting at? Thoughts sparked and swallowed the day before made their way up from her gut. Gram promising it to each of them, changing the story with each promise. Vanished. Dead. Erased. Happy. There was something there...

"I'm not sure," she said at last. "I'll figure it out, though."

* * * *

"It was right, for a while, and then it was too late."

"It is better not to know such things."

"It is always best to know."

Chapter 10

Three French Hens

"We were able to obtain the accident report from the Danbury Police Department."

Dr. Chowdary met the three of them at the door to Julietta's room. His voice was hushed but clear.

Her sister slept on in the bed, as she had the last two visits.

"Computers, thank goodness, made this possible." He held up the printout in a manila folder. "Before scanning capabilities, they destroyed everything after twenty-five years. But this is only the accident report. I've put in a request for any information about Carolina Coco Anker and Johan Anker with the hospital, and with the police department."

Anker.

Then they had been married, after all. Which meant…

Johanna Anker.

Until that moment, she hadn't even thought about her father's surname. Her grandparents were Coco, she and her sisters were Coco. They had all been Anker once, at least in some respect. There had been no birth certificates until Gram and Poppy took them in. The name on hers was Johanna Elsbet Coco.

"Would you ladies like to look it over together?"

All eyes turned to Dr. Sam.

"Have you read it yet?" Nina asked.

"I have."

"How bad is it?" Emma held out her hand, held the file against her chest when he handed it to her. "Should we sit?"

"There are some things that may come as a shock," he answered. "I am happy to sit with you, even to summarize it for you."

"No," Nina said. "We can manage."

"Julietta?" Johanna managed to croak.

"She is resting. She woke a little while ago, but did not stay awake long. It is the first time she did not require a sedative. This is good news. The nurse will come for you if she wakes again. Please, feel free to use the conference room. You will not be disturbed."

* * * *

The conference room smelled of lavender, not the nauseatingly floral scent that never quite masked the hospital odors of urine and antiseptic. Johanna could not decide if it soothed or unnerved her. The file folder pressed tight to Emma's chest confused whichever it might be.

They sat together at the small, round table. Emma slid the folder to the center. "We ready?"

Nina nodded, but she crossed her arms and slumped back in her chair. Emma made no move to open it.

Johanna reached out, relieved and surprised her hands did not shake, and pulled the folder closer. "There's a whole lot of technical stuff." Photos of the accident scene appeared three pages in. Her stomach heaved. Johanna closed her eyes tight, closed the folder. "And pictures."

"I don't want to see those," Emma said.

"I'll take a pass too." Nina tapped the front of the folder. "There should be a narrative on the last page. Why not start there?"

Johanna waited for the gurgling in her stomach to subside. She could not unsee what she'd seen—the wreck, the blood, the broken glass, the empty car seat Julietta had been cut from, the crushed car. Tears welled. She brushed them aside, and slid her finger to the last sheet in the folder.

"On October 11, 1983, I was first responder to a motor vehicle accident on 4th and Valley View, Danbury, CT. Four-door (vehicle 1, V1) vs. semi (vehicle 2, V2.) Called in a Code 3. Called for ambulance. Fire Department had already arrived at that time. V1's back end was half-way underneath V2. Truck could not be moved without risking further injury. Tried to make contact with vehicle occupants. Driver, Caucasian male (D,) approximately forty-five, non-responsive. First passenger, Caucasian female (P1,) approximately thirty-five, non-responsive. Caucasian male (P2) in back seat, non-responsive, age, indeterminate. Two little girls, approximately six (P3,) and two years of age (P4.)

*P3, non-responsive. P4 conscious, but non-responsive.
Jaws necessary to extricate back seat passengers.
Ambulance arrived to take D and P1. D awake and
combative. Needed restraining. Minor injuries, TBD.
P1 in and out, but cooperative, taken to CCU. P3
extricated first, slightly responsive. Minor injuries—
to be determined. Second ambulance took her to ER.
Approximately one hour necessary to cut and extricate
adult male P2, dead at scene, decapitated—"*

Her sisters gasped. The glands in Johanna's jaw watered, preparing for the gurgling in her belly to spew out.

"I need to stop." Emma bolted out of her chair but Nina held her back.

"Emma, what—"

"Let me go, Nina." She yanked free. "You don't get it. You weren't there. Dad…" She closed her eyes tight. "He wasn't the driver, Nina. Dad was P2."

This time, Nina did not stop her. She sat down again, ashen and trembling. Soul-tearing sobs seeped through the closed bathroom door. Emma needed her. She needed them, but Johanna could not force herself to her feet.

Mommy. I didn't mean to. I pushed him and it fell off.

"Are you okay, Jo?"

She blinked, forced her mind to close off the images forming so she could get through the rest, because avoiding it seemed worse than cowardice. It was betrayal. She opened the file.

"I can read to myself, if you prefer."

"No," Nina said. "Finish."

*"—decapitated. P4, injuries could not be ascertained
at scene. Too much blood. Ambulance three took her to
ER. Ambulance four arrived shortly thereafter for P2.
Grisly. Just grisly. This officer has never seen such a
thing, and hopes never to again."*

Nina slid a glass of water to Johanna. She took a sip.

*"Witnesses questioned. Detail noted in report.
Consensus the same. V1 was traveling at an excessive
rate of speed towards intersection. Light was red.*

*Showed no sign of stopping even as V2 came through the
light. Last minute, D cut the wheel and slid backwards
underneath V2's trailer. P3 and P4 survived due to their
size. P2 did not because of his.*

*"Driver of vehicle 2 was questioned and released—
no fault, but will be further questioned. Respectfully
Submitted, Officer R. José Ortiz."*

"I don't know if I can bear it," Nina said. "Not for me. It's gruesome
and sad and horrifying, but it didn't happen to me. Jules and Emma..."

Nina looked to the bathroom door, where the hollow, heartbreaking
sobs continued to pour out of their sister. Her jaw clenched. She pushed
to her feet and banged on the door.

"Emma. Let me in. Now."

Johanna was surprised but glad to hear the lock click open. And she
was alone. With the folder. And the pictures.

She started at page one.

Facts, diagrams, witness statements. They all blurred, but she knew
what they said. Officer Ortiz had been thorough. Her fingers shook, but
she pressed them to the page, the one separating her from the grisly scene
the responding officer hoped never to see the like of again.

"Perhaps that is not the best idea." A dark hand came gently to rest
upon hers. Dr. Sam sat beside her. "I know it feels like dishonor to shield
yourself from their pain, but that is not a reason to subject yourself to
something you cannot unsee, no matter how much psychotherapy you
undergo, as you can observe quite clearly by Julietta's current state."

"Did you look at them?"

"I did. But I can do so with a clinical eye. You cannot."

"Were there photos of...of him?"

"Yes. In a case of possible vehicular manslaughter, it is required.
Because she was the last taken from the car, Julietta is in some of them,
but only little legs and feet, a glimpse of her head."

I pushed him and it fell off.

"Dr. Sam," she began, but her mouth filled with saliva. She took another
sip of water. "The report said Julietta's injuries could not be ascertained at
the scene because of all the blood. I know two things—one, she came to
us with a bandage on her forehead, and a broken arm, and two..."

Dr. Sam touched her shoulder. "You don't have to—"

"No, I do have to." She took a deep breath. "In the other hospital,
Julietta thought I was our mother."

"Yes. Efan told me."

"What he could not have told you is what she whispered to me. Knowing all this"—She placed her hand upon the folder—"I understand it now, and it's something, as her doctor, you should know."

"All right. When you're ready."

Another, deeper breath. "She said she was sorry. That she pushed him and it fell off. She must have been talking about our dad. He, or part of him, must have been on her and she pushed him off. When she did, his head—" Johanna put her own head in her hands, fingers pressed to her eyes. Within the sparkles there, her father's headless corpse spurted blood on her baby sister, like a hose on a summer day. "She was covered in so much blood, Dr. Sam. So much the EMTs couldn't see if she was injured or not. Can you imagine what happened? Can you imagine what she saw?"

Dr. Sam did not answer. He seemed to go into himself, his eyes staring. Then he picked up the folder, leaned back in his chair and opened it. Johanna watched his eyes dart back and forth. Something of the photos reflected in his glasses. Her brain conjured those hints and blurs into imagines assisted by the one photo she did see. He closed the folder again, and did not put it back onto the table.

"Thank you for that, Ms. Coco. I know it was difficult for you."

"Johanna, please."

He nodded acknowledgement and rose from his chair. "I will be back shortly. It is my hope more reports have become available since I got this earlier. For the time being, Johanna, I advise you not to mention this to your sisters. It may become inevitable they learn this grisly truth, but it may also be it is a detail they never need become aware of."

"I don't know that I could anyway."

Dr. Sam left her with a grim smile and a firm squeeze to her shoulder. He could be no older than she, and was probably younger, but he exuded the sort of kind wisdom she associated with her grandfather. Poppy's quiet love had come, at least partially, from being deaf in one ear. Until now Johanna hadn't understood it also came from a sorrow so deep that silence was the only weapon against it. It made her wonder if Dr. Sam Chowdary had such a sorrow in his own life, or he absorbed what his patients gave him to hold.

* * * *

They should have been destroyed. They should never
have been seen. They show surface truths of blood and
horror and death. They speak nothing of the love. Did

anyone record arms shielding? The hands reaching?
Did anyone hear voices cry out? To slow? To mind the
crying children, so frightened? Only recorded is the bad
choice, the fear, the minds not quite centered in reality.
Those are facts, and facts deal little with the heart.
It is ever the clearest moment. The smell of the tires
burning on the asphalt. The taste of tears. The children's
cries and the mad laughter. 'I love you' moving heart
to heart, through those hands reaching. And the impact
that shattered us all.

* * * *

Julietta woke, confused but very much herself, at precisely six o'clock
the next morning, just as she did every day of her life prior to New Year's
Eve. Johanna could barely understand a word Efan spewed into the phone,
his accent suddenly heavy with those Welsh tones otherwise and usually
tamed. He was there. He was not going to move from her side. That much
she understood. After waking Nina and calling Emma, Johanna got in the
shower and let the hot water fall.

Behind eyes closed against the running water, she glimpsed the photo
images, and the conjured ones that taunted her through the night. She
wished she'd gone out with Charlie, as he asked. Dinner and a movie
would have done her good. Perhaps it would not let her unsee those
things, but she might have forgotten for a while.

Johanna told herself she would see him later in the day, after visiting
Julietta, even if it felt like a lie. Everything changed along the dark stretch
of road on New Year's Eve that not even baking cupcakes with his kids
had soothed. Day followed day and the hollow place got bigger instead of
smaller. She saw Charlie less and less. Until she figured it all out, Johanna
simply did not know what to say to him.

Dried and dressed, Johanna scrunched her wet hair into tighter curls
and slipped the locket over her head. As always, she started to tuck it
underneath her shirt and only fleetingly wondered why she still did so.
Not only did everyone know she had it, Johanna was close to certain she
no longer wanted it. But for the wish…

I wish. I wish.

She clutched the cold metal in her hand, quelled the urge to speak the
words. What would it hurt? If she spoke the wish, they all wanted and it
came true, her sisters would be happy. And if she spoke the wish and it
didn't, then it was as big a lie as the stories Gram told about it.

Johanna tucked the locket into her clothes. Gram had a reason for what she did, for all the things she said. Now was not the time to test the boundaries of what might or might not be true. She had enough truth the last few days.

She and Nina picked up Emma and headed out to the hospital. Her older sister had to take a conference call with Gunner and the realtors at two-thirty. Emma had sent Gio to a friend's house for the morning, but had to be home to get him off the bus by three. Johanna would stay at the hospital until four, when Julietta had her first official session with Dr. Sam.

And then Charlie was coming to pick her up, and she would have the rest of the day with him.

The happy thrill came before the anxiety—a good sign even if the bakery, Cape May, and a solitary life among acquaintances still beckoned.

"There's Efan," Nina said as they hurried down the hall. He stood outside the door of Julietta's room, his arms crossed and his head leaning toward the hushed voices inside.

"What's going on?" Emma asked as they neared.

"She doesn't want me here," Efan answered. "At first, she seemed happy to see me. She hugged me so tight. When she finally let me go, she said, 'We went off the road.' A moment later, she threw me out. Threatened to have me escorted back to Wales."

"She's embarrassed," Johanna offered. "I know my sister. She would hide for days after an anxiety attack."

"Give her some time," Nina soothed. "She's probably really confused. Does she know why she's here?"

"I don't know. She refuses to speak to me."

Dr. Sam came out of the room. His smile was tight. Forced. "Good morning, ladies. You must be anxious to see her."

"Very." Johanna started for the entrance, but he stopped her.

"Don't tell her anything, let her tell you."

They all nodded.

"Excellent. When the nurse comes in to help her bathe, find me in my office. We have a few things to discuss. Efan?" He turned to his friend. "You going back to school?"

"I will not leave her, not even to eat."

"You have classes to teach."

"Let them fire me. I'm not leaving her."

"Efan." Nina put her hands on his shoulders. "Don't lose your job. Julietta will be asking for you before you know it."

"Do you really think so?"

"Well, maybe not that fast. But she will."

"Come." Dr. Sam motioned to his friend. "You can walk me to my office."

"You have my cell number," Efan said as he hurried after him. "If she asks for me, call. I will be here in moments."

Johanna waited in the silence following the men down the corridor. Finally, Emma spoke.

"Are we ready?"

Nina nodded. Johanna said, "Ready."

First Emmaline, then Nina, and finally Johanna filed into Julietta's room. Always-instant tears welled in Johanna's eyes. Her youngest sister sat propped against the pillows, hair poking up and cheeks pink as a blossom. She smiled as they came to stand around her, the awkward angles of her skinny shoulders and knees shifting under the blankets.

"I'm sorry," was the first thing she said. "I ruined New Year's Eve."

"Don't be silly." Emma sat on the mattress, smoothed Julietta's hair. "It was a wonderful night, no matter what happened after. And as for that, you've nothing to be sorry about."

"It's all still such a blur." Julietta grimaced. "Dr. Sam said I have no physical injuries."

"Not even a bruise," Nina said.

"Then why can't I go home?"

"Dr. Sam just wants to see you awake for a little while," Emma answered. "That's all."

"That's not all. I'm not an idiot. What happened?"

The women exchanged glances. Nina asked, "Can't you tell us?"

Julietta's gaze went beyond them, focused on a point somewhere near the ceiling. "Efan's car hit a patch of ice and we went off the road. I remember...I remember freaking out—"

"You had an anxiety attack—"

"Let her talk, Emma," Nina hushed her. "Go on, Jules."

"I woke up here. This morning. But—"

"But?" Johanna prompted.

Her eyes blinked. She looked at Johanna. Tears welled. "I called you Mommy."

"I do look like her."

"I thought you were her. I thought it was...was then. I remember that night."

"Maybe we should get Dr. Sam."

"No, I…it's all so foggy, like trying to remember a dream after being awake a few minutes. I can get bits and pieces, but none of it is of now. It's of then. Going off the road must have triggered memories." Julietta looked up. "How long have I…what's the date?"

"January sixth," Johanna said. "Six days since New Year's Eve."

"January sixth…" Julietta blinked, and blinked again, thoughts processing behind her eyes. A slow smile made its way to her lips, and with that smile, tension scattered. "It's Little Christmas."

"Oh, wow," Nina said. "It is."

"It's been a while," Emma said. "Remember how Gram used to make such a thing of it?"

"I think that's when I baked my first cake." Johanna stuck out her tongue. "And if I remember right, it wasn't very successful."

"She'd make us sing the Twelve Days of Christmas before we got our gifts," Nina added. "I don't know if I could remember all of them now."

"We each sang three days," Julietta said. "I always got calling birds, maids milking, and the drummers."

"I always wanted the golden rings and the partridge in a pear tree," Johanna added. "Nina, you could never hold the notes without cracking…"

* * * *

It was almost noon when the nurse arrived to help Julietta to the shower. Dr. Sam had left the building for lunch by then and was unavailable until after one o'clock. She thought she saw him pass by while the sisters talked and laughed together, but wasn't certain. It was going to be difficult to meet with him before Emma and Nina had to leave.

While Julietta showered and her other two sisters went to the commissary to bring back food, Johanna waited by herself in the hospital room. Standing at the window overlooking a snowed-over courtyard, she imagined it in the spring, green and flowered. She missed the Berkshires in the spring when the mountains shrugged off their mantle of grey. Evergreens slipped into the background, giving way to the deciduous varieties that washed the skyline in a more muted version of autumn before bursting green. Cape May was lovely, but it got hot, fast. In the mountains, worn down and ancient, everything was slower. She could almost feel it in her pulse.

Her phone buzzed. She pulled it from her pocket to find a text from Charlie.

Still on for four?

Johanna answered, *yup*. Sliding the phone back into her pocket, she felt bad about creating doubt where there hadn't been a shred. He feared she would bolt again. He feared what happened with Julietta had frightened her enough to pull her away from him, send her back into a simpler life where love existed at a distance. She knew his fear, because it was her own.

"Much better," the nurse helping Julietta back to the bed said.

Johanna turned from the window.

Wet hair plaited, dressed in her own clothes, Julietta looked like herself rather than a hospital patient. But for the IV still in her arm, she looked ready to go home.

"Your lunch will be up shortly," the nurse told her. "And Dr. Chowdary will be in later."

"Great, thanks."

When the nurse was gone, Johanna moved to sit beside her sister, put her arm around her. Julietta's head rested instantly to her shoulder. "Why do you think we stopped celebrating?"

"Celebrating what?"

"Sorry. Little Christmas. It was such a big deal to Gram, and then we just…stopped."

"I guess we were getting a bit old," Johanna said. "Was that the year Poppy died?"

"I thought about that, but no. It was the year before." She felt silent, then, "I've always remembered."

Johanna shifted so her sister had to look her in the eyes. "You need to stop assuming I know where your thoughts are coming from, sweetheart. What have you always remembered?"

Julietta's uncanny eyes did not blink. They held Johanna's gaze like magnets gripping metal.

"The accident," she said at last. "Not the details, just…it. I suppose that's what happened when Efan and I went off the road. The details just popped out of where they are stored in my brain. But I've always remembered some of…I guess it must have been the impact. Mom in the front seat, reaching back for Emma. Dad covering me with his whole body. I remember feeling safe and not at all afraid, because he was there. Because he would never let anything bad happen to me."

Johanna took her sister's hand. "Emma remembers a different Daddy."

"She was older. Like Nina. You and I were both small enough to remember him in better ways. Mom, too. What did we know about madness as long as we had food and shelter and love?"

"We didn't always have food and shelter, or them around to watch over us."

"That's what we know now," Julietta said. "It's not what we knew then. We weren't old enough."

That is what you told yourself as you got older, as you remembered it. A child of three has no real sense of such dire consequence.

Dr. Sam's words whispered back to soothe in ways they hadn't then, because Julietta said them too.

"I know Dad died in the accident," Julietta's voice brought Johanna back to the present. "But Mom…I can't believe she'd have vanished forever unless she died too. I wish I knew what happened to her, Jo. I feel like a lot of what's wrong with me would ease up if I did."

I wish. I wish.

A sound like chimes twinkled in Johanna's ears. Her head felt suddenly full of cotton that forced the twinkling from her head to her fingers to her toes, through her blood crackling like pop-candy in cola. Her hand went to her chest, slid to the locket hidden in her clothes. Then it was in her hand, her mouth was opening to tell Julietta they all had the same wish, that Gram must have known, and somehow it all came together to help them find Carolina.

Nina and Emma flew into the room, cooing and clapping over Julietta's transformation. They spread the food from the commissary out on the tiny hospital tray, called Johanna to them with voices she could not hear, because the chimes still rang.

"Jo?" Nina's hand on her arm silenced the twinkling. "Are you all right?"

"I'm fine. I…" She gripped the locket tightly. "I think I know why Gram—"

"Ah, good." Dr. Sam and his manila envelope fluttered into the room. Efan hovered at the door. "Ladies Coco, you are all here. I returned from lunch to find this on my desk."

"What is it?" Emma asked. "The hospital records?"

"It is, and better." He looked to Julietta. Before he could ask, she said, "Whatever you tell them, you tell me too. I can handle it."

He nodded, a smile twitching at the corner of his lips. "Right, then," he said, and opened the folder. "Not only do I have the hospital records from the accident, but a letter from the attorney who handled your adoptions. She also oversaw the power of attorney granted, and commitment papers for one, Carolina Coco, to a psychiatric rehabilitation hospital in New Hampshire in March of 1984."

Chapter 11

Two Turtle Doves

Their father's death certificate showed that Johan Finn Anker was approximately six-foot-four, and one hundred eighty pounds, blond-haired, blue-eyed, and dead on impact. The official cause of death was a severing of the brain stem. His parents were Johan Anker and Agata Raske Anker.

From his death certificate, they also discovered he graduated high school, attended college but did not finish, and that he and Carolina Valentine Coco were, in fact, married. She was listed as his surviving spouse on the document, as well as the informant for the document itself. Johanna was not sure how reliable the information her mother gave might be, but it was officially documented, stamped and dated as fact.

Other hospital records showed that Adelina and Giovanni Coco were contacted. Emmaline was treated for minor bruising and lacerations but remained in the hospital with Julietta, whose age was noted as forty-eight months, not twenty-four. Her injuries were more extensive—a broken arm, concussion, stitches in her scalp and forehead. Other than that, her physical injuries were minor. Emmaline was allowed to stay in the pediatric ward with her, notes said, to keep the toddler from screaming. According to hospital records, their grandmother arrived the day following the accident, and took them home, appropriate documents in hand, four days later.

Of Carolina's injuries and hospital stay, there were no records. She appeared only as informant, wife to, mother of—until the lawyer's letter.

...Power of attorney granted to Adelina Coco for Carolina Coco, 10/18/83.

Minors: Nina Carol Anker, Johanna Elsbet Anker, Emmaline Prudence Anker, and Julietta Agatha Anker given over to the temporary custody of Adelina (Fiore) Coco and Giovanni Coco as of 12/27/83. Custody relinquished 4/22/84. Adoption finalized: 6/18/84. ...5/22/85. Settlement against Bruce Johnson, driver of the car, $1.5 million, awarded in civil proceedings. Extensive info on civil as well as criminal proceedings. Request for full access will take some time to fulfill. Advise if required.

...Carolina Valentine Coco willingly committed to Cully Mountain Psychiatric Convalescent Facility: 3/26/84.

"There is way too much information here," Nina, who had been searching the documents, set them down again. "Did you find Cully Mountain yet, Emma?"

"Nothing's coming up for a psych facility named Cully Mountain in New Hampshire." Emma did not look up from her tablet. "But I did find a Cully Mountain. It's in Killian, New Hampshire."

"It was thirty years ago." Johanna picked up the folder, started flipping through. "The facility must not exist anymore."

"But we know she survived," Julietta said. "She gave up her parental rights to us in April, and went to Cully Mountain in March. She must have been injured really bad to need so much recuperation time."

"Or she was temporarily committed in some other hospital," Nina told them. "Gram had power of attorney."

"Does that mean she could be committed her against her will?"

"I'm not sure."

Johanna paged through the attorney's report full of numbers and dates and events that told them almost nothing they wanted to know. Had Gram and Pop ever seen a dime of the money awarded? It would explain why the house in Bitterly never had a mortgage, and how they afforded the hospital bills including—at least for a little while—Cully Mountain.

Gram had a job, when she wanted one, making homemade pasta for D'Angelo's, as well as with the florist during holidays. Johanna remembered helping in the garden, selling the vegetables they grew at the Farm Market every Saturday through the summer months. Hard as she tried, she could not remember Poppy ever having a regular job outside of plowing roads in winter. And yet they never did without. In fact, now that she thought about it, they'd lived relatively comfortably. She looked up from the folder.

"Did Gram leave a will?"

Nina and Julietta looked her way. Emma still searched her tablet.

"I haven't found one," Julietta said. "Nina?"

"Nope, me either."

"What about a bank account?"

"She had one," Julietta answered. "The book would be in her desk, I guess."

"Gram had a desk?"

"Well, not a desk. The drawer in the kitchen. It was her desk. Kind of. Why?"

"Because if Gram and Pop got anything of the settlement from that Bruce Johnson person, there has to be—"

"Uncle Boo..."

All eyes turned to Emma, her fingers frozen mid-tap above her tablet.

"Emma?" Johanna asked.

"Bruce Johnson. We called him Uncle Boo. Do you remember, Jules?"

Julietta frowned. She shook her head.

"He was a friend of Dad's. He used to bring us those strands of lollipops with the smiley-faces on them. Oh, wow. I never realized that was him. I never thought of it at all, really." She shook herself out of memory, closed the cover over her tablet. "It's getting late. I have to go home and get my boys off the bus."

"Dammit." Nina looked at the clock on the wall. "I missed the conference call. I have to call Gunner."

Emma gathered her things while Nina fished her phone out of her purse, cursing over the number of voice messages and texts she found waiting.

"Aren't you going with them?"

Johanna sat on the bed next to her youngest sister. "Nah. I'm going to hang here with you a while, if that's okay. Charlie's coming to get me at four, when you have your session with Dr. Sam."

Julietta went silent, head bowed and picking at her fingernails. Emma and Nina whirred about, gathering coats and papers and clearing garbage. The excitement and energy upon gaining news of their mother had not abated even a little since Dr. Sam first told them.

"I'll be back in the morning." Emma kissed Julietta's cheek. "I'll keep trying to find out about Cully Mountain."

"Gunner and I will be by this evening." Nina kissed her next. "Any books you want? Games? Your laptop?"

"All three." Julietta smiled. "But I might come home tomorrow."

"You'll still want those things tonight. Have a good session with Dr. Sam, and I'll see you later."

In moments, Johanna and Julietta were alone in the hospital room.

"She's only humoring me."

"Who is?"

"Nina. She doesn't think I'll come home tomorrow. She thinks I need to stay here."

"She's just overly protective. You know that."

"But I feel fine," Julietta insisted. "I'm not stupid. I know I'm not, and I need Dr. Sam's help to work through it all so it doesn't happen again, but I feel like...me."

"Jules." Johanna shifted closer, nudged her with her knee. "You were out of it for six days. It's going to take a little longer than a few hours for everyone to feel safe."

"I suppose." She sighed. "I'm scared, Jo."

"Of remembering?"

Julietta looked up. "No, not really. I mean, yeah, but that's not it. I'm afraid nothing will ever be the same again."

"Was it so great before?"

"Maybe not, but it was safe. It's what I knew."

Johanna heard her own thoughts, once again, from her youngest sister's mouth. They could not be more different from the outside looking in, but from the inside looking out...

"Is that why you won't you speak to Efan?"

Julietta shrugged. "I don't want to talk about him."

"Honey, don't be embarrassed. He's been waiting since——"

"I mean it, Jo."

"All right, Jules. Fine. Don't get upset."

"And don't talk to me like I'm some wild dog about to bark itself mad."

"Hey, what's this about? I didn't——"

"I want to rest." Julietta leapt off the bed, went around to the other side. "See if you can catch Emma and Nina before they leave."

"You kicking me out?"

"I just want to rest, Jo." Julietta hit the nurse-call. "Please!"

Johanna gathered up the papers. The nurse came in as she left, folder clutched to her chest and uninterested in catching up with her sisters.

They would only worry that Julietta was still too fragile to be released, and argue it come morning. The nurse's hushed voice, her sister's shrill but subdued one, barely reached her ears. She had an hour and some to wait until Charlie got there. Johanna thought about calling him. Instead she bought a soda from the machine in the conference room and sat at the round table with the thrown-together folder of printouts.

She read again the lawyer's letter, highlighting those events handled by the firm. For how much more information she had now that she never did before, Johanna's brain bubbled with more questions than she ever thought to ask. Were her paternal grandparents still alive? Did they even live in America? She remembered her father having an accent. Perhaps he was the first to leave Norway. What college did Johan attend? Why did he drop out? What had he been studying? Question begat question, all of them about her father. For how much she now knew about him, Carolina remained a big mystery.

She pulled the lawyer's letter from the pile, and read it again. Sunlight coming through the window showed writing on the other side they had not noticed earlier. Johanna turned it over, and found a handwritten endnote.

> *But for the final transfer of funds from the estate of Bruce Johnson in 1993, the records for this family end when Carolina was committed to Cully Mountain. I have done a rudimentary search but can find no such facility at this time. If this office is able to attain any more information on that matter, we will forward it on to you.*
>
> *I remember this case well. It was one of my first. If I can be of any assistance, feel free to call my personal number...*

A cell number. A name—Willa Germaine. Someone who had details Johanna was not certain she wanted. She set the paper down, pulled her cell from her pocket. Fingers poised. Breath held. Instead of dialing the number, she looked up Bruce Johnson. The number of hits was overwhelming. She narrowed the search. Danbury, 1983. Vehicular manslaughter. 4th and Valley View.

She found newspaper coverage of the accident, and a headline reading: Eccentric Computer Genius To Be Tried For Murder. Johanna was able to follow a trail, both forward and back, chronicling Bruce Johnson's rise to fame in the early days of modern computers. Eccentric behavior once excused as genius became speculation about his mental health. And then all news of Bruce Johnson vanished along with the man, popping up again in 1983 when he appeared as the driver in an accident that killed a man.

Johanna skimmed through the news coverage more concerned with sensationalizing a computer-genius-millionaire-gone-mad than it was about her family tragedy. In the end, he'd been tried in criminal court, and again in a civil proceeding. Bruce Johnson died in a psychiatric correctional facility in 1992, and according to the obituary, "Though his contributions to computer science continue to impact the field, he left not a single living soul behind."

Johanna set her phone down and slumped back in her chair. She pulled the locket out, clicked it open.

Carolina Valentine Coco.

Gram and Poppy had honored their Italian heritage when they named their only child, while keeping it American. It was *Carolina*, like the state, not *Caroleena*. *Valentine*, like the holiday, not *Valenteena*.

When had she started showing signs of mental illness? Was she once wild Carolina, like Johanna and her sisters had always been the wild Coco sisters? Was she involved in drugs? Was that why her parents first put her into a psychiatric facility? Her mother never lived in Bitterly. Gram and Pop bought the house when they suddenly had two little granddaughters to raise, but where had they lived before? Where was Carolina's hometown? Did Gram and Pop buy the house on County Line Road because Bitterly was a nice small town? Or so their daughter's daughters would not grow up in the shadow, with the stigma, of a girl gone wrong?

There was no one left to ask, and for the first time, Johanna was angry. Tracing her mother's face when it was smiling and young and free of all things still to come, Johanna refused to cry. Not this time. No way. But she did anyway.

The nurse came out of Julietta's room, gestured to Johanna that her sister was sleeping. Reaching for the box of tissues, Johanna nearly jumped out of her skin when one was handed to her.

"My apologies." Efan scooted onto the chair beside her. "I thought you saw me enter. Are you all right, Johanna?"

"Thank you." She blew her nose. "I'm just a bit overwhelmed at the moment. And Julietta kicked me out."

"You too? Why?"

"I tried to get her to see reason about you."

"Oh. Well. Thank you."

"She'll come around, Efan. Give her time."

He moved some of the papers on the table without reading them, his eyes unfocused and his mouth chewing on words he was not speaking. "My name isn't Efan," he said at last. It took a moment for his gaze to shift from the papers. "I should say, it is, but it's pronounced more like Ivan, not Evan. Ee-van."

"It is?" Johanna sat up straighter. "But Julietta made it a point to correct us when we called you Evan. Efan, she said."

"It's what everyone calls me here in the States. I never correct them. You see, I was instantly smitten with your sister." His smile crinkled the corners of his eyes. "I was introduced to her as Efan and by the time I noticed, I didn't have it in me to correct her. It used to bother me, no one getting it right. Outside of Wales, people call me Efan and believe they've done me the honor of pronouncing it correctly. I do appreciate the effort, truly, and life has been so transitory since I left home. What did it matter the name I was called by people I would only know for a little while and never again? But with Julietta, with you and your sisters, it matters to me, Johanna. Very much."

Johanna. Like he did the *tt* in Julietta, Efan enunciated the *h* in Johanna the way only those in Bitterly did. Customers and acquaintances in New Jersey mostly called her Joanna. She never corrected them, like Efan never did, and only now did she understand—Cape May was a place she never meant to stay.

"I don't know what I'll do if she doesn't relent."

Johanna blinked.

Efan, head in hands, disheveled as the papers on the table. Adorable. She leaned forward to rub circles between his shoulder blades.

"She will."

"I have never loved anyone before, Johanna." His voice was thick and catching in his throat. "And I truly mean never. I believed I would be one of those infamous bachelor scholars Great Britain seems so fond of producing. Perhaps I'd marry when I was an old man too afraid of dying alone to put it off any longer. I actually looked forward to it. No wife. No children to take me from my pursuit of knowledge. But then I met Julietta."

He sat up straight, wiped his eyes and sniffed loudly and took the tissue Johanna handed him.

"I was hers, whether she wanted me or not, from the moment I saw her in the school library, knocking books off the desk and nearly toppling a shelf more trying to help the librarian pick them up. She struck me so dumb I didn't even realize I had no way of contacting her. The day I got your note? I nearly burst. I did. Ask young Steven, who handed it to me."

"What would you have done if I didn't get to you first?" she asked.

"I have no idea, Johanna. None. But I would have found her. Somehow." He blew his nose. "I cannot live without her. I know it sounds trite and dramatic, but it is true. She is perfect and precious and has cast all the things I ever thought I wanted so far away I can barely remember what they were. She is all I want. Julietta, and however many children she would consent to give me."

"What if I don't want children?"

Both Efan and Johanna spun in their chairs to see Julietta standing in the doorway of her hospital room. Arms wrapped tight around her middle, hair spilling from her braid, cheeks pink and eyes wide, she was more fairy than woman in that moment, and Johanna's love for her sister seeped out of her heart. Gripping the arms of her chair so she would not fly across the room, she stayed back so Efan could instead. Julietta pressed her hands to his chest, but did not push him away.

"Then I will spend my life worshipping only you."

"Did you mean all that?"

"Yes," he said softly. "Yes, Julietta. To everything."

"Even after—"

"If your troubles could scare me away, I would not be worthy of you to begin with. I beg of you, *cariad*, never ask me again."

Julietta lifted her gaze. "I'm never going to be normal."

"Normal doesn't exist, *cariad*. It is simply the middle point between two extremes. You are Julietta, and that is far more extraordinary."

Long moments passed while Julietta studied Efan's face, while he waited patiently, while Johanna held her breath.

"I love you, Ee-van."

He gathered her close and kissed her tenderly. "Marry me," Johanna thought he said, her hope confirmed by Julietta's eager nod. Her sister backed through the door to her hospital room, taking Efan with her. The door closed. The lock clicked. Johanna glanced at the clock and hoped they had enough time to…celebrate…before Dr. Sam arrived.

* * * *

The short drive from Bitterly to Great Barrington did not give Charlie the time necessary to gather all his thoughts. Johanna's manner towards him had definitely changed since New Year's Eve, though he could not pinpoint exactly how. They talked. They saw one another—less and less, but they did.

Charlie was no fool, and he did what a considerate man should and gave her the space she needed to deal with her sister's episode. In the days between then and now, he began to fear he'd backed too far off, given her time to rethink what was happening between them, given her anxiety room to spread and grow. By the time he reached the hospital, not only did his thoughts remain ungathered, Charlie had added to them.

He parked in the lot, grabbed the flowers he bought for Julietta and got out of the car. He tried to tell himself, as he had since finding her nearly frozen in the cemetery, that whatever happened, happened. He and Johanna would finally make it, or they wouldn't. One way or another, he would survive. He had five great kids, and a good life he existed in for many years before she blew back into it.

Charlie stopped short at the hospital door sliding open at his approach. Existed in.

The words echoed ear to ear. He took a deep breath, let the notion settle. Existing was not living. He existed with Gina, for children who would grow up and leave him wondering what, exactly, he'd do without them to fill his days. Everything he did was for them. What did he do for himself? Until Johanna arrived in Bitterly, the answer had been nothing. He'd been sleepwalking through his own life for years. Now he was awake and he wasn't going back to sleep again.

"Could you step through, sir?" the receptionist called from her desk. "That's a lot of January coming in."

"Oh, sorry." Charlie strode forward, each step more determined than the last. Johanna might be afraid. She could well choose to go back to Cape May and her anonymous life there, but this time, he would fight for her. For them.

"Can you tell me how I reach Julietta Coco's room?" he asked the receptionist.

"Are you a family member?"

"I'm Charlie McCallan," he said. "Her sister's...husband. She's waiting for me to pick her up."

* * * *

The elevator door slid open to reveal Johanna sitting at a table, squinting at a pile of papers there and sipping at a can of soda. The ding of the doors lifted her head and she was smiling, rising to greet him. Charlie tried to measure his steps and failed. Lifting her playfully off the ground, he kissed her and set her back onto her feet.

"How's Julietta?"

"Aside from kicking me out earlier, her old self. Are those for her?"

"I thought it would be a nice gesture," he said. "Where is she?"

Johanna grinned evilly. "In there." She pointed. "With Efan."

"Eevan?"

"Long story short, we've all been calling him by the wrong name. Efan is actually Eevan and he just asked my baby sister to marry him."

Charlie's jaw dropped. "No way."

"And she said yes. But don't tell my sisters. Let Jules."

"It's so...soon."

"Not everyone takes twenty years to figure things out." Johanna laughed and pulled out of his arms. "I'll leave those with the nurse's station, and then we can go."

"Oh, the flowers. Yes." Charlie handed them to her. "Want me to gather these papers up for you?"

"Sure, thanks. I'll be right back."

Charlie gathered the printouts. Johanna hadn't kissed him the way he hoped she would, but she didn't pull away from his embrace either. The nebulous grasp he had on whatever was going on between them slipped but he grabbed it back again. Slow and steady wins the race. He focused on the file of hospital records and legal proceedings, and pictures he quickly covered as Johanna approached. He closed the folder, tucking it under his arm so he could help her on with her coat.

"So, what is all this?" he asked as they walked. "Anything useful?"

"Yes and no," she answered. "There's a whole lot of information, but most of it raises more questions. There's so much more to tell you, Charlie, like my mother didn't die in the accident, but ended up in a psychiatric facility in New Hampshire that no longer exists."

"That's big."

"I know, and there's more. Gram and Poppy got a huge settlement from the man who caused the accident that killed my father."

"How huge?"

"$1.5 million. And there's more."

"More?"

"So much more. I'll tell you about it on the way home. Actually..." Johanna looked up at him, a little of the mischief that had been turning him to mush since they were kids flashed in her eyes. "What do you have planned for the rest of the day?"

"Nothing. Well, eating at some point. I'm all yours."

"How do you feel about doing some detective work?"

"Sounds like more fun than watching a movie."

"Good. Because I'm pretty sure there are a few answers hiding in the house, and I want to start with finding a checkbook Julietta mentioned. You can help me."

"I live to serve."

Charlie offered her his hand. Johanna looked at it a moment, then took it, her fingers meshing with his like puzzle pieces fitting.

* * * *

Johanna picked up the note from the table.

I had to go back to New York. Please tell Jules I'm sorry. Bring her her computer, books, and some cards or something over to her tonight. If you need me, call. Otherwise, I'll see you in a day or two. Love you, Nina.

Johanna put the note back onto the table and finished shucking off her coat. When she asked Charlie to come home with her, she thought Nina would be there too. Being alone with him was dangerous. When she saw him at the hospital, the instant joy overwhelmed her—until he lifted her in his arms and kissed her the way she'd been longing for since midnight on the rooftop in Great Barrington. The instant saturation of lust and love made caution a notion too ridiculous to contemplate, but one she forced to see reason. Once she gave into it, there was no going back, and Johanna needed the option kept open.

Charlie ducked into the bathroom while she hung their coats up. Glad as she was that Emma's coat wasn't there too, Johanna couldn't help selfishly wishing her sister would show up unannounced and save her from succumbing to an empty house, the man she loved, and a whole night of both. Would it be so bad to pull her away from her husband? Her boys? To ask for help searching for clues? She dug her phone from her pocket.

"Damn," she whispered when the message kicked on. The bathroom door opened. Her heart banged with it. Who would save her now?

"Hey, Emma," she said. "It's Johanna. Call me when you get this message."

"The boys have a soccer club meeting today," Charlie told her as she hung up. "I got Charlotte to take Tony for me."

"Oh, Charlotte's home?" Johanna busied herself putting the kettle on. "When did she get back from New Paltz?"

"Yesterday."

Tea bags. Sugar. Milk. Or did he prefer lemon? Did he even like tea? Johanna's brain whirred. He was so near, so dear, so damned irresistible. And soccer-club meeting or not, why the hell didn't Emma answer her phone?

"Johanna." He leaned elbows to the counter. "Jo?"

She stopped fiddling and looked at him.

"It's fine," he said.

"What's fine?"

"I didn't come here expecting anything more than digging into your grandmother's old bank statements and maybe some dinner."

The teakettle whistled. Johanna took it off the heat, grimacing. "I'm that obvious?"

"I'm not used to seeing you flustered." He came to her side of the counter, took her hands and kissed first one, then the other. Charlie looked at them a long time before meeting her eyes. "It's good to know I have that effect on you."

"You have no idea."

He laughed softly. "I think I might. Look, Jo. I know everything changed after New Year's Eve—"

"It didn't change," she said. "It's just…"

"I know what it's just. Reality's a bitch, Jo, but you keep letting it spin you rather than you spinning it." He laughed softly. "Wild Johanna Coco. Who would have ever thought you could be so cautious?"

Cautious?

Of all the adjectives in the English language, caution was never one in her own lexicon. She was one of the wild Coco girls. Wildest of them all, by popular account. She'd gone skydiving for her thirtieth birthday, for heaven's sake. And there was the whole living in Brooklyn, Boston, even Austin, Texas, for a little while, travelling all over Europe in between moves with only a backpack and enough money for a plane ticket home.

She opened her mouth to tell him he was mistaken, but Charlie kissed her and the words caught in her throat. Her body relaxed even as the desire intensified. Johanna trembled with wanting, and still she felt the fight or flight reflex battling to be obeyed.

Charlie's hands drifted lazily from face to breasts to waist. He drew her closer, kissed her harder, and let her go.

"To be continued," he said. "Where do you want to start looking for the checkbook?"

* * * *

Utensils. Flatware. Pens and pencils and sticky-notepads. The kitchen drawers were crammed full of stuff Johanna was close to certain no one used anymore. Thumbtacks. Old batteries. Razor blades in their paper and cardboard shrouds that never saved anyone from being sliced. She found a calculator they'd gotten free when Gram took them to buy notebooks Johanna's senior year in high school, still in the package. Pulling out the dish towels for the third time, Johanna's hand landed on something squished up and halfway caught in the back of the drawer. Not hidden, just haphazard. Gram's checkbook.

"Charlie, look." She held it up. He abandoned the plastic bin of old paint sample cards and receipts he'd been going through and scrambled to his feet.

"Open it."

"I'm...kind of scared."

"Of what? Being rich?"

She laughed. "Well, if you put it that way..." Johanna opened the checkbook, scanned the register and the numbers there. "Holy shit."

"What?"

She handed him the register, pointed to the last balance.

"Holy shit."

"How does a sweet old lady in Bitterly, Connecticut hide that kind of cash?"

"By not keeping it in Bitterly." Charlie showed her the checks. "The account was opened in Danbury. That's a lot of money to keep in a checking account."

"Where else is she going to keep it?"

"Stocks? Bonds? Some kind of mutual fund? I don't know. There has to be an accountant involved somewhere."

"Knowing Gram, she just put it all in a checking account and let it go at that."

"That does sound like Addie." Charlie blew out a deep breath, thumbed through the register. "This account doesn't look like it was used much. See that? First page of the register goes all the way back to 1999."

Johanna took the checkbook back. "You're right. The most recent entries are..."

November 14, 2013. $549. Memo: water heater.
September 12, 2013. $316. Memo: trees...

All the hair on Johanna's body stood on end. Her cheeks burned. Farther back, a few entries for odd amounts, random purchases, as if Gram only used the account to keep it active. Until March, 2005.

March 15, 2005. $4,265. WML.
February 15, 2005. $4,265 WML

"Charlie?"

January, December, November. 2005, 2004...03...02...all the way back to the very first entry in the register. The amount lowered as it went back in time. $3,565. $3,065. $2,765. There were other checks in between, written for other amounts, but in the memo, it was always the same: WML.

"This isn't the checkbook Julietta was talking about," she said. "What is WML?"

"We might be able to call the bank." He looked at his watch. "Well, tomorrow."

"Would it say on a bank statement, or...the canceled checks."

"Johanna, hang on!"

But she could not wait. She flew down the basement steps. Something was building, like a wave or an explosion. WML. Payments, the same day every month, like rent. Whose rent would Gram and Pop be paying? For who else but Carolina?

She found the boxes of canceled checks she and her sisters had put in the throw-it-out pile. Charlie came more slowly down the steps. Johanna handed him several boxes.

"These aren't the same bank account," he said after checking each one. "These are from the bank in town."

"How many bank accounts did they have?" She showed him the box in her hand. "This one is some bank out in Michigan."

"Just look for checks from Danbury Savings."

They sifted through boxes. The dust made Johanna's eyes itch and her nose stuff up.

"Here it is." Charlie motioned her closer. He showed Johanna the check on top. It was old. Older than the checkbook and register she'd found in the drawer.

"1992," she said. "Look, Charlie. It's made out to the Cully Mountain Convalescent Facility. $698. This must be for my mom's rent. Is it called rent?"

"I have no idea. Here." He handed her another box. "This one is more recent. Check it."

The canceled check on top was dated January 15, 2001. It was made out to Wolf Moon Lodge, in the amount of $1,985. Johanna's breath caught. "WML," she said. "Wolf Moon Lodge. This is it." She sifted through them, went back in time. 2001. 2000. 1999. 1998. Every month on the fifteenth, another check to Wolf Moon Lodge, until—

June 26, 1997. A check for $885, made out to Cully Mountain.

"It must have changed names," Johanna said aloud. "She was there. All along. So many years. For all I know, she's there still. Oh, Charlie."

Johanna buried her face into his chest, oblivious to the dust in his clothes. He held her close, rocked her gently. In the darkness behind her lids, she saw her mother. Alone. Lonely. Wondering why her daughters never came to see her. Had she thought them dead, as they all suspected she was?

"Why didn't they ever tell us?" she choked. Why didn't we ever ask?

"I wish I knew." He put her from him, bent to her level. "I think we have enough for now. Let's go upstairs and get on-line, see if Wolf Moon Lodge still exists."

* * * *

Vanished. Dead. Erased. Happy. Stories told. Wishes made. All the same wish. And separate. Not the kind that sparkles up from a well for the price of a penny, or one granted by stars and birthday candles. This requires a different kind of magic. The rarest kind. It needs hope and love and sacrifice. Like Tinkerbelle, it needs belief. It demands truth, that hardest of things, that cannot remain buried forever, only long enough.

Chapter 12

A Partridge in a Pear Tree

Johanna called Nina first.

"I found Mom," she said, and the rest spilled out. Next she called Emma, and, thank goodness, reached her. The three of them went to the hospital the following afternoon and, after consulting with Dr. Sam, told Julietta what they knew.

"Is she still there?" Julietta asked.

"We didn't call," Johanna answered. "We thought it would be best to find out together. But Charlie looked the place up. It still exists as a well-respected facility."

"It is," Dr. Sam agreed. "I wondered if Wolf Moon Lodge was the place you were looking for when Julietta told me Cully Mountain was in Killian. I was going to call, see what I could discover. You beat me to it."

"I would wonder where Gram and Poppy got the money to keep her there so long," Nina said, "but I guess I don't have to."

"There's more money left than there should be," Emma said. "Either they invested well or got an infusion of cash from someplace else, but even a million and a half doesn't last that long when you're keeping your daughter in a long-term care facility and raising her four girls."

"Willa Germaine, the lawyer in Danbury, said she would look into the banking stuff for us," Johanna said. "Right now, the most important thing is getting to Killian. She was so nice on the phone. She actually remembered all of us from the adopt—"

"Johanna." Nina halted her with a light touch to her arm. Johanna's cheeks instantly warmed. They were all looking at her. She could feel it without looking, but she did. One at a time. Nina and Emma wore the same incredulous expression. Julietta, of course, smiled.

"You can't possibly mean for us to drive all the way up there," Nina began, "and face whatever it is we must face without warning."

"Let's do it," Julietta said. "Today. Tomorrow. Before we chicken out."

"There's no chickening out of something we never agreed to do in the first place." Emma shook her head. "I won't be shamed into this."

"Just hear me out, will you?" Johanna waited for them to quiet. "Worst case scenario, we call and find out she's not there, that she died, that she's lost in the system. We're still going to go up there because that's where she was. Maybe we'll never see her again, but we can see where she lived. We can ask staff what she was like. Or maybe, maybe she's still there. If she is, she might not know who we are, or she might weep with joy to see us again. Whatever the scenario, finding out beforehand isn't going to make it easier. Isn't it better to drive up there with hope?"

"You've not taken one thing into account," Emma said. They all waited. "Maybe there's no hope, Jo. Either she's dead, vanished, or erased, just like the women in Gram's stories about the locket."

"What about the happy one?"

"If it were a possibility, she wouldn't be in Wolf Moon Lodge in Killian, New Hampshire," Nina put in. "I'm with Emma. Let's call first."

"That's your decision," Johanna said. "But I don't want to know what they say. I'm going up."

"I'm going with you," Julietta said. "As long as Dr. Sam says I can leave the hospital."

"Your release papers are already signed and dated," he said. "But I must caution you on taking unnecessary risks."

"See?" Emma gestured to the doctor. "He agrees. This is a dumb idea."

"I did not say that, Mrs. Chambers." Dr. Sam held up a finger. "I said no unnecessary risks, but if Julietta goes to Killian understanding what she might find there, I see no risk. In fact, I think discovering what happened to your mother after the accident is a very good thing. A healing one. For all of you."

"We will have each other," Johanna pressed. "The truth can't hurt us. Only pretending it's not there can. And if any of us has a problem—"

"She means me," Julietta interjected.

"Fine, if Julietta has an issue of any kind, we'll be in a place able to deal with it."

"That's true." Nina chewed at her lips. "I don't know. Emma?"

Emma fidgeted, her gaze darting from face to face. Of all her sisters, she was the one Johanna was least close to. Though they looked most alike, they were furthest apart in personality. Caution to Johanna's wild, Emma had always played it safe.

Who would have ever thought you'd be so cautious?

Charlie's words came back to hit her, suddenly and pitilessly, square between the eyes. Johanna's whole body flushed. All the travel, all the moving, all the floating through life, through relationships. Even the bakery. Johanna skimmed the edges of life with a caution she had never recognized for itself, hiding it behind a shield called wild. Wild Johanna Coco would take any dare, run any risk whether financial or physical, but she had run away from Charlie when she was just a girl and had not risked her heart again. She distanced herself from the sisters and grandmother she loved, never even asked about the mother who disappeared not once but twice, or the father who died protecting his baby girl...

"Emma." Nina moved closer to her sister. "We're all scared."

"What if I just don't want to know?"

A tear rolled down Emma's cheek. Another followed. Johanna felt her own eyes well, her throat start to close.

"Is that what you really want?"

"Yes. No. I just...I just want this not to be."

"But it is," Nina said. "Listen, little sister. Come with us. We'll make it the road trip we never took during our college years. If you don't want to go in, you don't have to. Just come with us. No pressure. I swear to you."

Emma put her head in her hands and cried. Nina was first to take her into her arms. Julietta and Johanna huddled around them, a knot of sisters, sorrow and tears. Dr. Sam's chair scraped along the floor. Then he was gone. Johanna could almost feel a shift in the air with his leaving, the sort of cool drifting in from an open window in January. The chill crept up her back. She held her sisters tighter and the chill became warmth easing through her blood. The sorrow ebbed, making way for something more. Something better. Johanna could not quite define it, but it made her smile.

"All right," Emma said when they broke apart. "I'll come. But I'm not making any promises about getting out of the car."

* * * *

The tense, four-hour car ride was only halfway over. Getting Julietta home, packing an overnight bag, and getting back into the car happened in less than twenty-four hours. Now, two hours closer to the answer they'd all been wishing a lifetime for, the anticipation was like ants under Johanna's skin. When her phone rang, she hit her head on the car window, but answered it gratefully.

"Hello? This is Johanna."

"Hello, Johanna. This is Willa Germaine. I have some news that might come as a bit of a shock."

"Who is it?" Emma whispered. Johanna mouthed, *attorney*, and put a finger to her lips.

"Well, I'm sitting. What do you have for me?"

"Good news. I found out where the money came from…"

Five minutes later, Johanna tapped out of the phone call. Her sisters waited silently. Even after shaking her head clear, it took another few seconds for her to find her voice.

"The account I found in the drawer," she began, "was the one Gram and Pop used for Mom's expenses. The account in town has a good amount in it, but nothing like the one in Danbury or Michigan. That one seems to have only been used for our college educations since it was opened in 1993."

"What?"

"Where'd it come from?"

"Why did they never tell us?"

Her own questions coming out of their mouths had Johanna holding up her hands in surrender.

"Two words," Johanna said, "Bruce Johnson."

"Uncle Boo?" Emma asked.

Johanna nodded. "First there was the settlement apparently awarded to Gram and Pop and put in the Danbury bank account back in the 1980s. Remember I told you Bruce Johnson was some kind of big deal in the computer world? Apparently, he had a lot of money stashed away. The Michigan account was set up in 1993 with money bequeathed to them for the sole purpose of taking care of our mother and us."

"But…there were no trust funds set up?" Nina asked. "That doesn't seem likely."

"Attorney Germaine said the same thing. The civil court award went directly to Gram and Poppy. This she knows because her firm did the whole thing. The inheritance, she believes, must have gone directly to them, too, because otherwise there would have to be trusts. She's going to look further into it."

"So the one in town," Nina said, "must have been what money they earned over the years. Social Security checks and that sort of thing. Smart old birds. No money, no gossip. I wonder why no one ever questioned how two elderly people on Social Security raised four girls and put them all through very expensive colleges."

"We never asked," Johanna reminded them.

"True."

"As with all things, Gram had a reason for keeping her secrets," Julietta said. "I always knew there was something going on behind that sassy smile."

"Poppy, too," Johanna added. "He must have been in on all of it."

Julietta shifted in her seat. "He was, sure, but Gram called the shots. I always thought of Poppy as being quiet, and figured it was because he couldn't hear very well. But finding out all this? Pop was sad. Really sad."

Johanna got a flash of her grandfather's face, of the always-smile on his lips. Sweet. Kind. Gentle. And sad. Yes, sad. How had she never noticed?

"Gram hid her secrets in the everyday," Nina said. "We never questioned anything because we never had to. How did she do it? How did she live her life on top of all these secrets, and do it so well no one ever suspected a thing?"

"Now it's all coming out," Johanna said. "All her secrets unraveling bit by bit."

"And still in her way." Nina laughed. "Don't you see? The locket, the stories, the wish. She orchestrated the whole thing so we would do exactly what we are doing. She made us ask the right questions that would lead to all the answers."

"I think you're giving our dear grandmother a bit too much credit," Emma said. "We didn't ask because, deep down, we didn't want to know. We've lived on the edge of all this our whole lives, and now we're diving headfirst into the deep end."

"A little dramatic, Emma, don't you think?" Nina asked.

"And you making Gram out to be some sort of mastermind isn't?" Emma stretched. "Whatever. I have to pee. Let's stop at the next coffee place or something."

Standing in line for coffee while her sisters used the ladies' room, Johanna tried once again to get Poppy's sad smile out of her head. Gram soothed her grief by making sure her granddaughters would never feel any, but her grandfather drifted from day to day, his thoughts most likely never far from the daughter he'd lost to tragedy, and mental illness. Had they seen her in all that time? Or simply sent checks to the facility keeping her? Hard as she tried to remember a weekend taken here or there, Johanna could not nail down a memory to fit properly.

"You're far away."

Julietta's whisper in her ear startled Johanna to the present. She kissed her sister's cheek. "Just thinking about Poppy."

"I miss him."

"Yeah, me too."

"And Gram."

Johanna winced. "I haven't even had a chance to miss her yet. It's been a little nuts since I got home."

"And you hadn't really seen her in eight years," Julietta said. "I guess it's going to take a while for it to sink in that you never will again." Straightforward. Blunt. Brutally so. Johanna could neither be upset by her sister's honesty nor by her lack of understanding how much the truth hurt to hear. Right was right, and denying it didn't make it less painful. Johanna linked their arms.

"You want a donut with your coffee?"

"No, thanks. I've had yours. I can't eat this crap anymore."

Moving forward in the line that never seemed to get any shorter, Johanna waved to Nina in the dining section of the rest area. "Emma and Nina got a table, if you want to sit. I don't mind waiting alone."

"I'll stay with you." Julietta stared straight ahead, eyes unfocused.

"You okay?"

"Just thinking about what Nina said about Gram setting all this up for us to figure out."

"You don't agree?"

"To an extent, but there's more to it, Jo. There has to be."

"What are you saying?"

Julietta turned to face her. "The wish, Jo. It isn't just part of the story. It's—"

"Can I help you, ladies?"

The line that never seemed to get any shorter was suddenly gone. Julietta's lips pressed into a thin line. Ordering their coffee, paying, bringing it to their sisters served to further them from Julietta's unspoken assertion, but Johanna did not forget it, any more than she could forget the sound like chimes, the head like cotton, and her blood crackling like pop-candy when Julietta had said, *I wish.*

* * * *

The sprawl of Wolf Moon Lodge appeared along the country road like the mushrooms Poppy used to gather in the woods. White. Rustic. Sufficiently New Age while maintaining a quintessential New England feel. The facility seemed more spa than psychiatric hospital. Johanna, having taken her turn at the wheel for the last hour of their journey, pulled into the drive curving through the outbuildings and ended at the oversized French doors of the Welcome Center.

"We should have called in advance," Nina leaned front to say. "We probably need permission to enter or something."

"Then we check into the bed and breakfast and come back tomorrow," Johanna said. "Come on. Let's go in."

Julietta was already out of the car. So, too, was Emma. Johanna slipped an arm about her waist.

"You sure?"

"No." She smiled. "But I'm here. We're in this together."

They climbed the wide stairs, pushed through the French doors, and entered the main lobby. Nina rang the little bell on the front desk.

"Good afternoon, ladies." A tall, thin man stepped through the open door behind the desk. His hair was graying and his face was lined, but he did not appear old as much as tired. "Can I help you?"

"We hope so"—Nina squinted at his nametag—"Darren. I'm Nina Coco-Allen. These are my sisters, Julietta, Emmaline, and Johanna. Our mother was, maybe is, a patient here. Carolina Coco?"

"Coco. The name is familiar, but…" He smiled and suddenly, he seemed younger. "Ah! The mystery is solved. If you would wait here, I'll be right back."

Darren returned moments later, large envelope in hand and trailed by several other staffers all looking to the sisters expectantly. He reached into the large envelope and pulled out a smaller one.

"This arrived shortly before the holidays," he said, "along with the necessary legal documents and a note asking that we hold this letter until one or all of you showed up to claim it."

Nina took it from his hands.

"This is Gram's handwriting." She showed it to her sisters. Their names were scrawled across the front. "But…how?"

"We do not normally agree to such requests," Darren told them, "but it seems there was precedent, and for the same family. Carolina Coco was a special case, in many respects, or so I understand. I wasn't here when she was, but we all know the lore."

"The lore?" Johanna shook her head. "I am very confused."

"Is our mother here or not?" Emma asked. "Can you please tell us what's going on?"

"Perhaps you should start with that." He pointed to the letter. "And we'll go from there. Feel free to use the gathering room. The fire is crackling and the couches are very comfortable. I'll have someone bring you herbal tea. We grow the chamomile ourselves."

The sisters moved to the gathering room in silence. Eyes watched them, ears listened. The air buzzed with curiosity. Nina made no move to open the letter once they were seated.

"It's not very thick," she said. "Too thin for any real explanation."

"Open it, Nina." Emma wrung her hands. "I can't take it anymore."

Nina tapped the letter, tore off the edge, and pulled the single sheet of paper from within. She read aloud.

Halloween 2006
Girls,

If you are reading this, you are in New Hampshire, at Wolf Moon Lodge where, you know by now, your mother spent most of her life. It also means I'm gone.

As I write this, children are trick-or-treating down at the Green, like you used to. The moon is bright. The air is a perfect sort of cool. And I am mourning the loss of your grandfather. Perhaps that's why I do this now, because I hadn't the heart to do it while he was alive. He loved you girls so much, just like he loved Carolina. She was his heart, and she broke it. Over and over, she broke it. He never gave up on her. He never turned his back on her the way his family did his own mother, and his sister. But then you came to us, in pairs. He wanted you to grow up innocent and free, especially after what you all suffered when you were so very young. We had to make some very difficult decisions.

That you are reading this now means I stuck to the decision we made, and so I will say here—your mother lived her life as happily as she was able, and died in November of last year. I will tell you that sometimes she remembered her little girls, but most of the time, she thought only of Johan. She got stuck in the moment he died, and never left it. Your grandfather and I hoped she would come back to us, to you, and had she, we would have told you about her. I think so, at least.

The lawyer who released this letter upon my death arranged for all the legal paperwork necessary for you to get at your mother's records. There is a box being held for you, of Carolina's personal things. I asked for it to be kept there so you would never accidentally come across it at home. The staff at Wolf Moon has always been very good to Carolina, and to Poppy and me. She was a favorite there.

In case you are wondering what would have happened had you never sought your mother, and found her in a wish you all shared, I will tell you. The lawyer in Michigan has instructions to contact you if you did not contact him within six months of my death. He will tell you all the legal things you need to know regarding your inheritance. What I will tell you of that is it came from a man named Bruce Johnson. He was not a bad man, girls, even if he was ultimately responsible for your father's death. He was ill, like your parents, and not getting the proper care. He paid a terrible price for that, and got the help he desperately needed to find his mind again while incarcerated. He loved your parents, and he loved Emmaline and Julietta. Through me and Poppy, he came to love Nina and Johanna as well. He bequeathed all he had left into my care, for you. I will leave that there. You have gotten this far, you will be able to discover more on your own. This letter is already longer than I meant it to be.

I will not ask your forgiveness. I did what I did and I have no regrets. You were all raised in love, and with the best intentions. I need no forgiveness for that. I can't know what would have happened had you known your mother's whereabouts, but I am as certain now as I was when we decided to keep her from you—nothing good would have come of her being in your lives. The cycle needed to be broken and, heartbreaking as it was, we broke it.

I love you to the moon and back,
Gram

Silence. Absolute and electrified. Johanna took the letter from her sister's unresisting hand. Adelina Coco's tight, tiny letters pecked across the page. Running her fingers along the line of her words brought tears to her eyes. For the first time since standing in the cemetery, in the snow, Johanna wept for her grandmother.

"He died of a broken heart." Julietta was first to speak. She blinked and tears rolled down her cheeks.

"Who did, love?" Emma asked.

"Poppy. Don't you see? I can remember so clearly now, looking back. I thought it was him getting old, but it was Mom's death that took the life from him. He died less than a year after she did."

"I remember, too," Emma said. "I made him go to so many doctors that year."

"Why didn't she tell us then?" Nina asked. "Why didn't they tell us before it was too late?"

"They did what they thought was right," Johanna answered. "To protect—"

"When we were kids, but we didn't stay kids, Jo. Do you know how many times I walked the streets in New York City, fearing I'd find our mother living in an alley? Hungry? Alone? Afraid?"

"But she wasn't," Johanna said. "There is always going to be the way things didn't happen."

"Telling us came with a whole different sort of heartache." Emma sighed. "They did their best, Nina. We can't dwell on what might have been."

"There were years and years we might have known her. Maybe we could have brought her back. Maybe seeing us would have—"

"It would have made no difference." The sisters turned as one to the older woman entering with a tea tray. Though it was January, she wore flip-flops, and a peach-colored unitard that accentuated her extraordinarily shapely form, offset the darkness of her skin. Only the lines in her face, part sorrow and part time, showed her age. "Forgive me for eavesdropping. I'm afraid I'm not the only one. There are many of us here who remember Carolina, or know of her. She is somewhat of a celebrity here at Wolf Moon Lodge."

"And you are?" Nina asked.

"Penelope Pitstop," the woman answered. "But you may call me Penny. I was a friend of your mother's."

"You...work here?" Emma asked.

"They give me odd jobs." Penny smiled. "But you are asking if I am an employee or if I am a resident. The answer is, resident. May I pour for you?"

Penny served the tea. They helped themselves to sugar and lemon, looking to one another, at a loss for words.

"Darren is getting a box of Carolina's things," Penny told them. "It's been waiting for you since she died. I imagine you have many questions about her, and her life here."

"Just a few," Nina drawled. She sipped her tea. "The man at the desk—Darren—said something about there being some kind of lore about our mother?"

"Yes, yes. Well, goodness, where to start?" Penny cocked her head, gaze on the ceiling as if the answer could be found there. "I know. Come with me."

Penny rose and gestured them to follow. Johanna pulled up the rear, looking behind to see if anyone would stop them entering the facility itself. The curious still trailed, but no one called them back. Penny led them through a corridor of offices, and beyond it to a casual dining room. Round tables. A coffee and tea station piled with fruit, packages of nuts, and brownies that looked freshly baked.

Residents talking and snacking looked up as they came through. Johanna was struck by their normalness. If she did not know better, she would have thought she was in an upscale resort, not a mental rehabilitation facility, and then she chastised herself for her clichéd assumptions that had more to do with old movies than it did her experience in such matters.

"Here we are."

Penny had stopped before a rather large and faded photo. She waited, smiling, for them to gather around. Residents, obviously, posed at some kind of outdoor event. Johanna scanned the faces in the photo, wondered about their lives, and spotted her mother a moment before Penny pointed her out.

"There she is, see? And that's me standing to her right. Oh, my. Why did no one tell me I was too old for cornrows even then?"

"What year was this taken?" Nina asked.

"2002," Emma answered, showing her the sign a resident sitting cross-legged in the foreground held. "Three years before she died."

"She let her hair go white." Julietta touched her own hair. "That's what you'll look like someday, Jo."

"Beautiful to the day she died." Penny sighed. "But that's not why I am showing you this." She moved in closer, wiped a film of dust from the glass with a perfectly manicured finger. "What do you see?"

Johanna squinted, leaned in as her sisters leaned in. Carolina, standing just off-center in the back row, wore a plaid button-down shirt and cargo shorts. Her hair was loose and long, and wispy-white like Poppy's had been. She smiled serenely, and Johanna wondered if it was a medicated serenity, or innate. Whatever Penny was trying to make her see, however, she was missing completely.

"She's alone," Julietta whispered.

"There are about fifty people all around her," Emma said.

"No, but look." Julietta drew a circle around their mother. "See how close everyone else is standing? Mom's got nearly an arm's length on either side of her."

"We always saved room for Johan." Penny smoothed a hand along her salt-and-pepper hair. "Bless her heart but she never went anywhere without him."

"Our dad was the schizophrenic," Johanna said. "Mom was bi-polar."

"Labels, labels. We don't like labels here. They tend to define us rather than help us. Carolina didn't see manifestations born out of faulty wiring in her brain. Johan was with her. He was...well, real isn't quite the right word, but that's close enough. We could feel him. Even some of the doctors admitted to an uneasy feeling when he was around."

"Yeah, right." Nina chuffed. "The cold air thing? Hair standing on end?"

"Oh, no." Penny waved her off. "When Johan was around, the air was charged with...with...I don't know. Energy, I suppose. 'Passionate in life, passionate in death,' Carolina used to say."

"All right, I've had about enough of—"

"Stop it, Nina." Julietta snapped. Nina paled, even shrank back a little. Julietta turned back to Penny. "Please go on."

Penny glanced Nina's way, pursed her lips. "I am not a madwoman making things up," she said. "You asked for the story behind Carolina's legend. I am giving it to you. You can do with it what you wish."

"I'm sorry," Nina murmured. "Please, I'm listening."

Penny turned back to the photo. "Your mother and father had the sort of love only possible in the movies. It transcended life and death. It knew no boundaries. She said he was with her, and we all believed, because we could sense him there. Waiting. Watching over her. There were times I was envious, and there were times I felt pity for her. To have such a love only to lose it so tragically." Penny tsked. "But she had it, and it is more than some of us get."

"Did she talk about us?" Emma asked. "Ever?"

"She did." Penny patted Emma's hand. "But she always spoke of you in the past tense. I thought she was like me—a mother who lost her children and could not speak of it, could no longer cope in the world. I didn't learn you girls were still living until after she died."

"How did she?" Johanna forced the words through the constriction of her throat. "Die, I mean. Do you know?"

"Well, now, that is part of the lore," Penny said. "About, oh, a week or so before Carolina died, she told me she had a secret, and this secret made her happier than I had ever seen her in all the years we were friends. It took some prodding, but she told me Johan was coming for her, just like he always promised. " She bit her lip. "You do know your parents fled the institutions they had been committed to not once but twice, yes?"

"We were born after the first escape." Nina pointed to herself and Johanna, then to Julietta and Emma. "And they were born after the second."

"Ah, I did not know. Carolina told me that Johan vowed he would always come for her, no matter who tried to separate them. And now he was going to fulfill his promise. I admit I got a little scared. I told her doctors, fearing it was going to be a suicide attempt. They did not seem overly concerned. Carolina lived her life somewhere between this one and the next. She was mostly sweet and mischievous, but there were times she would go into herself for days. Weeks. She didn't know me, or anyone else. Only Johan. Sometimes your grandmother."

"Gram came here?" Emma blurted. "And Poppy?"

"I only knew Addie," Penny answered. "I was under the impression she was a widow."

Johanna looked from sister to grim sister. Had Pop ever gone to see her? Or had it only been those later years he could not bring himself to do so? And then she died, and he faded away.

"How did she die?" Julietta asked. "Can you tell us?"

"She just did." Penny snapped her fingers. "Like that. When she didn't come to breakfast, I went to wake her. She was fond of sleeping in, but it was getting quite late, and I didn't want her missing out altogether. I went to her room." Penny's voice hushed. "And there she was sitting beside an open window, Johan's urn clutched in her arms. Gone."

"Did she have a stroke?" Nina asked. "A heart attack?"

"She was young," Penny said. "Well, too young, and too healthy for anything like that. I cannot say what the actual cause of death was. The doctors don't share such information with us. But I can tell you what the residents say."

They waited. Penny crooked her finger and they all leaned in.

"Johan came for her, just as he promised."

Eavesdropping residents were scattering, breaking the spell of Penny's story. Darren-at-the-desk hurried into the dining room, making a beeline for them.

"I've been looking all over for you," he said breathlessly. "I'm sorry, but you can't be back here."

"I was only showing them a picture of Carolina," Penny said. "Telling them a little bit about her. They know nothing. At least I knew her for a few years."

"It was very kind, but you know the rules. I'll escort them back." He looked her up and down. "Aren't you supposed to be leading the afternoon yoga session?"

"Hell's bells, yes, I am. Forgive me, ladies. It was so nice to meet you. I hope I have been helpful." She waved as she scurried away. "Please come back to visit me. I will tell you more about your mother."

"This way, if you would." Darren gestured them ahead. "Forgive me for being so lax. I assure you, we are not in the habit of allowing strangers into the residence. We value our patients, and their privacy. I should have known how quickly gossip would spread, and leaving you to find the box was not a good idea. The other person at the front desk had to leave unexpectedly."

"It's okay," Nina said. "And we're the ones who should apologize."

"Yes," Johanna agreed. "Chalk it up to a very long car ride, and too much curiosity. We should have waited for you."

"I hope Patricia didn't upset you." Darren held open the door leading back into the front lobby. "She's very sweet, and quite harmless."

"Patricia?" Julietta asked. "She said her name is Penny. Penelope..."

"...Pitstop," they all said together.

"Like the old cartoon." Johanna shook her head, more than a little sad that the story warming her heart suddenly chilled. "Was anything she said true?"

"I suppose it depends upon what she told you," Darren said. "But if it was about Carolina and her ghost, and that he came from the grave to get her? That's the lore I mentioned earlier. It's the story the residents tell, anyway. If there is any truth to it, I can't say. I wasn't here then. But here." He pointed to a plastic bin on the low table beside the abandoned herbal tea. "Your mother's things. Take your time. Look through it here or take it home to do so. Her medical records are on a flash-drive in there somewhere, if you want to see them. Just please don't wander off again. If you'd like to make arrangements to return and speak with Patricia or some of the other residents, we need a week to make it happen."

"What about her doctors?" Emma asked. "Can we see any of them?"

Darren grimaced. "I'm pretty certain most of the staff here back then have since retired or moved on. They will be listed in the files on the flash-drive. Perhaps we can help you find them."

"Thanks, anyway."

Darren-from-the-desk returned to his station. Johanna looked from sister to sister, each of them doing the same. The bin sat untouched, waiting. She said, "Here? Or home?"

"Let's take a quick peek." Julietta gestured to the bin.

Johanna reached for it, her fingers tingling. Inside were things once belonging to her mother. Things she had touched, used, cherished. Cracking the lid, she set it aside. The sisters leaned in. Julietta was first to reach inside. She pulled out a small, square book.

The hard, white cover had no title, no art. The handwritten pages were fragile, the edges crumbling as Julietta opened it.

"What does it say?" Johanna asked.

"It looks like poetry." Julietta carefully turned to the first page. "Oh."

Half sob, half laugh, the sound caught in Johanna's heart. She slipped her arm around her sister's waist. "What is it, Jules?"

"Daddy must have written these for her," she said. "See?"

Julietta held the book open wider, pointing for all to see the inscription.

> *My most precious Carolina. Eternity is not enough,*
> *but it is what I give to you. I love you to the moon and*
> *back.*
>   *~Johan*

"That's what Gram always said," Emma murmured. "To the moon and back."

"Do you think she knew?" Nina asked.

"Now that I think about it," Julietta sniffed. "It really doesn't sound like Gram, does it?"

Johanna laughed. "No, not really. Do you…could she have known him? Maybe even loved him?"

The sisters fell silent then, in the face of all they would never know. Johanna always assumed her grandparents would have despised the man who led their daughter through such a chaotic life, that they would try to keep them apart, but perhaps the true story was different. She had no idea how long her parents were in the same facility as young people in love. It could have been years. Maybe Gram and Pop hoped they would get well, be released, and have a chance at a good life. Maybe it wasn't until Mom got pregnant and they became desperate that they disappeared. It would take a lot more digging into old, possibly non-existent records, and Johanna was not certain she even wanted to. The possibility of a different scenario to the one she'd assumed all her life was enough. For now.

She could not say who moved first, but they were taking things from the box—a porcelain fairy, a net bag of seashells, a leather pouch full of pretty stones and crystals, a deck of tarot cards. Among the various trinkets and mementos, they found the flash-drive. They also found a plastic zipper-bag marked: *Personal effects. Carolina Valentine Coco. November 9, 2005.*

Johanna opened it, tumbling the contents onto the table. Two wedding rings, a tiny diamond engagement ring, a gold horn on a thin, golden chain, and a pair of pearl earrings.

"Mom must have been wearing these when she died," she said. "I wonder why Gram didn't take them?"

"Probably for the same reason she didn't have this box stored in the basement," Emma answered. "So we'd never find them."

"We should each have something," Nina said. "Jules, you should have the wedding rings, if you want them. You're getting married soon. Is that creepy?"

A sob burst from Julietta and was quickly quelled. "It's not creepy, but...does anyone mind?"

Julietta took the wedding rings, Emma, the engagement ring, and Nina the pearls. Johanna reached for the golden horn—a *cornicello*—and remembered she still wore the locket. She lifted it out of her clothes, over her head, and put it into the now-empty zipper bag. Its magic spent. Its origins unclear. A lie that brought the truth, and granted their wish nonetheless. Johanna didn't know what else to do with it.

"Ladies?" Penny—Patricia, hurried into the lobby, a towel around her neck and flip-flops hooked over her fingers. "I was afraid I'd miss you. Darren, oh, Darren!"

He came scurrying out from behind his desk, but Patricia did not give him a chance to scold her.

"I wanted to make sure you direct Carolina's daughters out to the cemetery. They should know where their mother is buried."

"Oh, well," Darren flustered. "I didn't know she was buried in the Lodge cemetery. Thank you, Patricia."

"Penny," she wagged a finger at him, then to the sisters, "Patricia is long gone, but he forgets. It's all right. He has so many of us to remember."

It took some time, but Darren was able to give them a plot location, and directions to the cemetery a few miles from Wolf Moon Lodge itself. The sisters took the box, and got back in the car. They found it without incident, but it was getting quite late. A sign on an otherwise deserted guard station said it closed at sunset. The heralding pink and purple dusk gave just enough light to find their mother's resting place by. They stood before the simple stone with, not one, but two names engraved on the face.

Johan Finn Anker

March 26, 1953 ~ October 11, 1983

*

Carolina Valentine Coco

January 6, 1953 ~ November 9, 2005

"They buried them together," Nina said. "Gram and Poppy did."

"They must have loved him to do that," Julietta muttered. "Don't you think?"

"This is right," Emma added. "It's perfect. I'm glad we came."

Johanna could not speak her own thoughts jumbling and jumping through her head. She could only stare at the names, the dates, thinking the old saying about a lifetime existing in the dash between. Her father's brief one. Her mother's sorrowful one. Lives impacted by mental illness, but a love not defined by it, a love that eclipsed all, including the children love brought into the world. Standing at their grave, knowing some of what existed in the dash between, Johanna understood her grandparents and the decision they made. She not only understood, she was grateful.

She bent to the stone, traced her father's name, then her mother's. She traced the dates they were born, and when they died, realizing that until recently, she hadn't known her father's birthday, and until today, hadn't known her mother's. Her fingers memorized the feel of the inscription, punctuated it at the end. Not a period or an exclamation point, but a question mark she was content to let stand. Rising, she kissed her fingertips and touched the stone.

"Oh," she gasped. Her sisters quieted. "I just realized...Mom was born on January 6."

Silence but for their breathing that drifted as clouds over their heads.

"Little Christmas?"

Her sisters gasped.

"That's why we stopped celebrating," Emma burst. "It was the year she died."

"The cake, the gifts." Nina shook her head. "No wonder Gram and Poppy made such a big deal about it. We celebrated her birthday every year and didn't know it."

"But knowing it now changes everything," Emma said. "In a good way. Like, she wasn't completely absent from our lives, or us from hers."

Arms around one another, the sisters stood together before the grave, alone in their thoughts. Johanna closed her eyes and tipped her face to the darkling sky, breathing deeply of the January cold. Her head felt suddenly light. Her heart followed suit. Amid all the sorrow the weeks since leaving Cape May for Bitterly bestowed, she had also found great happiness. She found her parents, answers to questions she never realized she had, and the peace that came from knowing. She found her sisters again, home again.

And Charlie.

A chill streaked up her back, became joy bursting in her brain and trickling through her body. Charlie. Charlie-freaking-McCallan. Like she could not mourn the decisions her grandparents made, neither could she lament her own. They took her on the journey of her life, and brought her here, to this present. For the first time in all the years she could think back upon and remember, Johanna Elsbet Coco did not regret a thing.

* * * *

He had no idea how long he'd been waiting.

Twenty minutes.

Twenty hours.

Twenty days.

Twenty years.

Charlie leaned his head to the steering wheel, closed his eyes. When Johanna called and told him what happened in New Hampshire, she sounded...different. She bubbled, the same way she did back when they were kids. He'd bubbled too, in a thirty-something-guy-way, of course. She hadn't asked him to meet her at home, but she did make it a point to tell him when she'd arrive. Charlie took it as a sign, a good sign.

He shaved his beard. All of it. Charlie saw his face for the first time in over a year, astounded by the transformation facial hair had hidden. The face that looked back at him was older, but somehow closer to who he had been before the years of responsible apathy changed him. He could not go back to being the young man who first loved Johanna, but neither would he return to who he'd become when he married Gina. Between the two versions of himself was who he wished most to be—the man who loved Johanna, and the father devoted to his children. Even Gina had a place in that man's life, as a friend who had once been his wife, the mother of his children, and essential as anyone else he cherished.

He checked the dashboard clock, the rearview. Three o'clock and still no sign of her. And he'd drunk a whole thermos of coffee.

The key-alarm dinged as he got out of the car. Charlie pulled out the keys and tossed them onto the passenger seat. He dodged behind the garage but couldn't bring himself to take a piss at the side of the building like a stray dog marking territory. Instead he trudged into the woods where the snowdrifts made the going a bit tougher. Instinct or memory took him to the little clearing where he and Johanna used to spread their quilt and make out for hours, the place where he'd nearly lost his virginity, the place she'd run away from and set them both onto separate paths.

Charlie moved further into the woods, relieved himself in some bramble no one would accidentally trudge through. He thought about avoiding the clearing—no good could come of dwelling on the past—but once again found himself there, remembering all those extraordinary days before that last one.

Johanna hadn't just been the girl he was in love with, she was the person he most enjoyed spending his time with. That was how they started out—pals exploring the woods and building forts while their schoolmates played video games.

They had been seventeen, and it was the best summer of his life.

The sound of snow crunching underfoot jarred him out of memory. Johanna stepped into the clearing, a bundle in her arms. She smiled a tired smile, dropped the bundle, and closed the space between them.

"You shaved." She took his face in her small hands.

"Like it?"

"I do. I like the beard too, though. I wouldn't care if you dyed your hair green and tattooed your cheekbones."

"Tempting," he laughed. "But I'll pass. How'd you know I was out here?"

She shrugged. "You weren't in your car. I just…knew."

Charlie held her a little closer. "Good trip?"

"Amazing trip. I have so much to tell you."

"Then let's go back to the house and—"

She placed a warm finger to his lips. "Not yet. First—"

Johanna kissed him softly, her lips teasing his, her arms reaching around his neck. Charlie held her closer. He met each kiss, matched her tenderness, and then her hunger. Backing up without leaving their embrace, Johanna let him go only long enough to grab for the bundle she had earlier dropped.

"I came prepared," she said, and spread a blanket onto the snow. "Just like old times."

Kneeling on the blanket, she smiled up at him, waiting. Charlie's blood surged, his body prickled desire like electrical charges along his skin. He knelt on the blanket. He took her into his arms. "Not like old times, Johanna. I want now. I want new. I want the rest of my life making memories that have nothing to do with the past."

"The past is part of who we are," she said. "But just a small part. I love you, Charlie. I'm scared of how much I do, but going back to the life I was living before all this isn't going to make me love you less. It'll just mean I don't get all the good stuff that goes with it."

Johanna unzipped his coat as she said this, unbuckled his belt, pulled his shirt from the waistband, her eyes never once leaving his. Desire. Fear. And the love he had for her reflected back at him. Something like surprise burst in him like the fireworks on New Year's Eve. Even when they were kids, he always assumed he would love her more. He stopped her hands.

"Say it again. Tell me you love me."

"I love you, Charlie." Brimming tears rolled. "To the moon and back."

He kissed the corners of her eyes, her nose, her lips.

"To the moon and back," he whispered against them, drawing her to the blanket in the January snow, in this clearing where it once ended, and now began again.

* * * *

"To the moon and back."

"To the moon and back."

"Enough of that now. It's time, at last, to rest."

Chapter 13

My True Love Gave To Me

"Do I look all right?"

Johanna tucked a curl behind her baby sister's ear. Julietta wore no veil, no garland in her hair. She had never worn make-up a day in her life, and did not on this day of days either, although every awkward angle of her body sparkled with the fairy-dust sheen Charlotte had given her at her bachelorette party. She wore a dress of elegant-and-unadorned red, the only color acceptable for a Valentine's Day wedding. In her long, pale fingers, she carried a single white rose.

"You are perfect," Johanna told her. "But you need one last thing."

She reached into her cleavage, the only place she had to put anything, and drew out the locket Gram had promised to each of them, the locket that started it all.

I wish, I wish. I wish you had another one in you.

She chuckled to herself. As it had always been, Johanna knew the exact wish she would make, but no amount of magic was going to somehow make Bitterly closer to Cape May. She slipped the chain over Julietta's head.

"We all agree, you should have it," she said. "You believed the most."

Eyes welling, Julietta only hugged her, nearly breaking the rose's long stem in doing so. Johanna held her all the tighter. The youngest of them all had, in fairytale fashion, truly believed the most, but Johanna would never forget the chimes and the pop-candy feeling when her sister made her wish, even if she would never tell anyone about it.

"I didn't think I could be this happy," Julietta whispered, drawing away. "Is that cliché for a bride to say on her wedding day?"

"Probably, but who cares?"

"This is how Mom felt about Dad. This is what was at the root of it all. Their life together couldn't be all bad, could it?"

"No. It couldn't."

Julietta leaned back against Johanna, their gazes meeting in the mirror. "I just wish they had it better."

"They had what they had. Don't fret about what was or wasn't. You and Efan are going to live happily-ever-after in Great Barrington among all those books and students and knowledge. I can't imagine anything better."

Julietta's gaze dropped.

"Jules?" Johanna turned her sister around. "What's wrong?"

Julietta shrugged.

"Are you afraid about moving out of Bitterly? Of leaving home?"

"Of course I am." Julietta laughed softly. "But Sam says the more I cling to everything staying the same, the more I'm going to need it to. So I'm going. I have to. I want to. Efan will be my something familiar. That's what I keep telling myself, anyway. It's going to take a little while to start really believing it."

A light tap on the door turned their attention. Julietta nodded, and Johanna answered it. "Ready for us?"

"Ready." Darren-at-the-desk answered. "If we don't start this soon, I believe we're going to have to tie the groom down so he doesn't float off like a helium balloon."

Johanna checked her hair and dress in the mirror. "This is it, baby-sis."

"You have the rings?"

Johanna pulled the little pouch out of her dress.

Julietta laughed. "Please don't keep it in there during the ceremony. Emma will have a cow."

Kissing her sister's cheek, Johanna gripped the rings in one hand. She offered her sister the other and together, they left the office serving as the bridal dressing room.

There was no house of worship at Wolf Moon Lodge, only a sanctuary to serve as a place of peace for the residents to take refuge in. Julietta's request to be married there, in that place her mother lived and died, had first been met with friction. Penny, as she insisted they call her, had advocated on her behalf, dragging Darren into the appeal and ultimately winning permission. Johanna was close to certain Nina pulled strings only their warrior-sister had the connections and fearlessness to pull, but she denied it. Gunner only winked and smiled the way Poppy always did when Gram was up to something he would not tattle on, and for that, Johanna loved her brother-in-law even more.

Walking into the sanctuary together, Julietta gripped her hand tighter when Johanna would let her go.

"Walk with me," she said.

Heart swelling, pride welling, Johanna Elsbet Coco accompanied her baby sister down the aisle, through whispered encouragement, teasing, and love, from one life into another.

"*Cariad*," Efan whispered, taking Julietta's hand. Sam, no longer Dr. Sam or Dr. Chowdary, left his place beside Efan and offered Johanna his arm. She took it and stepped away, knowing already she was forgotten, and happy to be so. She slipped onto the bench beside Charlie, leaning into him when his arm went around her shoulders. He kissed her temple.

"You okay?"

"I am spectacular," she whispered back.

"Yes, you are." Charlie kissed her neck, and thankfully, let it go at that. They had been going at one another like porn stars since the first time in the woods. Johanna kept waiting for it to mellow into something more rational, but even after being caught mauling one another, in the car outside the movie theater, by Caleb who would not get into the car with his new girlfriend until all the windows had cleared of steam, it didn't. She wasn't sure if age or exhaustion would kick in first. Johanna hoped neither.

Efan wept through his vows, unembarrassed sobs that elicited tears from almost everyone witnessing, even Charlie's older boys, who pretended itchy eyes rather than admit it. Julietta wiped away her almost-husband's tears with her thumbs. She kissed him tenderly, and promised her love without a single hitch in her voice. Darren-at-the-desk, who also happened to be a justice-of-the-peace, pronounced them husband and wife. The gathering cheered. Millie tossed rose petals behind the departing bride and groom.

"Tony, Henry, no," the little girl wailed. "Gio, don't eat them!"

"Knock it off, guys," Ian scolded his younger brothers, and Millie's twin. "You're such babies. Come on, Millie. You toss. I'll make sure they leave them be."

Emmaline's oldest held out his hand to Charlie's youngest. Millie gazed up at him with little-girl-worship Ian didn't seem to notice. He led her to the front of the sanctuary, glaring the other boys motionless.

Johanna nudged Emma who had come to stand beside her. "We might have a problem there in a few years."

"It wouldn't be the first time a McCallan fell for a Coco," Charlie said, burying his face in Johanna's curls.

"You two are like cats in heat." Emma laughed. "Charlie, get off my sister and go help Gunner and Mike shepherd everyone to the dining room. Please."

Emma batted her lashes playfully. Charlie leaned in and kissed her cheek. "Hint taken. I'll see you ladies inside."

Emma's eyes stayed on Charlie's back until he was gone. She took Johanna's hand and led her away from the aisle where people were still filing out.

"Something wrong?" Johanna asked quickly. "You okay?"

"I'm fine, actually. I just wanted a minute with you."

"All right. What's up?"

Emma shifted from foot to foot. "We Cocos are very close," she began, "but we all know Nina and I are closer, and you and Jules are closer. No, don't protest." She held up her hands when Johanna opened her mouth to do just that. "It's nothing to do with love and everything to do with personality. I'll fly to the sun for any of you. This is not what I wanted to say."

"Start again, then. Take your time."

Emma took a deep breath, let it go slowly. "Remember the talk we had, about me and Mike and all that?"

"Of course."

"I took it to heart, Jo. I wanted you to know, you were right. Mike and I were in a terrible cycle of misunderstanding and, well, rebellion is probably the best word for it. We haven't been happy in a long time. Me wanting babies and him having a vasectomy are symptoms to something bigger."

"What are you saying?" Johanna grasped both her sister's hands. "Divorce?"

Emma did not answer right away, and Johanna's heart sank. Her eyes welled.

"Don't start crying." Emma hugged her quickly. "That's what I have been thinking about, Jo, right up until today when Julietta and Efan said their vows. It's hard to explain."

"Well, try."

"I am. Before Gram died and all this started, I would have divorced him if I had the money. I was furious, but I was also unhappy, and so was he. On New Year's Eve, I thought everything could be good again, and then all that happened with Jules and we found Mom and I realized what real, eternal love actually was, and I wanted that. But…"

"But? Emma, come on."

"I have the money now, Jo," she said. "The inheritance would allow me to start over again, buy the house on County Line Road and raise my boys where I was raised. I could go back to college and never have to worry about where the money for bills would come from. I can have all I ever thought I wanted, but sitting here today, watching Julietta and Efan promise their love to one another, I looked at Mike. He looked at me. I saw it in his face, Jo. He's afraid."

"He loves you."

"I know he does, but I don't think he remembered until the possibility of losing me hit him. We've been butting heads for so long, we forgot how to love one another, that we do love one another." Emma sighed. "It might not be what Mom and Dad had, or what Jules and Efan do, but it is what we have. And it worked once. Now that I have the cushion I'd need if it doesn't, it makes me want to make it work instead of have to. I'll tell you, Jo, it makes a huge difference to me. It really does."

"I'm not sure what to say about all this?" Johanna wiped her eyes carefully so her mascara wouldn't smudge. "Why are you telling me now, of all days?"

"Because you're going to get home to a message on the voicemail saying to take the house off the market because I want to buy it." Emma laughed. "I told you, I thought my mind was made up. I left a message on the house phone so I couldn't chicken out."

"Does he know?"

"Mike? No. Let's keep it between us, all right?"

"Maybe you should tell Nina then," Johanna said. "She's liable to get to the phone messages before I will. Or Gunner. They check incessantly. One time a vendor left a message at the house was all it took. You know how Nina is."

"She always claims Gunner's the obsessive one."

"Gunner's hyper. She is obsessive. But it is a huge thing they're doing. I don't blame her for being a bit preoccupied with it."

"Leave it to Nina and Gunner." Emma sighed dramatically. "Sailing the world, collecting oddities. It's going to be years before they come home to set up shop. They make me feel so mundane."

"Be honest, Emma. You are no more interested in her life than she is yours."

"True enough, if not completely. I think Nina wanted kids, but time got away from her. From them. Now kids just don't fit into their life."

"Maybe. I don't think it's a regret, though. Do you?"

"In passing, like I'll always think about traveling the world as casually and carefree but never actually want it enough to make the effort."

Arms around one another's waists, Johanna and Emma followed the last of those leaving the sanctuary for the dining room.

"So what about you, Jo?" Emma asked.

"What about me?"

"Any thoughts about adding a sixth to Charlie's brood?"

"I'm a little old, don't you think?"

"You're thirty-eight."

"It sounded good." Johanna blew a breath through her lips. "We still haven't addressed our living situation. I have to go back to Cape May eventually. He can't uproot the kids. I don't want to simply throw away what I've built down there."

"But you want to be in Bitterly."

Johanna groaned. "It feels so much like caving in to a life I spent trying to avoid."

"Do you hear how ridiculously babyish that sounds?"

"I'm not a baby, you are." Johanna grinned.

Emma gave her a squeeze. "You had reasons before. Those no longer exist. And there's one of them."

Emma pointed to Charlie helping Charlotte position the wedding cake. Johanna closed her eyes to the thrills racing along her skin. Was it caving to give up something you kind of like at the moment for something you never-in-a-bajillion-years thought you could have? Was it betraying her sex to want a home, a man, a family when she had built a successful career on a whim?

Johanna kissed her sister's cheek and headed for the cake table. Charlotte fussed over the cake. The decoration she had spent painstaking hours on the day prior faced the wall.

"Oh, Johanna! Yoohoo!"

Johanna halted halfway across the dining room full of family, friends and residents. She spotted Penny waving, weaving her way through the guests finding tables and chattering excitedly.

"I'm so glad I caught you before you got too busy." Penny patted her chest, caught her breath. "It was so nice of you to invite those able to attend. It's not often we have such a happy occasion to celebrate here."

"Well, thank you for going to bat for us."

"It's the least I can do for Carolina's darling girls." Penny wiped a tear from the corner of her eye before it could fall. "I dream of her sometimes. More since you girls came into my life. I feel like she is with me, just like old times. Would it be overstepping my bounds to tell you I believe she is so happy and proud?"

"Of course not. We are all grateful to you for the friendship you gave our mother. And for the memories you've shared with us."

Penny reached up tentatively then, touched Johanna's cheek when she smiled instead of pulling away. "You know, Johanna, I had a son once. He would be your age now. I came here because I lost him, and no one in my life understood that the world was just too big a place without him. Carolina understood, because it was how she felt after Johan died. I would have done anything for her. I'm glad I was able to do something, at last."

Penny let her hand fall and walked away. What a terrible waste it was, when sorrow consumed a whole life. How close she had come to being Penny, to being Carolina. How terrifyingly close.

"Dad, be careful."

"I didn't even touch it."

Charlie stood back, hands up in surrender while Charlotte fussed over the cake she and Johanna spent the last several days baking, icing, decorating. Charlotte's off-hand artistry was not something to be learned, but an unexplainable instinct shared by artists of all kinds. Johanna was already planning the display window in CC's, ripe and ready for June weddings, with cakes never before seen in Cape May. Whether the town knew it or not, their favorite local bakery was about to go up a notch on the swanky scale.

She closed the gap to slide her hand into Charlie's. "Shall I rescue you?"

"Rescue him?" Charlotte pursed her lips. "He nearly dumped the cake. Twice."

"You need to relax, Char." Charlie said. "It's a cake."

"I'll pretend you didn't say that." She turned to Johanna. "Is it as beautiful as I think it is?"

"Probably more so," Johanna answered. "You did take a picture, right? To add to your portfolio for school?"

"I didn't think of that." Charlotte fished her phone out of her pocket. "Will you take it dad? I want Jo in the pic too. I can't take all the credit."

They posed. Charlie took the picture and handed the phone back to his daughter. The conspiratorial look passing between the two was as good as words. Almost.

"Okay, you two, what's up?"

"Nothing," Charlotte said quickly, but her father leveled another glance, and her shoulders slumped a little. "Well, I was wondering about something."

"I'm getting a little nervous here."

"So am I." Charlotte scooped her into a hug and let her go just as quickly. "Okay, I'm just going to say it. What if you and I went down to Cape May and opened CC's for Easter. You can teach me the ropes and then..."

"And then?" Johanna prodded when she fell silent. Charlotte's cheeks blotched crimson.

"It's okay if you say no," she said. "I mean it, Johanna. Seriously." "Just tell me."

"Okay, it's...see, there isn't...I know this is presumptuous but..." She let go a deep breath. "I have been thinking that Bitterly needs a bakery. A real bakery and not the gross grocery store one that never used real cream or butter ever in its life. Ever. With all the revitalization going on in town, a bakery would do really well and you just got all that money and dad can do the work, for free, considering...you know. And I thought I could help manage CC's down in Cape May, and you could start work on opening another CC's in Bitterly. Then you get to keep the first CC's and Dad, and it'll be a success, I just know it." Charlotte fell suddenly silent, then, "What do you think?"

Words buzzed like bees in Johanna's mouth. Old fears battled and lost fairly quickly. Opening another CC's. In Bitterly. The notion of a baker having her cake and eating it too was entirely too ridiculous to make it out of her mouth. Instead she said, "I think you're as good a businesswoman as you are a baker."

Charlotte clapped her hands, squealing. "It's kind of perfect, don't you think?"

"What about school?"

"I still want to go to school," Charlotte answered. "I know how to do things, but I don't know why they work. I want to learn the chemistry of it all. It's a lot of going back and forth between New Jersey and Connecticut, but it's only two years and then, if things work out between you and my dad. Notice I said if? See, I'm not taking anything for granted. So if you and Dad work out, it will be a family business. You, me, dad. Who knows? Maybe even the boys and Millie one day. And if it doesn't work out, then you can sell the Bitterly place, to me, and call it a day. See? I thought of everything."

Johanna's belly fluttered. She did not ask herself why she never thought about opening a CC's in Bitterly. The reasons were far too easy to pick out, one by one, and groan over. She thought of Penny again, and Carolina, and the lives they gave over to sorrow and fear and loss. Pretending to brush crumbs from the tablecloth, Johanna let the idea settle into her brain. Life changed so quickly, became unrecognizable in an instant. CC's and Cape May seemed like a lifetime ago. If she went back now, there would be no pretending Gram's death and all that came after hadn't happened. All the secrets were spilled. All their lives had changed. She had changed, or perhaps, shed the masquerade. Nina was off to travel the world. Emmaline was reinventing herself. Julietta was stepping out into a new life.

And I am going home.

Home. Johanna felt it in her core. It was not just Bitterly and the house on County Line Road. Not her sisters and Charlie and his kids. Home was the past, and it was the future. Home was the present she made rather than the one fear and sorrow choose for her. It was not a place or people, but the amazingly chaotic, sometimes frustrating, always beloved mishmash of all.

Charlotte stood waiting. Charlie did too. Johanna held out her hand for his and the ghosts of her past settled into their proper places. In her heart. In her memory. Always there, but no longer haunting.

* * * *

The dead do not haunt the living; it is the living who do the haunting. They hold with memory and bind with grief, unmindful that there are no boundaries, shadowy and vague. No beginnings, no ends. Just a continuous road through a yellow wood, one tread together for a time, and then as way leads on to way—parts beloved company.

We do not haunt, we watch. We do not grieve, we wait. For that new road lovely, dark and deep, and the promises we keep, and the miles we go before we sleep...

Meet the Author

Terri-Lynne DeFino lives in a log cabin in Connecticut, but she's a Jersey girl at heart. Writer, mother, cat wrangler, and self-proclaimed sparkle queen, Terri began writing when she was seven. Though that first story remains locked away in her parents' attic, some of her works include *Finder*, *A Time Never Lived*, and *Beyond the Gate*. *Seeking Carolina* is her first step into contemporary romantic fiction. Visit her blog at: Modestyisforsuckers.com, or contact her at: terrilynnedefino@aol.com.

Keep reading for a sneak peek at book two of Terri-Lynne DeFino's
Bitterly Suite Romance

DREAMING AUGUST

Some spirits cannot be broken...

Benny Grady never expected to fall in love with Dan Greene, her late-husband's best friend—or become pregnant. Caught between the joy of living again and the guilt such happiness brings, she closes herself off and keeps her feelings and the baby to herself; but it's getting harder. Bitterly is a small town. She sees Dan everywhere, and each time she does, her feelings for him become impossible to ignore.

A Lyrical Press romance coming March, 2016

Learn more about Terri-Lynne DeFino at
http://www.kensingtonbooks.com/author.aspx/31624

Chapter 1

when evening falls

"*You sure you want to do this?*"

"*Very sure, Harriet. I must.*"

"*That's not exactly true. You could just stay here.*"

"*That is your choice, not mine.*"

"*I never stepped foot outside of this town. Don't 'spect I ever will.*"

"*Then you can?*"

"*'Course I can. And so can you. You don't have to bedevil that young woman. Just go.*"

"*Bedevil? Harriet, I would never.*"

"*August, you miscreant, you bedevil me constantly.*"

"*Then you should be glad I seek her assistance. You'll be rid of me for all eternity.*"

"*Lot'a 'nonsense, far as I'm concerned.*"

"*Only because you are more stuck than you want to believe.*"

"*Stuck? Bah! I'm just waiting...*"

* * * *

Dirt helped.

Cold earth. Fragrant, moist earth. Under-her-nails, in-the-cracks-of-her-chapped-hands earth. It smelled of snowmelt and leaf mold and worms. Black and rich and crumbly, it was the perfect medium for the colorful pansies planted among the forget-me-nots just starting to pop. Sitting back on her heels, Benny inspected her work.

"What do you think, Henny?" she asked. "Better than impatiens, right? This spot is way too sunny. Maybe we'll do some morning glories this year. I still have that little wooden trellis in the shed. I love morning glories. The blue ones with yellow centers. Yeah, let's do it. I'll stop for seeds on the way ho——"

The nausea she thought banished by dirt swished through her again. She shoved her hands back into the churned-up earth, let the cool fragrance soothe her belly. Swallowing, swallowing, swallowing until it passed, Benny turned to the neighbor. "What do you think, Mrs. Farcus? You like the pansies?"

Again the swell of nausea. Four months. This was supposed to be over. But it hadn't just come in the morning, so why should it stick to the first three months? She'd ask Mrs. Farcus, but she didn't know Benny was pregnant. No one did. And no one would. Yet.

Benny dusted her hands off on the front of her jeans and pushed to her feet. She picked up her trowel and the empty bag from the soil, bent again to grab the plastic potting containers and nearly vomited right there in the garden she'd just spent the last hour planting. Leaning heavily upon the tombstone, she screwed her eyes tight until it passed.

"Hey, Benny? You okay?"

Her eyes flew open and she was grateful for the dark fringe of hair obscuring her face. It gave her a moment to hide all she did not want anyone else to see. Straightening, she waved to the man standing with one foot in and one foot out of his truck.

"I'm fine, Charlie. No worries. Just hungry. I think I forgot to have lunch."

Instead of waving back and moving on, Charlie McCallan closed the door and started up the rise towards her. Benny choked down the panic. Could he see? Did he know? But Charlie was squinting into the sunlight, smiling the same smile she'd known since they were young and she was his best pal's pesky kid sister. Benny quelled the panic and tried to relax.

"It gets more extravagant by the year," Charlie said when he reached her. He bent down to brush dirt from the grey stone. "I see you did up Mrs. Farcus's plot too."

"She's an old friend."

"She died nearly a century before you were born, Benny." Charlie laughed softly. "Did you know she's my great-whatever grandmother?"

Benny looked up. "Really?"

"Didn't know my family went back so far, huh? Harriet was one of three daughters, so the name Gardner died out here in Bitterly, but I have Farcus cousins somewhere."

"I wonder why she's buried alone."

"Her husband, I think his name was Josiah, died out west somewhere. She didn't even know he was dead for about six months. That's the story, anyway."

"So sad."

"It's nice of you to pretty-up her grave too."

Benny shrugged. "I always bring too many flowers."

"You okay?"

Her gaze moved to the tombstone easier to look at than Charlie's familiar concern.

Henderson Parker Fredericks
June 3, 1976 ~ August 20, 2010
Beloved Husband

Benny-and-Henny—a joint moniker earned in high school that carried through to the day he crashed his motorcycle barely a mile from their home. Now she was Benny-without-Henny, and the hole he left in her gaped just as wide and as deep as it had six years ago.

"I'm okay, Charlie. Really."

"Why not come to the bakery with me? Johanna's still got some shepherds-pie-pies left from lunch. You'd be doing us a favor if you take some. They're not as good the next day. The crust gets soggy."

"I'm sure you and your ridiculously large family will find use for them."

"Do you know how often we eat shepherds-pie-pies?"

They laughed together. Benny's belly churned. "I'll have to pass," she told him. "You know my mother. She's already made dinner enough to feed the whole town. But thank you. And say hi to Johanna for me."

"Will do." He started back to his truck. "And say hey to your brother for me. Tell him to come home once in a while. I haven't seen him since the reunion."

"He is home," Benny called. "In North Carolina."

"Bitterly is home. Always. Whether he likes it or not."

Benny shook her head, waved him off and finished tucking her tools into the daisy-dotted canvas carrier she bought two years ago and subsequently had inked into the tattoo covering most of her right arm. Her trowel. The forget-me-nots. The always-reliable marigolds and snapdragons. Last year's impatiens. This year she would add the pansies, thus marking her gardening calendar as only Benedetta Marie Grady would, no matter what her mother thought of tattoos.

She pushed back her sleeve, peeking at the first tat inked, on the first anniversary of Henny's death—a little blue forget-me-not, there on the underside of her wrist. In the six years since her husband's death, Benny added steadily to her "mural." A tribute to Henny, and the garden she kept for him, there on her arm. Forever.

"Forever, baby," she told the tombstone. "I promised you forever, and I meant it."

Her hand nearly moved to her still-flat belly, but she stopped herself, closed her eyes to the impulse until it passed. A promise was a promise, and Benny knew straight down to her superstitious Italian soul that breaking this one was even less of an option than stepping on a crack in the sidewalk, or refusing to wish on birthday candles.

"Ah, Henny…" She squatted on her haunches again, pinching off a spent flower she hadn't earlier noticed. "You make it very hard to leave Bitterly, but I have to. If I stay, everyone will know, and…well, anyway. I won't be gone long, and it'll be winter, so it won't matter so much, right? I'll come back after I figure things out. I just want to do it without everyone hovering. You know how my family is. And then there's Dan—"

Benny felt tap on her shoulder, spun and thumped flat onto her bottom, looking for Charlie or whoever had snuck up on her while she confided in her dead husband, Benny found herself alone but for the tombstones. She looked narrowly in Mrs. Farcus' direction.

"Are you playing games with me, you old trickster?"

No answer. Of course. Mrs. Farcus never answered, not once in all the years Benny had been talking to her grave. Neither did Henny, for that matter. Benny's laughter sounded hollow, even to her own ears. She pick herself up, brushed herself off, and hurried to her motor scooter before either of them decided to finally oblige.

* * * *

Benny twirled her spaghetti with no intention of eating it. Tomato sauce gave her the worst heartburn in the history of heartburn. When she thought no one was looking, she shoved a forkful into her mouth as she rose from the table and headed straight for the garbage can in the corner of the yellow kitchen.

"Don't even think about it, young lady." Clarice Irene Grady descended upon her daughter with all the intensity of an Italian-mama intent upon feeding her young. She yanked the full bowl of spaghetti and meatballs from Benny's hand. "You hardly touched it."

"I'm not hungry. I—I went to CC's on the way home from the cemetery. Charlie said there were a whole bunch of pie-pies left over. You know how I love them. I'm sorry, Ma. I couldn't resist."

"Ah, you should have brought one home for me." Peadar Grady gazed heavenward, his hands patting his paunch. "There's no bit of heaven like one of Johanna Coco's pie-pies. You make me jealous, girl."

"I'm sorry, Daddy." Benny kissed his forehead. "Next time. I promise."

"What am I to do with all of this?" Clarice held up the plate. "I cook a good meal and you stop on the way home for—"

"Give it here, Ma." Benny's brother Peter held out his hand. "I'm ravenous."

"And if you don't stop eating like a horse you'll be as big as your father."

"Then throw it away. See if I care."

Clarice plonked the plate in front of her son, glared at her daughter and huffed to the stove, muttering. Benny mouthed, thank you to Peter. He winked and tucked into her uneaten meal. Tall and lean and muscular, her baby brother didn't have an extra ounce on his body and never had. Neither had their father, as Clarice was fond of reminding him. Still she fed him as if he'd been starved half his life, and would continue starving for the rest of it if not for her efforts.

Benny headed for the back stairs leading up to the second-story of the two-family house, to the apartment she and Henny had lived in all seven years of their married life.

"It's movie night," her mother called after her. "You coming back down?"

"Sure, Ma." If having her way were actually an option, Benny would take a long bath, curl into bed, and be asleep before dusk gave way to dark. But—

All ways here you see, are the Queen's ways.

The urge to push against every one of Clarice's shoves had diminished. Benny just didn't have it in her anymore. After a shower, Benny would be downstairs again, plopped on the couch she'd been plopping into all her life, to watch a romantic comedy starring one of the British Dames her mother was so fond of. Resistance was futile, and often not worth the guilt.

In the privacy of her own apartment, Benny smoothed her hands over her belly. She could imagine it rounding, swelling, exploding, but not her mother's joy. Clarice had been dreaming of grandchildren since her own brood turned from childhood to adolescence. Grandchildren provided within a year of a wedding and at a rate of every other year thereafter. But Tim married and moved to North Carolina before the first was born. Peter hadn't even had a serious girlfriend yet. And in the seven years of Benny's marriage, there had not even been a suspected oops. She and Henny wanted to see the world first. They planned to backpack across Europe, to book passage on a cargo vessel sailing from California to Japan, to work the vines in Napa a full season. Seven years of planning adventures they never took.

Then he died.

No Henny. No adventures. No baby.

Until now.

Letting her hands drop, Benny moved like a ghost through her apartment, closed all the windows. The beautiful day was becoming a chilly dusk. Nights were usually cold in Bitterly, even when summer days spiked in the nineties. The trees, the river, the sheltering Berkshire Mountains absorbed the heat, stored it away for the long winter—a winter she would miss. Along with the autumn splash in the mountains. She would be in North Carolina with her brother, Tim, and his family. Where it was hot. Even at Thanksgiving and Christmas. And she would have a newborn Clarice didn't even know about. A baby born in sorrow, whose daddy was not Henny...

Benny could not breathe. Grasping for the door, she yanked it open to pound down the exterior stairs leading to the yard. She jammed the helmet on her head, kicked her scooter to life, and sped off before her mother could shout her name, even if Benedetta saw her at the back screen door.

* * * *

The bakery was still open. During the summer months, CC's North often hopped long after the posted six o'clock closing. It was only June and unseasonably cool, but it was still light enough to pass for daytime. The doors of the bakery were open wide.

Benny slipped off her scooter. Adjusting her getting-tight jeans, she followed the scent of baking into CC's and stopped dead in her tracks.

"Oh." She forced her feet to walk her into the bakery. "Hey."

"Hey, yourself."

"How are...what have...Valentine's getting so big."

"Yeah, I hear kids do that."

Benny felt the color rising in her cheeks, quelled the need to press her palms to them. Dan Greene shifted the toddler in his arms. Waiting? What could he be waiting for? Benny pretended she didn't know exactly what and instead moved to the counter, her back to him.

"Jo!" he called, startling both her and the baby. "Come get your kid. I have to go home."

Johanna Coco McCallan pushed through the swinging door, arms outstretched. Flour on her cheek, long hair in a knot on top of her head, she swooped past Benny with a look of surprise and a wave before scooping her daughter from Dan's arms.

"Sorry, Dan. I didn't realize—"

"No worries." He kissed the baby's round cheek. "See you and Charlie for my niece's graduation party?"

"We'll be there. Caleb will be watching the bakery, but we'll have Tony and Millie with us."

"I'll let my sister know. See you, Jo. Benedetta."

Benny waved over her shoulder, eyes resolutely on the menu board.

"Curiouser and curiouser."

Johanna's voice turned Benny around, and only then did she realize there were others in the bakery. They sat at tables, sipping coffee out of to-go cups from the coffeehouse next door. It was a deal Johanna struck when first she opened her bakery in Bitterly. She wouldn't serve coffee if the coffeehouse didn't serve baked goods. The result was a sort of co-op suiting not only the two businesses, but the town as well.

"What's strange?" Benny held out her arms for Valentine, a chubby little cherub as fixed an icon in CC's as Johanna's mud cookies and shepherds-pie-pies. Johanna handed her over.

"Dan. I usually have to pry Valentine from his arms before he'll give her up."

"She's a special girl." Benny's heart pounded, her face burned. "I don't blame him."

"Well he was sure in a hurry to hand her off just now." Johanna pulled the elastic from her hair, piled it high again and secured it in place. "Did someone say something to him?"

"I only just walked in." She bounced the baby, avoiding Johanna's eyes. "Dad was hoping for some of your pie-pies. Any left?"

"One or two. Charlie said you turned him down."

"I did. Out at the cemetery. When I got home, Dad was inconsolable that I would pass up a pie-pie."

"Then I'll go grab one for him. You mind holding her?"

Benny clutched Valentine closer. "Try taking her."

Johanna scooted around the counter and into the back. Valentine watched her mother vanish, but did not cry. Smiling a wet, baby smile, she reached for Benny's turquoise pendant.

"No you don't." She tapped it away from the baby's mouth, but not out of her hand. Valentine studied the blue stone, her baby brow furrowed with thoughts Benny couldn't begin to guess at. Would she dream in blue that night? Holding the baby closer, Benny closed her eyes and allowed her own tremulous joy rumble through her.

A boy. She was positive. Already, she loved him so much.

"Here you go." Johanna came at her, the bagged pie-pies outstretched and already spreading buttery patches in the paper sack. "Tell him he got the last two."

"I'll trade you." She offered Valentine, who reached for her mother with a little squeal. Benny grabbed the sac. "Crap. I didn't bring any money."

"I'm not charging you for leftovers, Ben."

"They're not leftovers until tomorrow."

"They're leftovers the minute lunch is over. Seriously, don't be weird."

"Thanks, Jo."

Johanna waved away her thanks. "Now if I can get these laggers out of here, I can go home. I should have gotten Dan to do it before he left. He's good at clearing a room."

Benny laughed along with Johanna, even if it made her woozy. Funnyman, Dan Greene. Always joking, lightening even the darkest moments. Dependable. Loyal. Kind. Everyone's favorite plow-man in winter, landscaper the rest of the year even if he liked to pretend he was an ornery old bachelor and dedicated grouse. It was part of his charm, and Benny had always liked that about him—until she more than liked him for it, which was unacceptable.

"How are you doing, Benny?" Johanna asked

Startled, Benny bit her lip. "I'm okay. Just—you know. Same old, same old. I—I hear Nina is coming back to the States for the holidays."

"You heard right. And she's bringing back a surprise."

"Nina? A surprise? That doesn't sound like her."

"I know, right?" Johanna laughed. "But she's not talking. I'm dying of curiosity."

While those stragglers finished up and left, while Johanna tidied up the front and her stepson did the same in back, Benny listened to her talk and talk and talk. About Nina and the Curiosity Shop that would finally open in New York City. About the honeymoon Johanna and Charlie finally took, meeting her sister and brother-in-law in Bora Bora, sailing those South Seas islands that never stopped being exotic. As long as Johanna kept talking, Benny did not have to. Any wondering about Daniel Greene was safely off topic, even if the conjured image of him so tenderly holding Valentine would not quit. Then there was the way he looked at her the moment she first walked in...

She rode her scooter home in the dark, the only light coming from the stars overhead.

Star light, star bright,
First star I see tonight.
I wish I may, I wish I might,
Have this wish I wish tonight.

Benedetta revved the tinny engine, pretended the tears instantly drying on her cheeks came from forgetting her goggles in her rush to be out of the house. They had nothing to do with Dan, or the gentle way he held Valentine, or how her heart had stuttered that moment before she forced it to still.